W9-AMB-444

white rabbit

white rabbit

A Psychedelic Reader

EDITED BY JOHN MILLER
AND RANDALL KORAL

CHRONICLE BOOKS
SAN FRANCISCO

Compilation copyright ©1995 by John Miller and Randall Koral. All rights reserved. No part of this book may be reproduced in any from without written permission from the publisher.

Page 281 constitutes a continuation of the copyright page.

Printed in the United States of America.

Library of Congress Cataloging-in-Publication Data:
White Rabbit: a psychedelic reader / edited by John Miller and Randall Koral.
p. cm.
ISBN 0-8118-0666-9 (pbk.)
1. Drugs—literary collections. I. Miller, John, 1959–
II. Koral, Randall.
PN6071.D77W48   1995
808.8'0355—dc20   94-7317
CIP

Editing and design: Big Fish Books
Composition: Jennifer Petersen, Big Fish Books

Distributed in Canada by Raincoast Books,
8680 Cambie Street, Vancouver, B.C. V6P 6M9

10 9 8 7 6 5 4 3 2 1

Chronicle Books
275 Fifth Street
San Francisco, CA 94103

SPECIAL THANKS TO

KIRSTEN MILLER

AND RUTH MARSHALL

CONTENTS

INTRODUCTION

❊

"THE OTHER DAY I discovered, dusty and neglected on one of the upper shelves of the local bookshop, a ponderous work by a German pharmacologist [Louis Lewin's Phantastica]. The price was not high; I paid and carried home the unpromising-looking treasure. It was a thick book, dense with matter and, in manner, a model of all that literary style should not be. Strictly an unreadable book. Nevertheless, I read it from cover to cover with a passionate and growing interest. For this book was a kind of encyclopedia of drugs. Opium and its modern derivatives, morphia and heroin; cocaine and the Mexican peyotl; the hashish of India and the near East; the agaric of Siberia; the kawa of Polynesia; the betel of the East Indies; the now universal alcohol; the ether, the chloral, the veronal of the contemporary West—not one was omitted. By the time I had reached the last page, I knew something about the history, the geographical distribution, the mode of preparation and the physiological and psychological effects of all the delicious poisons by means of which men have constructed, in the midst of an unfriendly world, their brief and precarious paradises.

The story of drug-taking constitutes one of the most curious and also, it seems to me, one of the most significant chapters in the natural history of human beings. Everywhere, at all times, men and women have sought, and duly found, the means of taking a holiday from the reality of their generally dull and often acutely unpleasant existence. A holiday out of space, out of time, in the eternity of sleep or ecstasy, in the heaven or the limbo of visionary phantasy. "Anywhere, anywhere out of the world."

Drug-taking, it is significant, plays an important part in almost every primitive religion. The Persians and, before them, the

*Greeks and probably the ancient Hindus used alcohol to produce
religious ecstasy; the Mexicans procured the beatific vision by eating
a poisonous cactus; a toadstool filled the Shamans of Siberia with
enthusiasm and endowed them with the gift of tongues. And so on.
The devotional exercises of the later mystics are all designed to
produce the drug's miraculous effects by purely psychological means.
How many of the current ideas of eternity, of heaven, of supernatural
states are ultimately derived from the experiences of drug-takers?*

*Primitive man explored the pharmaceutical avenues of
escape from the world with a truly astonishing thoroughness. Our
ancestors left almost no natural stimulant, or hallucinant, or
stupefacient, undiscovered. Necessity is the mother of invention;
primitive man, like his civilised descendant, felt so urgent a need to
escape occasionally from reality, that the invention of drugs was
fairly forced upon him.*

*All existing drugs are treacherous and harmful. The heaven
into which they usher their victims soon turns into a hell of sickness
and moral degradation. They kill, first the soul, then, in a few years,
the body. What is the remedy? "Prohibition" answer all contemporary
governments in chorus. But the results of prohibition are not
encouraging. Men and women feel such an urgent need to take
occasional holidays from reality, that they will do almost anything to
procure the means of escape. The only justification for prohibition
would be success; but it is not and, in the nature of things, cannot be
successful. The way to prevent people from drinking too much
alcohol, or becoming addicts to morphine or cocaine, is to give them
an efficient but wholesome substitute for these delicious and (in the
present imperfect world) necessary poisons. The man who invents
such a substance will be counted among the greatest benefactors of
suffering humanity."*

—ALDOUS HUXLEY, 1931

ON APRIL 16, 1943, Swiss researcher Albert Hofmann accidentally dosed himself with LSD-25, an experimental compound he had synthesized from ergot fungus. A few hours later, he was home in bed, experiencing "a not unpleasant state of drunkenness . . . characterized by an extremely stimulating fantasy." In drug lore, these events—the world's first acid trip—are on a par with Caesar crossing the Rubicon.

Outside the realm of drug lore, however, there are no monuments to Albert Hofmann, no streets named after him, no postage stamps depicting the Jonas Salk of psychedelia. In medical texts, he barely ranks. His employer, Sandoz Pharmaceuticals, was decidedly uncomfortable with LSD, marketing it (under the trade name Delysid) only to a chosen few researchers. The company proved even less enthusiastic about Hofmann's second Promethean breakthrough—in 1958, he succeeded in synthesizing psilocybin, the active ingredient in the magic mushrooms of Huatla de Jimenez. "LSD and everything connected with it were scarcely popular subjects to the top management," Hofmann recalled.[1]

The gulf between drug lore and straight history is vast. This is not surprising if you consider that drug lore is compiled pretty much exclusively by people who once used or continue to use drugs, whereas straight history is compiled by . . . straight people. If the latter were to acknowledge Hofmann at all, he would be portrayed as Dr. Frankenstein to the monster of the whole Day-Glo, instant-nirvana-seeking Sixties drug underground. With Tim Leary as Igor, scrounging the countryside for fresh brains, flipping the levers of the P.R. machinery . . .

Where straight history is concerned, drugs are no minor threat. Ethnobotanist Wade Davis offers this explanation: "Biodynamic plant preparations, be they poisons or hallucinogens, are inherently subversive—the poisons because they kill surreptitiously and the hallucinogens because they expose the frail, ambivalent position of man, perpetually on the cusp between nature, society, and the spirit world." [2]

Drugs, particularly hallucinogens such as LSD and psilocybin, don't just create a separate reality for the individual user. They create a separate reality that is *collective*. Drugworld, located somewhere off the coast of Western society, is not to be confused with Wonderland. Drugworld has patron saints (Hofmann; mycologists Gordon and Valentina Wasson), but it also has schisms and theological disputes. It has its clergy (underground chemists, contraband farmers) and its apostates (authors of self-help books). It has a Great War (America's "War on Drugs"), resistance heroes (William S. Burroughs), legions of nostalgic veterans, and too many walking wounded to count.

And of course, Drugworld has its own storehouse of art. Peter Max's butterflies hang next to Van Gogh's absinthe drinkers, Gauguin's Buddah and Dali's everything. Robert Heinlein and Herman Hesse share a shelf with Aldous Huxley. Carlos Castenada is over there by Cocteau. If a visitor scratches his head, wondering how these works came to co-exist within the same theme park, well, that head may need more . . . *expanding*.

But what happens when we leave Drugworld as, sooner or later, most of us must? We shrink back to earthly proportions and the visions vanish. We look back at the art and, sure enough, it's still there, and some of it is magnificent. But much of it isn't. The no-longer-altered consciousness is embarrassed. Read any good Heinlein lately?

Art is long, drugs wear off quickly. It is a mistake, we realize, to assume that a marriage between drugs and mind will beget lasting art, or an appreciation for worthwhile art. Yet the assumption persists, fueled by some powerful evidence: Coleridge attributed "Kubla Khan," his best poem, to the influence of laudanum. Milton "Mezz" Mezzrow, the bebopper whose name became a slang synonym for high-quality marijuana, insisted that pot "puts a musician in a real masterly sphere, and that's why so many jazzmen have used it."[3]

"I was convinced in advance," Aldous Huxley writes of his first mescaline experience, "that the drug would admit me, at least for a few hours, into the kind of inner world described by Blake."[4] Once the drug tourist has gained entry to that inner world, what's to say his visions won't be every bit as interesting as the "memorable fancies" of the poet? They might well be—but chances are they will lose something in the retelling. "Nothing in the world bores me more," Salvador Dali once said, "than people with the habit of recounting their dreams or their hallucinations, since not one of them is capable of bringing to life either."

"If you have no imagination," quips the dope dealer in Laurie Colwin's short story, "a Swiss pharmaceutical company will supply one for you. Isn't that wonderful what modern science does?" The writers represented in this anthology have no such lack of imagination. In the selections that follow they avail themselves of cocaine, moonshine, yage, eboka, opium, DM cough syrup—a thorough sampling of the pharmacopoeia. The Fang people, the early Indo-Europeans, and Tim Leary supply the scripture. Lewis Carroll and Philip Dick offer inspirational parables. Huxley and Robert Gilbert-Lecomte provide early warnings of drug hysteria. Thomas De Quincey and Jean Cocteau provide early warnings of, respectively, opium addiction and recovery. Bayard Taylor gets high. William Burroughs gets sick.

In each case, these writings stand the tests of time and sobriety. Preconceptions wither. Great minds—Baudelaire, Freud—are moved to write elegies to their preferred substance. One drug sends an Amazonian shaman into a trance. Another sends Hunter Thompson over the speed limit.

Viewed from the proper distance, the shores of Drugworld sparkle with genius.

— **RK**

Introduction

1. Albert Hofmann, *LSD: My Problem Child*, Tarcher, 1983

2. Wade Davis, *The Serpent and the Rainbow: A Harvard Scientist Uncovers the Startling Truth About the Secret World of Haitian Voodoo and Zombies*, Warner Books, 1985

3. Milton Mezzrow and Bernard Wolfe, *Really the Blues*, New Directions, 1946

4. Aldous Huxley, *The Doors of Perception*, Harper & Row, 1954

WILLIAM S. BURROUGHS

❊

IN SEARCH OF YAGE

APRIL 15

HOTEL NUEVO REGIS, BOGOTA

Dear Al:

Back in Bogota. I have a crate of Yage. I have taken it and know more or less how it is prepared. By the way you may see my picture in *Exposure.* I met a reporter going in as I was going out. Queer to be sure but about as appetizing as a hamper of dirty laundry. Not even after two months in the brush, my dear. This character is shaking down the South American continent for free food and transport, and discounts on everything he buys with a "We-got-like-two-kinds-of-publicity-favorable-and-unfavorable-which-do-you-want,-Jack?" routine. What a shameless mooch. But who am I to talk?

Flashback: Retraced my journey through Cali, Popayan and Pasto to Macoa. I was interested to note that Macoa dragged Schindler and two Englishmen as much as it did me.

This trip I was treated like visiting royalty under the mis-apprehension I was a representative of the Texas Oil Company travelling incognito. (Free boat rides, free plane rides, free chow; eating in officers' mess, sleeping in the governor's house.)

The Texas Oil Company surveyed the area a few years ago, found no oil and pulled out. But everyone in the Putumayo believes the Texas Company will return. Like the second coming of Christ. The governor told me the Texas Company had taken two samples of oil 80 miles apart and it was the same oil, so there was a pool of the stuff 80

1

miles across under Macoa. I heard this same story in a backwater area of East Texas where the oil company made a survey and found no oil and pulled out. Only in Texas the pool was 1,000 miles across. The beat town psyche is joined the world over like the oil pool. You take a sample anywhere and it's the same shit. And the governor thinks they are about to build a railroad from Pasto to Macoa, and an airport. As a matter of fact the whole of Putumayo region is on the down grade. The rubber business is shot, the cocoa is eaten up with broom rot, no price on rotenone since the war, land is poor and there is no way to get produce out. The dawdling psychophrenia of small town boosters. Like I should think some day soon boys will start climbing in through the transom and tunneling under the door.

Several times when I was drunk I told someone, 'Look. There is no oil here. That's why Texas pulled out. They won't ever come back. Understand?' But they couldn't believe it.

We went out to visit a German who owned a finca near Macoa. The British went looking for wild coca with an Indian guide. I asked the German about Yage.

'Sure,' he said, 'My Indians all use it.' A half hour later I had 20 pounds of Yage vine. No trek through virgin jungle and some old white haired character saying, 'I have been expecting you my son.' A nice German 10 minutes from Macoa.

The German also made a date for me to take Yage with the local Brujo (at that time I had no idea how to prepare it).

The medicine man was around 70 with a baby smooth face. There was a sly gentleness about him like an old time junkie. It was getting dark when I arrived at this dirt floor thatch shack for my Yage appointment. First thing he asked did I have a bottle. I brought a quart of aguardiente out of my knapsack and handed it to him. He took a long drink and passed the bottle to his assistant. I didn't take any as I wanted straight Yage kicks. The Brujo put the bottle beside him and squatted down by a bowl set on a tripod. Behind the bowl was a wood shrine with a picture of the Virgin, a crucifix, a wood idol, feathers and little packages tied with ribbons. The Brujo sat there a long time without moving. He took another long swig on the bottle. The women retired behind a bamboo partition and were not seen again. The Brujo began crooning over the bowl. I caught 'Yage Pintar' repeated over and over. He shook a little broom over a bowl and made a swishing noise. This is to whisk away evil spirits who might slip in the Yage. He took a drink and wiped his mouth and went on crooning. You can't hurry a Brujo. Finally he uncovered the bowl and dipped about an ounce more or less of black liquid which he handed me in a dirty red plastic cup. The liquid was oily and phosphorescent. I drank it straight down. Bitter foretaste of nausea. I handed the cup back and the medicine man and the assistant took a drink.

I sat there waiting for results and almost immediately had the impulse to say, 'That wasn't enough. I need more.' I have noticed this inexplicable impulse on the two occasions when I got an overdose of junk. Both times before the shot took effect, I said, 'This wasn't enough. I need more.'

Roy told me about a man who came out of jail clean and nearly died in Roy's room. 'He took the shot and right away said, "That wasn't enough" and fell on his face out cold. I dragged him out in the hall and called an ambulance. He lived.'

In two minutes a wave of dizziness swept over me and the hut began spinning. It was like going under ether, or when you are very drunk and lie down and the bed spins. Blue flashes passed in front of my eyes. The hut took on an archaic far Pacific look with Easter Island heads carved in the support posts. The assistant was outside lurking there with the obvious intent to kill me. I was hit by violent, sudden nausea and rushed for the door hitting my shoulder against the door post. I felt the shock but no pain. I could hardly walk. No coordination. My feet were like blocks of wood. I vomited violently leaning against a tree and fell down on the ground in helpless misery. I felt numb as if I was covered with layers of cotton. I kept trying to break out of this numb dizziness. I was saying over and over, 'All I want is out of here.' An uncontrollable mechanical silliness took possession of me. Hebephrenic meaningless repetitions. Larval beings passed before my eyes in a blue haze, each one giving an obscene, mocking squawk (I later identified this squawking as the croaking of frogs)—I must have vomited six times. I was on all fours convulsed with spasms of nausea. I could hear retching and groaning as if I was some one else. I was lying by a rock. Hours must have passed. The medicine man was standing over me. I looked at him for a long time before I believed he was really there saying, 'Do you want to come into the house?' I said, 'No,' and he shrugged and went back inside.

My arms and legs began to twitch uncontrollably. I reached for my nembutals with numb wooden fingers. It must have taken me ten minutes to open the bottle and pour out five capsules. Mouth was dry and I chewed the nembutals down somehow. The twitching spasms subsided slowly and I felt a little better and went into the hut. The blue flashes still in front of my eyes. Lay down and covered myself with a blanket. I had a chill like malaria. Suddenly very drowsy. Next morning I was all right except for a feeling of lassitude and a slight backlog nausea. I paid off the Brujo and walked back to town.

PETER MATTHIESSEN

❅

WESTWARD

ON HER FIRST drug trip, D freaked out; that is the drug term, and there is no better. She started to laugh, and her mouth opened wide and she could not close it; her armor had cracked, and all the night winds of the world went howling through. Turning to me, she saw my flesh dissolve, my head become a skull—the whole night went like that. Yet she later saw that she might free herself by living out the fear of death, the demoniac rage at one's own helplessness that drug hallucinations seem to represent, and in that way let go of a life-killing accumulation of defenses. And she accepted the one danger of the mystical search: there is no way back without doing oneself harm. Many paths appear, but once the way is taken, it must be followed to the end.

And so, with great courage, D tried again, and sometimes things went better. I remember an April afternoon in 1962, when we had taken LSD together. She came out onto the terrace of a country house and drifted toward me, down across the lawn. D had black hair and beautiful wide eyes; in the spring breeze and light of flowers, she looked bewitched. We had been quarreling in recent days, and recriminations rose, tumbling all over one another in the rush to be spoken, yet as we drew near, the arguments aired so often in the past rose one by one and passed away in silence. There was no need to speak, the other knew to the last word what would be said. Struck dumb by this telepathy, our mouths snapped shut at the same instant, then burst into smiles at the precise timing of this comic mime of our old fights; delighted, we embraced and laughed and laughed. And still not one word had been spoken; only later did we discover that all thoughts, laughter, and emotions had been not similar but *just the same, one mind, one Mind*, even to this: that as we held each other, both bodies

5

turned into sapling trees that flowed into each other, grew together in one strong trunk that pushed a taproot deeper and deeper into the ground.

And yet, and yet . . . an "I" remained, aware that something-was-happening, aware even that something-was-happening because of drugs. At no time did the "I" dissolve into the miracle.

Mostly D went on long, gray journeys, plagued by fear of death. I had bad trips, too, but they were rare; most were magic shows, mysterious, enthralling. After each—even the bad ones—I seemed to go more lightly on my way, leaving behind old residues of rage and pain. Whether joyful or dark, the drug vision can be astonishing, but eventually this vision will repeat itself, until even the magic show grows boring; for me, this occurred in the late 1960s, by which time D had already turned toward Zen.

Now those psychedelic years seem far away; I neither miss them nor regret them. Drugs can clear away the past, enhance the present; toward the inner garden, they can only point the way. Lacking the temper of ascetic discipline, the drug vision remains a sort of dream that cannot be brought over into daily life. Old mists may be banished, that is true, but the alien chemical agent forms another mist, maintaining the separation of the "I" from true experience of the One.

NELSON ALGREN

❖

THE MAN WITH THE
GOLDEN ARM

THE CLOCK IN the room above the Safari told only Junkie Time. For every hour here was Old Junkie's Hour and the walls were the color of all old junkies' dreams: the hue of diluted morphine in the moment before the needle draws the suffering blood.

Walls that went up and up like walls in a troubled dream. Walls like water where no legend could be written and no hand grasp metal or wood. For Nifty Louie paid the rent and Frankie knew too well who the landlord was. He had met him before, that certain down-at-heel vet growing stooped from carrying a thirty-five-pound monkey on his back. Frankie remembered that face, ravaged by love of its own suffering as by some endless all-night orgy. A face forged out of his own wound fever in a windy ward tent on the narrow Meuse. He had met Private McGantic before: both had served their country well.

This was the fellow who looked somehow a little like everyone else in the world and was more real to a junkie than any real man could ever be. The projected image of one's own pain when that pain has become too great to be borne. The image of one hooked so hopelessly on morphine that there would be no getting the monkey off without another's help. There are so few ways to help old sad frayed and weary West Side junkies.

Frankie felt no pity for himself, yet felt compassion for this McGantic. He worried, as the sickness rose in himself, about what in God's name McGantic would do tomorrow when the money and the morphine both gave out. Where then, in that terrible hour, would Private M. find the strength to carry the monkey through one more endless day?

By the time Frankie got inside the room he was so weak Louie had to help him onto the army cot beside the oil stove. He lay on his back with one arm flung across his eyes as if in shame; and his lips were blue with cold. The pain had hit him with an icy fist in the groin's very pit, momentarily tapering off to a single probing finger touching the genitals to get the maximum of pain. He tried twisting to get away from the finger: the finger was worse than the fist. His throat was so dry that, though he spoke, the lips moved and made no sound. But Fomorowski read such lips well.

"Fix me. Make it stop. Fix me."

"I'll fix you, Dealer," Louie assured him softly.

Louie had his own bedside manner. He perched on the red leather and chrome bar stool borrowed from the Safari, with the amber toes of his two-tone shoes catching the light and the polo ponies galloping down his shirt. This was Nifty Louie's Hour. The time when he did the dealing and the dealer had to take what Louie chose to toss him in Louie's own good time.

He lit a match with his fingertip and held it away from the bottom of the tiny glass tube containing the fuzzy white cap of morphine, holding it just far enough away to keep the cap from being melted by the flame. There was time and time and lots of time for that. Let the dealer do a bit of melting first; the longer it took the higher the price. "You can pay me off when Zero pays you," he assured Frankie. There was no hurry. "You're good with me any time, Dealer."

Frankie moaned like an animal that cannot understand its own pain. His shirt had soaked through and the pain had frozen so deep in his bones nothing could make him warm again.

"Hit me, Fixer. Hit me."

A sievelike smile drained through Louie's teeth. This was his hour and this hour didn't come every day. He snuffed out the match's flame as it touched his fingers and snapped the head of another match into flame with his nail, letting its glow flicker one moment over that sievelike smile; then brought the tube down cautiously and watched it dissolve at the flame's fierce touch. When the stuff had melted he held both needle and tube in one hand, took the dealer's loose-hanging arm firmly with the other and pumped it in a long, loose arc. Frankie let him swing it as if it were attached to someone else. The cold was coming *up* from within now: a colorless cold spreading through stomach and liver and breathing across the heart like an odorless gas. To make the very brain tighten and congeal under its icy touch.

"Warm. Make me warm."

And still there was no rush, no hurry at all. Louie pressed the hypo down to the cotton; the stuff came too high these days to lose the fraction of a drop. "Don't vomit, student," he taunted Frankie to remind him of the first fix he'd had after his discharge but it was too cold to answer. He was falling between glacial walls, he didn't know how anyone could fall so far away from everyone else in the world. So far to fall, so cold all the way, so steep and dark between those morphine-colored walls of Private McGantic's terrible pit.

He couldn't feel Louie probing into the dark red knot above his elbow at all. Nor see the way the first blood sprayed faintly up into the delicate hypo to tinge the melted morphine with blood as warm as the needle's heated point.

When Louie sensed the vein he pressed it down with the certainty of a good doctor's touch, let it linger a moment in the vein to give the heart what it needed and withdrew gently, daubed the blood with a piece of cotton, tenderly, and waited.

Louie waited. Waited to see it hit.

Louie liked to see the stuff hit. It meant a lot to Louie, seeing it hit. "Sure I like to watch," he was ready to acknowledge any time. "Man, their *eyes* when that big drive hits 'n goes tinglin' down to the toes. They retch, they sweat, they itch then the big drive hits 'n here they come out of it cryin' like a baby 'r laughin' like a loon. *Sure* I like to watch. *Sure* I like to see it hit. Heroin got the drive awright—but there's not a tingle to a ton—you got to get M to get that tingle-tingle."

It hit all right. It hit the heart like a runaway locomotive, it hit like a falling wall. Frankie's whole body lifted with that smashing surge, the very heart seemed to lift up-up-up—then rolled over and he slipped into a long warm bath with one long orgasmic sigh of relief. Frankie opened his eyes.

He was in a room. Somebody's dust-colored wavy-walled room and he wasn't quite dead after all. He had died, had felt himself fall away and die but now he wasn't dead any more. Just sick. But not too sick. He wasn't going to be really sick, he wasn't a student any more. Maybe he wasn't going to be sick at all, he was beginning to feel just right.

Then it went over him like a dream where everything is love and he wasn't even sweating. All he had to do the rest of his life was to lie right here feeling better and better with every beat of his heart till he'd never felt so good in all his life.

"Wow," he grinned gratefully at Louie, "that was one good *whan.*"

"I seen it," Louie boasted smugly. "I seen it was one good *whan*"—and lapsed into the sort of impromptu jargon which pleases junkies for no reason they can say—"vraza-s'vraza-s'vraza—it was one good *whan-whan-whan.*" He dabbed a silk handkerchief at a blob of blood oozing where the needle had entered Frankie's arm.

"There's a silver buck and a buck 'n a half in change in my jacket pocket," Frankie told him lazily. "I'm feelin' too good to get up 'n get it myself."

Louie reached in the pocket with the handkerchief bound about his palm and plucked the silver out. Two-fifty for a quarter grain wasn't too high. He gave Frankie the grin that drained through the teeth for a receipt. The dealer was coming along nicely these days, thank you.

The dealer didn't know that yet, of course. That first fix had only cost him a dollar, and it had quieted the everlasting dull ache in his stomach and sent him coasting one whole week end. So what was the use of spending forty dollars in the bars when you could do better at home on one? That was how Frankie had it figured *that* week end. To Louie, listening close, he'd already talked like a twenty-dollar-a-day man.

Given a bit of time.

And wondered idly now where in the world the dealer would get that kind of money when the day came that he'd need half a C just to taper off. He'd get it all right. They always got it. He'd seen them coming in the rain, the unkjays with their peculiarly rigid, panicky walk, wearing some policeman's castoff rubbers, no socks at all, a pair of Salvation Army pants a size too small or a size too large and a pajama top for a shirt—but with twenty dollars clutched in the sweating palm for that big twenty-dollar fix.

"Nothing can take the place of junk—just junk"—the dealer would learn. As Louie himself had learned long ago.

Louie was the best fixer of them all because he knew what it was to need to get well. Louie had had a big habit—he was one man who could tell you you lied if you said no junkie could kick the habit once he was hooked. For Louie was the one junkie in ten thousand who'd kicked it and kicked it for keeps.

He'd taken the sweat cure in a little Milwaukee Avenue hotel room cutting himself down, as he put it, "from monkey to zero." From three full grains a day to one, then a half of that and a half of that straight down to zero, though he'd been half out of his mind with the pain two nights running and so weak, for days after, that he could hardly tie his own shoelaces.

Back on the street at last, he'd gotten the chuck horrors: for two full days he'd eaten candy bars, sweet rolls and strawberry malteds. It had seemed that there would be no end to his hunger for sweets.

Louie never had the sweet-roll horrors any more. Yet sometimes himself sensed that something had twisted in his brain those nights when he'd gotten the monkey off his back on Milwaukee Avenue.

"*Habit? Man,*" he liked to remember, "I had a great *big* habit. One time I knocked out one of my own teet' to get the gold for a fix. You call that bein' hooked or not? *Hooked?* Man, I wasn't hooked, I was *crucified.* The monkey got so big he was carryin' *me.* 'Cause the way it starts is like this, students: you let the habit feed you first 'n one mornin' you wake up 'n you're feedin' the habit.

"But don't tell *me* you can't kick it if you *want* to. When I hear a junkie tell me he wants to kick the habit but he just can't I know he lies even if *he* don't know he does. He *wants* to carry the monkey, he's punishin' hisself for somethin' 'n don't even know it. It's what I was doin' for six years, punishin' myself for things I'd done 'n thought I'd forgot. So I told myself how I wasn't to blame for what I done in the first place, I was only tryin' to live like everyone else 'n doin' them things was the only way I had of livin'. Then I got forty grains 'n went up to the room 'n went from monkey to nothin' in twenny-eight days 'n that's nine-ten years ago 'n the monkey's dead."

"The monkey's never dead, fixer," Frankie told him knowingly.

Louie glanced at Frankie slyly. "You know that awready, Dealer? You know how he don't die? It's what they say awright, the monkey never dies. When you kick him off he just hops onto somebody else's back." Behind the film of glaze that always veiled Louie's eyes Frankie saw the twisted look. "*You* got my monkey, Dealer? You take my nice old monkey away from me? Is that my monkey ridin' your back these days, Dealer?"

The color had returned to Frankie's cheeks, he felt he could make it almost any minute now. "No more for me, Fixer," he assured Louie confidently. "Somebody else got to take your monkey. I had the Holy Jumped-up-Jesus Horrors for real this time—'n I'm one guy knows when he got enough. I learned my lesson *good.* Fixer—you just give the boy with the golden arm his very latest fix."

"What time you have to be by Schwiefka?" Louie wanted to know.

Frankie brushed the hair, matted by drying sweat, off his forehead and glanced at his watch. Sweat had steamed the crystal, he couldn't read the hands. He dried it on the bedcover, for his shirt was still wringing damp. "Nine-thirty—I got an hour and a half. I'll make it."

"Crawl your dirty gut over to the table," Louie advised him. "Can you take coffee?"

Frankie thought it over carefully. "In a couple minutes," he decided. "Half a cup anyhow."

"You better," Louie counseled him, "You're likely to get so hungry around one o'clock you won't be able to steal enough for another fix."

Louie busied himself over the little gas plate in the corner and didn't look around till he heard the dealer move. Frankie was swaying but he was on his feet and he'd make it fine, all night. All night and maybe the whole week end. It was hard to tell with these joy-poppers. "That stuff cost me more than the last batch," he said indifferently.

"I know," Frankie grinned, "you told me," sounding bored while he used a dish towel on his chest beneath the soiled undershirt. "Keeps goin' up all the time, like a kite with the string broke off." His eyes were growing heavy, the towel slipped out of his fingers and caught under his arm, hanging there like a flag at half-mast. The junkies' flag of truce, to guard him as he slept. There beneath a single bulb, flat on his feet, the knees bending a little, the slight body swaying a bit, the flat-bridged nose looking peaked. Hush: he is sleeping the strange light sleep.

"I can't help it when they up the price on me," Louie added. "They got me, Dealer, that's all."

"The way you got me," Frankie murmured knowingly. Then he smelled the coffee, got down to the table in front of a cup, took one sip and, smiling softly, started to let his head fall toward his chest. Louie got the cup out of the way of that blond mop before it bent to the table.

"Now look at him sleep, with all his woes," Louie teased him almost tenderly; and Frankie heard from a dream of falling snow.

The snow fell in soft, suspended motion, as snow does in dreams alone. He coasted without effort around and around and down a bit and then up like that kite with the broken string and came coasting, where all winds were dying, back down to the table where Fixer sat waiting.

"I got no woes," he laughed among slow-falling flakes, seeing Louie smiling through the snow. "You got a woe, Fixer?" he asked. "It's what I been needin'—a couple good old secondhand woes."

"You'll have a couple dozen if you ain't boxin' that deck by Schwiefka's suckers in half an hour," Louie reminded him.

Frankie got the rest of the coffee down. "Squarin' up, Fixer," he assured Louie. He held the cup out at arm's length. "Look at that." Not a tremor from shoulder to fingertip. "The sheep 'r gonna get a fast shearin' t'night, Fixer," he boasted with a strange and steady calm.

"I think you're one of the weaker sheep yourself," Louie decided silently.

FLORENCE
NIGHTINGALE

❈

OPIUM

NOTHING DID ME any good, but a curious little new fangled operation of putting opium under the skin which relieves one for twenty-four hours—but does not improve the vivacity or serenity of one's intellect.

AMOS TUTUOLA

❊

THE PALM-WINE DRINKARD

I WAS A palm-wine drinkard since I was a boy of ten years of age. I had no other work more than to drink palm-wine in my life. In those days we did not know other money, except COWRIES, so that everything was very cheap, and my father was the richest man in our town.

My father got eight children and I was the eldest among them, all of the rest were hard workers, but I myself was an expert palm-wine drinkard. I was drinking palm-wine from morning till night and from night till morning. By that time I could not drink ordinary water at all except palm-wine.

But when my father noticed that I could not do any more work than to drink, he engaged an expert palm-wine tapster for me; he had no other work more than to tap palm-wine every day.

So my father gave me a palm-tree farm which was nine miles square and it contained 560,000 palm-trees, and this palm-wine tapster was tapping one hundred and fifty kegs of palm-wine every morning, but before 2 o'clock p.m., I would have drunk all of it; after that he would go and tap another 75 kegs in the evening which I would be drinking till morning. So my friends were uncountable by that time and they were drinking palm-wine with me from morning till a late hour in the night. But when my palm-wine tapster completed the period of 15 years that he was tapping the palm-wine for me, then my father died suddenly, and when it was the 6th month after my father had died, the tapster went to the palm-tree farm on a Sunday evening to tap palm-wine for me. When he reached the farm, he climbed one of the tallest palm-trees in the farm to tap palm-wine but as he was tapping on, he fell down unexpectedly and died at the foot of the palm-tree as a result of injuries. As I was waiting for him to bring the palm-wine, when I saw that he did not return in time, because he was not keeping me long like that before, then I called two of my friends to accompany me to the farm. When we reached the farm, we began to look at every palm-tree, after a while we found him under the palm-tree, where he fell down and died.

But what I did first when we saw him dead there, was that I climbed another palm-tree which was near the spot, after that I tapped palm-wine and drank it to my satisfaction before I came back to the spot. Then both my friends who accompanied me to the farm and I dug a pit under the palm-tree that he fell down as a grave and buried him there, after that we came back to the town.

When it was early in the morning of the next day, I had no palm-wine to drink at all, and throughout that day I felt not so happy as before; I was seriously sat down in my parlour, but when it was the third day that I had no palm-wine at all, all my friends did not come to my house again, they left me there alone, because there was no palm-wine for them to drink.

But when I completed a week in my house without palm-wine, then I went out and, I saw one of them in the town, so I saluted him, he answered but he did not approach me at all, he hastily went away.

Then I started to find out another expert palm-wine tapster, but I could not get me one who could tap the palm-wine to my requirement. When there was no palm-wine for me to drink I started to drink ordinary water which I was unable to taste before, but I did not satisfy with it as palm-wine.

When I saw that there was no palm-wine for me again, and nobody could tap it for me, then I thought within myself that old people were saying that the whole people who had died in this world, did not go to heaven directly, but they were living in one place somewhere in this world. So that I said that I would find out where my palm-wine tapster who died was.

One fine morning, I took all my native juju and also my father's juju with me and I left my father's hometown to find out whereabouts was my tapster who had died.

But in those days, there were many wild animals and every place was covered by thick bushes and forests; again, towns and villages were not near each other as nowadays, and as I was travelling from bushes to bushes and from forests to forests and sleeping inside it for many days and months, I was sleeping on the branches of trees, because spirits etc. were just like partners, and to save my life from them; and again I could spend two or three months before reaching a town or a village. Whenever I reached a town or a village, I would spend almost four months there, to find out my palm-wine tapster from the inhabitants of that town or village and if he did not reach there, then I would leave there and continue my journey to another town or village. After the seventh month that I had left my home town, I reached a town and went to an old man, this old man was not a really man, he was a god and he was eating with his wife when I reached there. When I entered the house I saluted both of them, they answered me well, although nobody should enter his house like that as he was a god, but I myself was a god and juju-man. Then I told the old man (god) that I am looking for my palm-wine tapster who had died in my town some time ago, he did not answer to my question but asked me first what was my name? I replied that my name was "Father of gods" who could do everything in this world, then he said: "was that true" and I said yes; after that he told me to go to his native black-smith in an unknown place, or who was living in another town, and bring the right thing that he had told the black-smith to make for him. He said that if I could bring the right thing that he told the black-smith to make for him, then he would believe that I was the "Father of gods who could do everything in this world" and he would tell me where my tapster was.

Immediately this old man told or promised me so, I went away, but after I had travelled about one mile away then I used of my juju and at once I changed into a very big bird and flew back to the roof of the old man's house; but as I stood on the roof of his house, many people saw me there. They came nearer and looked at me on the roof, so when the old man noticed that many had surrounded his house and were looking at the roof, he and his wife came out from the house and when he saw me (bird) on the roof, he told his wife that if he had not sent me to his native black-smith to bring the bell that he told the black-smith to make for him, he would tell me to mention the name of the bird. But at the same time that he said so, I knew what he wanted from the black-smith and I flew away to his black-smith, then when I reached there I told the black-smith that the old man (god) told me to bring his bell which he had told him to make for him. So the black-smith gave me the bell; after that, I returned to the old man with the bell and when he saw me with the bell, he and his wife were surprised and also shocked at that moment.

After that he told his wife to give me food, but after I had eaten the food, he told me again, that there remained another wonderful work to do for him, before he would tell me whereabouts my tapster was. When it was 6:30 a.m. of the following morning, he (god) woke me up, and gave me a wide and strong net which was the same colour as the ground of that town. He told me to go and bring "Death" from his house with the net. When I left his house or the town about a mile, there I saw a junction of roads and was doubtful when I reached the junction, I did not know which was Death's road among these roads, and when I thought within myself that as it was the market day, and all the market goers would soon be returning from the market—I lied down on the middle of the roads, I put my head to one of the roads, my left hand to one, right hand to another one, and both my feet to the rest, after that I pretended as I had slept there. But when all the market goers were returning from the market, they saw me lied down there and shouted thus:—"Who was the mother of this fine boy, he slept on the roads and put his head towards Death's road."

Then I began to travel on Death's road, and I spent about eight hours to reach there, but to my surprise I did not meet anybody on this road until I reached there and I was afraid because of that. When I reached his (Death's) house, he was not at home by that time, he was in his yam garden which was very close to his house, and I met a small rolling drum in his verandah, then I beat it to Death as a sign of salutation. But when he (Death) heard the sound of the drum, he said thus:—"Is that man still alive or dead?" Then I replied "I am still alive and I am not a dead man."

But at the same time that he heard so from me, he was greatly annoyed and he commanded the drum with a kind of voice that the strings of the drum should tight me there; as a matter of fact, the strings of the drum tightened me so that I was hardly breathing.

When I felt that these strings did not allow me to breathe and again every part of my body was bleeding too much, then I myself commanded the ropes of the yams in his garden to tight him there, and the yams in his garden to tight him there, and the yam stakes should begin to beat him also. After I had said so and at the same time, all the ropes of the yams in his garden tighted him hardly, and all the yam stakes were beating him repeatedly, so when he (Death) saw that these stakes were beating him repeatedly, then he commanded the strings of the drum which tighted me to release me, and I was released at the same time. But when I saw that I was released, then I myself commanded the ropes of the yams to release him and the yam stakes to stop beating him, and he was released at once. After he was released by the ropes of yams and yam stakes, he came to his house and met me at his verandah, then we shook hands together, and he told me to enter the house, he put me to one of his rooms, and after a while, he brought food to me and we ate it together, after that we started conversations which went thus:—He (Death) asked me from where did I come? I replied that I came from a certain town which was not so far from his place. Then he asked what did I come to do? I told him that I had been hearing about him in my town and all over the world and I thought within myself that one day I should come and visit or to know him personally. After that he replied that his work was only to kill the people of the world, after that he got up and told me to follow him and I did so.

He took me around his house and his yam garden too, he showed me the skeleton bones of human-beings which he had killed since a century ago and showed me many other things also, but there I saw that he was using skeleton bones of human-beings as fuel woods and skull heads of human-beings as his basins, plates and tumblers etc.

Nobody was living near or with him there, he was living lonely, even bush animals and birds were very far away from his house. So when I wanted to sleep at night, he gave me a wide black cover cloth and then gave me a separate room to sleep inside, but when I entered the room, I met a bed which was made with bones of human-beings; but as this bed was terrible to look at or to sleep on it, I slept under it instead, because I knew his trick already. Even as this bed was very terrible, I was unable to sleep under as I lied down there because of fear of the bones of human-beings, but I lied down there awoke. To my surprise was that when it was about two o'clock in the mid-night, there I saw somebody enter into the room cautiously with a heavy club in his hands, he came nearer to the bed on which he had told me to sleep, then he clubbed the bed with all his power, he clubbed the center of the bed thrice and he returned cautiously, he thought that I slept on that bed and he thought also that he had killed me.

But when it was 6 o'clock early in the morning, I first woke up and went to the room in which he slept, I woke him up, so when he heard my voice, he was frightened, even he could not salute me at all when he got up from his bed, because he thought that he had killed me last night.

But the second day that I slept there, he did not attempt to do anything again, but I woke up by two o'clock of that night, and went to the road which I should follow to the town and I travelled about a quarter of a mile to his house, then I stopped and dug a pit of his (Death's) size on the centre of that road, after that I spread the net which the old man gave me to bring him (Death) with on that pit, then I returned to his house, but he did not wake up as I was playing this trick.

When it was 6 o'clock in the morning, I went to his door and woke him up as usual, then I told him that I wanted to return to my town this morning, so that I wanted him to lead me a short distance; then he got up from his bed and began to lead me as I told him, but when he led me to the place that I had dug, I told him to sit down, so I myself sat down on the road side, but as he sat down on the net, he fell into the pit, and without any ado I rolled up the net with him and put him on my head and I kept going to the old man's house who told me to go and bring him Death.

PAUL GAUGUIN

❊

DRINKING ABSINTHE
WITH VAN GOGH

THAT SAME EVENING we went into a café. He ordered a light absinthe. Suddenly he flung the glass and its contents into my face. I managed to duck and grab him, take him out of the café and across the Place Victor Hugo. A few minutes later, Vincent was in his own bed and in a matter of seconds had fallen asleep, not to awaken until morning.

When he awoke he was perfectly calm and said to me: "My dear Gauguin, I have a dim recollection that I offended you last night."

JIM HOGSHIRE

❖

THE ELECTRIC COUGH SYRUP ACID TEST

THIS ISSUE'S PILL review is devoted to a chemical called Dextromethorphan Hydrobromide, the "DM" in DM cough syrups such as Robitussin Maximum Strength Cough. It's one of the most mystifying drugs in the pharmacopia. Even though it can be found in virtually every over-the-counter cold, flu, and cough remedy, most reference works hardly mention it; when they do, their information is sketchy and sometimes contradictory.

One reference book called it a "narcotic antagonist" with "very good analgesic" properties. Other descriptions say DM is a cough suppressant only and does not kill pain. It is supposedly non-addicting. And it's not supposed to get you high—though legions of high-school and college students have formed an entirely different opinion. DM produces "full warping of subspace," in the words of one experimenter, who took more than the recommended dosage. "Pin Head with expansive arms/legs. Incredible head size. Warping and folding of body. Incredible spatial distortions."

With this in mind, your faithful editor decided to carry out a Robitussin experiment of his own.

LAST NIGHT I drank about eight ounces of DM cough syrup. I was feeling kind of achy and wanted to see if it would kill pain. After a couple of hours all my pain had gone away, and I went to bed. It was midnight, but I felt neither awake nor asleep. It was like a typical narcotic high—mildly content, kind of nodding—but not as pleasant.

At four o'clock in the morning I woke up suddenly and remembered that I had to go to Kinko's copy shop and that I had to shave off about a week's worth of stubble from my face. These ideas were very clear to me. That may seem normal, but the fact was that *I had a reptilian brain.* My whole way of thinking and perceiving had changed. I had full control over my motor functions, but I felt ungainly. I was detached from my body, as if I were on laughing gas.

So I got in the shower and shaved. While I was shaving I "thought" that for all I knew I was hacking my face to pieces. Since I didn't see any blood or feel any pain I didn't worry about it. Had I looked down and seen that I had grown another limb, I wouldn't have been surprised at all; I would have just used it. Looking back, I realize that I had already lost all sense of time.

The world became a binary place of dark and light, on and off, safety and danger. I felt a need, determined it was hunger, and ate almonds until I didn't feel the need any more. Same thing with water. It was like playing a game. I sat at my desk and tried to write down how this felt so I could look at it later. I wrote down the word "Cro-Magnon." I was very aware that I was stupid. I think I probably seemed like Benny on *L.A. Law.*

I thought I would have trouble driving but I had none. I only felt "unsafe" in the dark street until I got into the "safe" car. Luckily there were only a couple of people in Kinko's and one of them was a friend. She confirmed that my pupils were of different sizes. One wasn't quite round. I was fucked up.

I KNEW THERE was no way I could know if I was correctly adhering to social customs. I didn't even know how to modulate my voice. Was I talking too loud? Did I look like a regular person? I understood that I was involved in a big contraption called civilization and that certain things were expected of me, but I could not comprehend what the hell those things might be.

All the words that came out of my mouth seemed equal. Instead of saying "reduce it about 90 percent" I could have said "two eggs and some toast, please." The whole world was broken down into elemental parts, each being of equal "value" to the whole—which is to say, of no value at all.

I sat at a table and read a newspaper. It was the most absurd thing I had ever seen! Each story purported to be a description of a thing or an event, or was supposed to cover "news" of reality in another place. This seemed stupid. An article on the war in Burma was described as "the war the West forgot." It had an "at-a-glance" chart that said Burma was approximately three times the size of the state of Washington. This was meaningless and I knew it. The story did not even begin to describe the tiniest fragment of the reality of what was happening in that place. Since I hadn't always been a reptile, I knew things were what they call "complicated" and that the paper's pitiful attempt to categorize individuals as "rebels" or "insurgents" or to describe the reasons for the agony was ridiculous. I laughed out loud.

I found being a reptile kind of pleasant. I was content to sit there and monitor my surroundings. I was alert but not anxious. Every now and then I would be a "reality check" to make sure I wasn't masturbating or strangling someone, because of my vague awareness that more was expected of me than just being a reptile. At one point I ventured across the street to a hamburger place to get something to eat. It was closed and yet there were workers inside. This truly confused me, and I considered trying to find a way to simply run in, grab some food, and make off with it. Luckily, the store opened (it was now 6 A.M.) and I entered the front door like a normal customer.

It was difficult to remember how to perform a money-for-merchandise transaction and even more difficult to put it into words, but I was eventually successful. I ate the hamburger slowly and deliberately. If I had become full before I finished the hamburger, I think I would have simply let it fall from my hands.

The life of a reptile may seem boring to us, but I was never bored when I was a reptile. If something started to hurt me, I took steps to get away from it; if it felt better over there, that's where I stayed. Now, twenty-four hours later, I'm beginning to get my neocortex back (I think). Soon, I hope to be human again.

JEAN COCTEAU

❖

DETOX DIARY

WITH OPIUM, EUPHORIA leads the way to death. The tortures come from going against the current back toward life. A whole springtime drives the veins to madness, sweeping along ice and molten lava.

I advise the addict who has been deprived for eight days to bury his head in his arm, to glue his ear to that arm, and to wait. Upheavals, riots, factories exploding, armies retreating, flood—in the starry night of the human body, the ear bears witness to an entire apocalypse.

DON'T EXPECT BETRAYAL from me. Naturally opium remains unique in offering a euphoria superior to that of sobriety. I owe it my perfect hours. It's a pity that instead of perfecting the process of detoxification, science doesn't endeavor to render opium harmless.

But here we come back to the problem of progress. Is suffering an obligation or something lyrical?

It seems to me that, on an earth so old, so wrinkled, so plastered over, so encrusted with compromise and laughable conventions, non-addictive opium would improve people's manners and cause more good than the fever of activity causes harm.

My nurse tells me: "You're the first patient I've seen writing by the eighth day."

I'm fully aware that I'm sticking a spoon into the soft tapioca of young cells, that I'm interfering with a step in the process, but I'm burning myself and will always do so. In two weeks, despite these notes, I will no longer believe in what I'm going through now. I must leave a record of this journey that memory moves past. When this is impossible, I must write, draw, without accepting the romantic invitations of pain, without enjoying suffering as if it were music, writing with my feet if necessary, to help doctors who would learn nothing from idleness.

CERTAIN ORGANISMS ARE born to become a prey for drugs. They require a corrective, without which they are unable to make contact with the outside world. They float. They vegetate in the twilight. The world remains a ghost until some substance can give it a body.

Sometimes these poor souls live out their days without ever finding the slightest remedy. Other times the remedy that they find kills them.

It's a lucky thing when opium can steady them and provide these souls of cork with a diver's suit. Because the harm caused by opium will be less than that of other substances and less than the illness they are seeking to cure.

THE PURITY OF a revolution can last but fifteen days.

That is why a poet, a revolutionary of the soul, limits himself to about-faces of the mind.

Every fifteen days I change the show. For me opium is a rebellion. Addiction is a rebellion. Detox is a rebellion. Forget my artworks. Each one guillotines the other. My sole working method: I aim to spare myself Napoleon.

WE ARE NO longer, alas, a race of farmers and shepherds. There is no doubting our need for another therapeutic system to defend the over-burdened nervous system. For that reason it is crucial that we discover a way to render harmless the beneficial substances that the body has such trouble eliminating, or to shield nerve cells.

Tell this transparent truth to a doctor and he shrugs his shoulders. He mentions literary devices, utopia, the ravings of an addict.

I contend, however, that one day we will use sedatives without danger, without addiction, that we'll laugh at the straw-man of Drugs, and that the newly tamed opium will assuage the evil of cities where trees once died on their feet.

THE FATAL BOREDOM of the recovering opium-smoker! Everything that happens in one's life, even love, happens on an express train racing toward death. To smoke opium is to jump off the moving train, to concern oneself with something other than life or death.

IF AN OPIUM-SMOKER, ravaged by the drug, questions himself honestly, he will always find he's paying the price of some misdeed or shortcoming, and that this is turning opium against him.

The patience of the poppy. He who has smoked will smoke. Opium knows how to wait.

ONE ALWAYS SPEAKS of the slavery of opium. Its organization of time imposes discipline, but also provides freedom. Freedom from callers, from people sitting around in circles. I must add that opium is antithetical to the Pravaz syringe. It reassures. It reassures by its luxury, by its rites, by the anti-medical elegance of its lamps, burners, pipes, by the ancient practice of this exquisite poisoning.

I'M NOT A recovering addict who is proud of his effort. I'm ashamed to be chased out of this world, next to which sobriety resembles those wretched newsreels in which politicians unveil statues.

PICASSO USED TO say to me: *The smell of opium is the least stupid smell in the world.* Only the smell of a circus or a seaport comes close.

Raw opium. If you don't lock it away in a metal safe and you make do with a simple box, the black snake will be quick to creep out. Be forewarned: It climbs walls, goes downstairs, floor after floor, turns, passes through the hall and the courtyard, under the archway, and will soon be coiled around the policeman's neck.

DURING MY STAY in this clinic I wanted to record these notations, especially the contradictions, in order to follow the stages of treatment. The idea was to speak of opium without shame, without literature, and without any medical knowledge.

The specialists seem unaware of the world that separates the opium addict from victims of other poisons—the drug from the Drugs.

I'm not trying to defend the drug; I'm trying to see it clearly in the dark, to walk forward on level ground, to come face-to-face with problems that are always approached from the side.

THE HALF-SLEEP of opium makes us turn down corridors and cross hallways and push open doors and lose ourselves in a world where people startled awake are horribly afraid of us.

THE OPIUM-SMOKER gets a bird's eye view of himself.

OPIUM IS THE only vegetable substance that speaks to us of the vegetable state. Through it we have an idea of this other speed of plants.

NORMAL MAN: Smoker of tree sap, why live this life? It'd be better just to throw yourself out the window.

SMOKER: Impossible: I'd just float away.

NORMAL MAN: Your body would get down quickly enough.

SMOKER: I'd arrive slowly after it.

OPIUM RELEASES THE mind. It never makes one witty. It lets the mind wander. It does not lead it to a point.

NOW THAT I am cured, I feel empty, poor, heartbroken, sick. I'm adrift. The day after tomorrow I check out of the clinic. Check out to where? Three weeks ago I felt a sort of happiness. I was asking M . . . about altitudes, about little inns in the snow. I was going to be released. In fact it was a book that was going to be released [*Les Enfants Terribles*]. It's a book that is going to be released, that is *due to be released*, as the publishers say. Not me. I could die and it would make no difference to the book. . . . The same trick happens over and over again, and we always let ourselves be taken in by it.

It was difficult to see how a book could be written in seventeen days. I might have thought it would have something to do with me. The work that exploits me needed opium; it needed me to give up opium; once more I am tricked. And I wonder: will I or won't I start smoking opium again? Useless to pretend nonchalance, dear poet. I'll start smoking again if my work wants me to.

AND IF OPIUM wants me to.

LAURIE COLWIN

❖

THE ACHIEVE OF, THE MASTERY OF THE THING

ONCE UPON A time, I was Professor Thorne Speizer's stoned wife, and what a time that was. My drug of choice was plain, old-fashioned marijuana—these were the early days when that was what an ordinary person could get. By the time drugs got more interesting, I felt too old to change. I stood four-square behind reefer except when a little opiated hash came alone, which was not often.

Thorne was an assistant professor when I first met him. I took his Introduction to Modern European History—a class I was compelled to take and he was forced to teach. Thorne was twenty-seven and rather a young Turk. I was twenty-one and rather a young pothead. I sat in the back of the class and contemplated how I could get my hands on Thorne and freak him out. I liked the idea that I might bring a little mayhem into the life of a real adult. Thorne was older and had a job. That made him a real citizen in my eyes. He also had an extremely pleasing shape, a beautiful smile, and thick brown hair. His manner in class was absolutely professional and rather condescending. Both of these attitudes gave me the shivers.

I employed the tricks childish adolescents use to make the substitute math teacher in high school nervous. I stared at his fly. Then at stared at him in a wide-eyed, moronic way. At a point of desperation when I felt he would never notice me, I considered drooling. I smiled in what I hoped was a promising and tempting fashion.

It turned out that Thorne was not so hard to get. He was only waiting for me to stop being his student and then he pounced on me. I was high during our courtship so I did not actually notice when things got out of hand. I was looking for a little fun. Thorne wanted to get married. I felt, one lazy afternoon when a little high-quality grass had unexpectedly come my way, that a person without ambition or goals should do something besides smoke marijuana, and marriage was certainly something to do. Furthermore, I was truly crazy about Thorne.

I got wrecked on my wedding day. I stood in front of the mirror in my wedding dress and stared intently at my stick of grass. You should not smoke this on this day of days, I said to myself, lighting up. Surely if you are going to take this serious step, I said, inhaling deeply, you ought to do it straight.

You may well imagine how hard it was for an innocent college girl to score in those dark times. You had to run into some pretty creepy types to get what you wanted. These types preferred heavier substances such as smack and goofballs. How very puzzled they were at the sight of a college girl in her loafers and loden coat. For a while they thought I was a narc. After they got used to me they urged me to stick out my arm and smack up with them, but I declined. The channels through which you found these types were so complicated that by the time you got to them you forgot exactly how you got to them in the first place, and after a while they died or disappeared or got busted and you were then left to some jerky college boy who sold speed at exam time as well as some sort of homegrown swill that gave you a little buzz and a headache.

Of course I did not tell Thorne that I used this mild but illegal hallucinogen. He would have been horrified, I believed. I liked believing that. It made me feel very free. Thorne would take care of the worrying and I would get high. I smoked when he was out of the room, or out of the house. I smoked in the car, in the bathroom, in the attic, in the woods. I thank God that Thorne, like most privileged children, had allergies and for a good half of the year was incapable of detecting smoke in the house. And of course, he never noticed that I was stoned since I had been stoned constantly since the day we met.

Thorne took me away to a pastoral men's college where there was sure to be no drugs, I felt. That was an emblem of how far gone I was about him—that I could be dragged off to such an environment. However, a brief scan of the campus turned up a number of goofy stares, moronic giggles, and out-of-it grins. It did not take me long to locate my fellow head.

In those days professors were being encouraged to relate meaningfully to their students. I did my relating by telephone. Meaningful conversations took place, as follows:

"Hello, Kenny. Am I calling too early?"

"Wow, no, hey Mrs. Speizer."

"Say, Kenny. Can't you just call me Ann." I was only three years older than Kenny but being married to a faculty member automatically made one a different species.

"Hey," said Kenny. "I'll call you Mrs. Ann."

"Listen, Kenny. Is it possible to see you today on a matter of business?"

"Rightaway, Mrs. Ann. I'll meet you at six in front of the Shop-Up."

That's how it was done in those days. You met your connection in an inconspicuous place—like the supermarket, and he dropped a nickel bag—generally all these boys sold—on top of your groceries and you slipped him the money. Things were tough all right. Furthermore, the administration of these colleges were obsessed by the notion that boys and girls might be sleeping together. Presumably the boys would have had to sleep with the drab girls from the girls' college ten miles away which had a strict curfew. Or they would be forced to hurl themselves at the campus wives who were of two varieties: ruddy, cheerful mothers of three with master's degrees, private incomes, foreign cars, and ten-year marriages. Then there were older wives with grey hair, grown sons, old mink coats, and station wagons. These women drank too much sherry at parties and became very, very still. Both kinds of wife played tennis, and their houses smelled evocatively

of a substance my ultimate connection, Lionel Browning, would call
"Wasp must." Both of these kinds of wives felt that students were
animals; and they didn't like me very much either.

I was quite a sight. I was twenty-three and I wore little pink
glasses. I wore blue jeans, polished boots, and men's shirts. For evening
wear I wore extremely short skirts, anticipating the fashion by two or
three years. I drove the car too fast, was not pregnant, and liked to listen
to the Top 40. Faculty wives looked at me with fear—the fear that I
knew something they did not know. When they had been my age they
had already produced little Amanda or Jonathan and were about to start
little Jeremy or Rachel. They wore what grown-up women wore, and
they gave bridge and tea parties. These women lived a life in which
drugs were what you gave your child in the form of orange-flavored
aspirin so they did not, for example, go rooting around the campus
looking for someone off of whom to score.

The older wives said to Thorne, whom they adored: "Gracious,
Thorne, don't Ann's legs get cold in those little skirts? Goodness, Thorne, I
saw Ann *racing* around in the car with the radio on *so* loud." These
women hadn't seen anyone like me before, but years later after a few
campus riots they would see a much more virulent and hostile form of me
in large numbers. From my vantage point between the world of students
and the world of faculty it was plain to see how much professors hated
students who, since they had not yet passed through the heavy gates of
adulthood, were considered feckless, stupid, with no right to anything.

It was assumed that Thorne was married to a hot ticket, but no
one was sure what sort. This pleased Thorne—he did not mind having a
flashy wife, and since I never misbehaved I caused him no pain, but I
looked as if I were the sort to misbehave and this secretly pleased him.
My image on campus however was not my overriding concern. I was
mostly looking for decent grass.

Connecting on the college campus of the day was troublesome.
Everyone was paranoid. I was lucky that I did not have to add money to

my worries—I had a tiny bit of inheritance, just enough to keep me happy. I was a good customer when I could find a supplier, mostly some volelike and furtive-looking boy. Those blithe young things who spent their high school days blowing dope in suburban movie houses had not yet appeared on campus—how happy we would all be to see them! One's connection was apt to flunk out or drop out, and once in a while they would graduate. As a result, I was passed hand to hand by a number of unsavory boys. For example, the disgusting Steve, who whined and sniffled and sold very inferior dope. Eventually Steve was thrown out of school and I was taken over by another unpleasant boy by the name of Lester Katz. He carried for Lionel Browning, and Lionel Browning was the real thing.

Lionel, who allowed himself to be called Linnie by those close to him, had laid low for his first three years at college. In his senior year he expanded from a self-supplier to a purveyor of the finest grass to only the finest heads—by that time there were enough to make such a sideline profitable. Lionel's daddy was an executive in a large company that had branches abroad. Lionel had grown up in Columbia, Hong Kong, and Barbados, three places known for fine cannabis. He was a shadowy figure at college. He lived off campus and was not often seen except by my husband Thorne, whose favorite student he was. I had never seen him—he sent Lester to bring me my dope, with messages such as: "Mr. Browning hopes you will enjoy this sampling." It killed Lester that he called Lionel "Mr. Browning." He said it killed Lionel that Professor Speizer's wife was such a head. When he said that, I looked into his beady little eyes and it seemed a very good idea for me to go and check out this Lionel Browning who very well might have it in mind to blackmail me. Or maybe he was the uncool sort—the sort who might sidle up to his favorite professor and say: "That dope I laid on your wife sure is choice."

Lionel lived off campus in a frame house. Only very advanced students lived off campus. On campus room were very plush—suites with fireplaces and leaded glass windows. But the off campus fellows considered themselves above the ordinary muck of college life. These boys were either taking drugs or getting laid or were serious scholars who could not stand the sight of their fellow boy in such quantities.

Lionel lived on the top floor and as I mounted the stairs—I had, of course, made an appointment—I expected that he would be a slightly superior edition of the runty, unattractive boys who sold dope. This was not the case at all. He looked, in fact, rather like me. He was blond, tall but small boned, and he wore blue jeans, loafers with tassels, a white shirt, and a blue sweater—almost the replica of what I was wearing. He smiled a nice, crooked smile, offered me a joint, and I knew at once that I had found what I was looking for.

LIONEL DID NOT fool around. He got bricks—big *Survey of English Literature*-size bricks of marijuana that came wrapped in black plastic and taped with black tape. Underneath this wrapping was a rectangular cake of moist, golden greenish brown grass—a beautiful sight. It was always a pleasure to help Linnie clean this attractive stuff. We spread newspapers on the floor and strained it through a coarse sieve. The dregs of these Linnie would sell to what he called the lower forms of life.

The lower forms included almost everyone on campus. The higher forms included people he liked. His own family, he said, was a species of mineral-like vegetation that grew on lunar soil. There were four children, all blond, each with a nickname: Leopold (Leafy), Lionel (Linnie), Mary Louise (Mally), and Barbara (Bumpy or Bumps). His family drove Linnie crazy, and the thought of their jolly family outings and jolly family traditions caused him to stay high as often as possible, which was pretty often.

In matters of dope, it depends on who gets to you first. I was gotten to in Paris, the summer before I went off to college. I looked up the nice sons of some friends of my parents, and they turned me on. I had been sent to practice French and to have a broadening cultural experience. I learned to say, among other things: "Yes, this African kif is quite heavenly. Do you have more? How much more? How much will you charge me per matchbox?"

The nice boys I looked up had just come back from Spain. They were giant heads and they had giant quantities. These boys were happy to get their mitts on such a receptive blank slate as me. Pot, they told me, was one of the great aids to mental entertainment. It produced unusual thoughts and brilliant insights. It freed the mind to be natural—the natural mind being totally open to the hilarious absurdities of things. It mixed the senses and gave flavor to music. All in all, well worth getting into. We would get stoned and go to the movies or listen to jazz or hang around talking for what may have been minutes and may have been hours. This was more fun than I ever imagined, so my shock when I went off to college and discovered my fellow head was profound. My fellow head was sullen, alienated, mute when high, inexpressive, and no fun at all. Until I met Lionel, I smoked alone.

Lionel was my natural other. Stoned we were four eyes and one mind. We were simply made to get high together—we felt exactly the same way about dope. We liked to light up and perambulate around the mental landscape seeing what we could see. We often liked to glom onto the Jill and Bill Show—that was what we called one of the campus's married couples, Jill and Bill Benson. Jill and Bill lived off campus, baked their own bread, made their own jam and candles, and knitted sweaters for each other. Both of them were extremely rich and were fond of giving parties at which dreadful homemade hors d'oeuvres and cheap wine were served. Linnie and I made up a Broadway musical for them to star in. It was called *Simple on My Trust Fund*. We worked mostly on the opening scene. Jill and Bill are in the kitchen of their horrid apartment. Jill is knitting. Bill is stirring a pot of jam. A group of ordinary students walks by the open window. "Jill and Bill," they say. "How is it that you two live such a groovy, cool, and close-to-the-earth life?"

Jill and Bill walk to center stage, holding hands. "Simple," each coos. "On my trust fund." And the chorus breaks into the lovely refrain. Once in the coffee shop Jill confessed to Linnie that she only had "a tiny little trust fund." This phrase was easily worked into the Jill and Bill Show.

Jill and Bill, however, appeared to be having something of a hard time. They were seen squabbling. Jill was seen in tears at the Shop-Up. They looked unhappy. Jill went off skiing by herself. I had very little patience with Jill and Bill. I felt that with all that money they ought to buy some machine-made sweaters and serve store-bought jam. Furthermore, I felt it was slumming of them to live in such a crummy apartment when the countryside was teeming with enchanting rural properties. The idea of a country house became a rallying cry—the answer to all of Jill and Bill's trouble.

Linnie mused on Jill and Bill. What could be their problem, he wondered, rolling a colossal joint.

"They're both small and dark," I said. Linnie lit up and passed the joint to me. I took a life-affirming hit. "Maybe at night they realize what they look like and in the morning they're too depressed to relate to each other. What do you think?"

"I think Jill and Bill are a form of matted plant fiber," said Linnie. "I think they get into bed and realize that more than any other single thing, they resemble that stuff those braided doormats are made of. This clearly has a debilitating effect on them. This must be what's wrong. What do you think, Mrs. Ann?"

"A country house," I said. "They must buy a lovely country house before it's too late."

That was the beginning of *Ask Mrs. Ann*, a routine in which Linnie and I would invent some horrible circumstance for Jill and Bill. Either of us could be Mrs. Ann. It didn't matter which. One of us would say, for instance: "Answer this one, Mrs. Ann. Jill and Bill have just had a baby. This baby is a Negro baby, which is odd since neither Jill nor Bill is Negro. Naturally, this causes a bit of confusion. They simply cannot fathom how it happened. At any rate, this baby has webbed feet and tiny flippers. Jill finds this attractive. Bill less so. Meanwhile Jill has bought a sheep and a loom. It is her girlish dream to spin wool from her own sheep, but the sheep has gone berserk and bitten Bill. In the ensuing melee the loom has collapsed, dislocating Jill's shoulder. Meanwhile, Bill, who has had to have forty stitches in this thigh as the result of violent sheep bite, has gone into the hospital for a simple tonsillectomy and finds to his amazement that his left arm has been amputated—he is left-handed as you recall. Jill feels they ought to sue, but to Bill's shock he finds that he has signed a consent to an amputation. How can this have happened? He simply can't fathom it. But there is relief in all this, if only for Jill. Jill, whose maiden name is Michaelson, suffers from a rare disorder called 'Michaelson's Syndrome," which affects all members of her family. This syndrome causes the brain to turn very slowly into something resembling pureed spinach. By the time she is thirty she will remember nothing of these unhappy events, for she will have devolved to a rather primitive, excrement-throwing stage. Whatever should they do?"

All that was required of Mrs. Ann was the rallying cry: a country house! Many hours were spent trying to find new awful tidings for Jill and Bill, and as those familiar with the effects of marijuana know, even the punctual are carried away on a stream of warped time perceptions. One rock-and-roll song takes about an hour to play, whereas a movement of a symphony is over in fifteen seconds. I felt that time had a form—the form of a chiffon scarf floating aimlessly down a large water slide; or that it was oblong but slippery, like an oiled football. I got home late, having forgotten to do the shopping. Since I had freely opted to be Thorne's housewife, he was perfectly justified in getting angry at me. My problem was, he thought I was having an affair.

It is one thing to tell your husband that you are sleeping with another man, and it is quite another to tell him that from the very instant of your meeting you have been under the influence of a mind-altering substance, no matter how mild. An astonishing confession next to which the admission of an afternoon or two in the arms of another man is nothing. Nothing!

What was I to do? My only real talent in life appeared to be getting high, and I was wonderful at it. Ostensibly I was supposed to be nurturing a talent for drawing—everyone had a skill, it was assumed. Every day I went upstairs to our attic room, lit a joint, and drew tiny, incoherent, and highly detailed black and white pictures. This was not my idea of an occupation. It was hardly my idea of a hobby. Of course it is a well-known fact that drawing while high is always fun which only made it more clear to me that my true vocation lay in getting stoned.

And so when dinner was late, when I was late, when I had forgotten to do something I had said I would do, Thorne liked to get into a snit, but he was terrified of getting furious with me. After all, my role was to look sort of dangerous. In some ways, Thorne treated me with the respectful and careful handling you might give to something you suspect is a pipe bomb: he didn't want to tempt fate because the poor thing was in some ways enraptured with me and he was afraid that if he got mad enough, I might disappear. That was the way the scales of our marriage were balanced. When he looked as if he were about to shout, I would either get a very dangerous look in my eyes, or I would make him laugh, which was one of my prime functions in his life. The other was to behave in public.

Since I was stoned all the time, I tried in all ways to behave like Queen Victoria. Thus I probably appeared to be a little cracked. At public functions I smiled and was mute—no one knew that at home I was quite a little chatterbox. The main form of socializing on campus was the dinner party. I found these pretty funny—of course I was high and didn't know the difference. Thorne found them pretty dull, so I tried to liven them up for him. If we were seated together at dinner, I would smile at the person opposite and then do something to Thorne under the table. I tended, at these parties, to smile a great deal. This unnerved

Thorne. He wore, under his party expression, a grimace that might have been caused by constant prayer, the prayer that I would not say something I had said at home. That I would not talk about how a black transvestite hooker should be sent as a present to the president of the college for his birthday. He prayed that I would not say about this gift: "With my little inheritance and Thorne's salary I think we could certainly afford it." Or I would not discuss the ways in which I felt the chairman of the history department looked like an anteater, or, on the subject of ants, how I felt his wife would react to being rolled in honey and set upon by South American fire ants. I did think that Professor X stole women's clothing out of the townie laundromat and went through the streets late at night in a flowered housecoat. I knew why Professor Y should not be left alone with his own infant son, and so on. But I behaved like a perfect angel and from time to time sent Thorne a look that made him shake, just to keep him on his toes.

I actually spoke once. This was at a formal dinner at the chairman of the department's house. This dinner party was so unusually dull that even through a glaze of marijuana I was bored. Thorne looked as if he were drowning. I myself began to itch. When I could stand it no longer I excused myself and went to the bathroom where I lit the monster joint I carried in my evening bag and took a few hits. This was Lionel's superfine Colombian loco-weed and extremely effective. When I came downstairs I felt all silvery. The chairman of the department's wife was talking about her niece, Allison, who was an accomplished young equestrienne. At the mention of horses, I spoke up. I remembered something about horses I had figured out high. Lionel Browning called these insights "marijuana moments"—things you like to remember when you are not stoned. Since no one had ever heard me say very much, everyone stopped to listen.

"Man's spatial relationship to the horse is one of the most confusing and deceptive in the world," I heard myself say. "You are either sitting on top of one, or standing underneath one, and therefore it is impossible to gauge in any meaningful way exactly how big a horse is in relationship to you. This is not," I added with fierce emphasis, "like a man inside a cathedral."

I then shut up. There was a long silence. I mediated on what I had said which was certainly the most interesting thing anyone had said. Thorne's eyes seemed about to pop. There was not a sound. People had stopped eating. I looked around the table, gave a beautiful, unfocused smile, and went back to my dinner.

Finally, the chairman of the department's wife said: "That's very interesting, Ann." And the conversation closed above my head, leaving me happy to rattle around in my own altered state.

Later, at home, Thorne said: "Whatever made you say what you said at dinner tonight?"

I said, in a grave voice: "It is something I have always believed."

THE NICE THING about being high all the time is that life suspends itself in front of you endlessly, like telephone poles on a highway. Without plans you have the feeling that things either will never change, or will arrange themselves somehow someday.

A look around the campus did not fill the heart of this tender bride with visions of a rosy adult future. It was clear who was having all the fun and it was not the grown-ups. Thorne and I were the youngest faculty couple, and this gave us—I mean me—a good vantage point. A little older than us were couples with wornout cars, sick children, and debts. If they were not saddled with these things, they had independent incomes and were saddled with attitudes. Then they got older and were seen kissing the spouses of others at parties, or were found, a pair of unassorted spouses, under a pile of coats on a bed at New Year's Eve parties. Then they got even older, and the strife of their marriages gave them the stony affection battle comrades have for one another.

There were marriages that seemed propped up with toothpicks, and ones in which the wife was present but functionless, like a vestigial organ. Then the husband, under the strain of being both father and more to little Emily, Matthew, and Tabitha plus teaching a full course load, was forced to have an affair with a graduate student in Boston whom he could see only every other weekend.

The thought of Thorne and my becoming any of these people was so frightful that I had no choice but to get immediately high. Something would either occur to me, or nothing would happen. Meanwhile, time drifted by in the company of Lionel Browning—a fine fellow and a truly great pothead for whom I had not one particle of sexual feeling. He was my perfect pal. Was this cheating? I asked myself. Well, I had to admit, it sort of was. Thorne did not know how much time I spent with him, but then Linnie was soon to graduate, so I had to get him while I could, so to speak.

In the spring, Thorne went off to a convention of the Historical Society and I went on a dope run to Boston with Linnie. I looked forward to this adventure. It did not seem likely that life would bring me many more offers of this sort. The purity of my friendship with Linnie was never tainted by the well-known number of motels that littered the road from school to Boston. Sex was never our mission.

We paid a visit to a dealer named Marv (he called himself Uncle Marv) Fenrich, who was somewhat of a legend. The legend had it that he had once been very brilliant, but that speed—his drug of choice—had turned his brain into shaving cream and now he was fit only to deal grass to college boys. He also dealt speed to more sinister campus types, and he had tried to con Linnie into this lucrative sideline. But Linnie wanted only quality marijuana and Uncle Marv respected him, although it irked him that Linnie was not interested. He sold what he called "The Uncle Marv Exam Special—Tailored to the Needs of the College Person." This was a box containing two 5 milligram Dexamyls, a Dexamyl Spansule (15 mgs), two Benzadrines (5 mg), and something he called an "amphetamine football"—a large, olive-green pill which he claimed was pure speed coated with Vitamin B$_{12}$. On the shelves of his linen closet were jar upon hospital-size jar of pills. But his heart, if not the rest of his metabolism, was in grass, and he never shut up.

"Man," he said, "now this particular reefer is very sublime, really very sublime. It is the country club of grass, mellow and rich. A very handsome high can be gotten off this stuff. Now my own personal favorite cocktail is to take two or three nice dexies, wash them down with some fine whiskey or it could be Sterno or your mother's French perfume, it makes no difference whatsoever, and then light up a huge monster reefer of the very best quality and fall on the floor thanking God in many languages. This is my own recipe for a very good time. I like to share these warm happy times with others. Often Uncle Marv suggests you do a popper or two if you feel unmotivated by any of the above. Or snap one under the nose of a loved friend. Believe me, the drugstore has a lot to offer these days. Now a hundred or so of those little Romilar pills make you writhe and think insects are crawling all over your body—some people like this sort of thing very deeply. I myself find it a cheap thrill. Say, Linnie, have you authentic college kids gotten into mescaline yet? Very attractive stuff. Yes, you may say that it is for people with no imagination, but think of it this way: if you have no imagination, a Swiss pharmaceutical company will supply one for you. Isn't that wonderful what modern science does? Let me tell you, this stuff is going to be very big. Uncle Marv is going to make many sublime shekels off this stuff as soon as he can set it up right. You just wait and see. Uncle Marv says: the streets of Boston and Cambridge are going to be stacked with little college boys and girls hyperventilating and having visions. Now this lysergic acid is also going to be very big, very big. God bless the Swiss! Now, Linnie," he began rooting in various desk drawers. "Now, Linnie, how about some reds for all those wired-up college boys and girls to calm down after exams? I personally feel that reds go very well after a little speed abuse and I should know. Calm you down, take the reptile right out of you. Uncle Marv is so fond of these sublime red tens." He paused. "Seconal," he said rather coldly to me, since it was clear even to a person who was out of his mind that I did not know what he was talking about. "I like to see a person taking reds. This is a human person, a person unafraid to admit that he or she is *very nervous*. You don't want any? Well, all right. But you and this authentic college girl have not come to pass the evening in idle drug chatter. This is business. Reefer for Linnie, many shekels for Uncle Marv. Now, Linnie, this reefer in particular I want you to taste is very sublime. You and this authentic college girl must try some this very instant. Now this is Colombian loco-weed of the highest order. Of Colombian distinction and extremely handsome. I also have some horse tranquilizers, by the way. Interested? Extremely sublime. They make you lie down on the floor and whimper for help and companionship. Uncle Marv is very fond of these interesting new pills."

He cleared a space on his messy kitchen table and proceeded to roll several absolutely perfect joints. It was extremely sublime grass, and Linnie bought a kilo of it.

"Linnie, it will not fail you," Uncle Marv said. "Only the best, from me to you." Linnie paid up, and Uncle Marv gave us each a bennie for a present, which we were very glad to have on the long ride home.

WHEN THORNE CAME back from his conference, the axe, which had been poised so delicately over the back of my neck, fell. This marked the end of my old life, and the beginning of the new. Thorne had called me from Chicago—he had called all night—and I had not been home.

"You are sleeping with Lionel Browning," he said.

"I never laid a hand on him," I said.

"That's an interesting locution, Ann," said Thorne. "Do you just lie there and let him run his grubby undergraduate hands all over you?"

This was of course my cue. "Yes," I said. "I often lie there and let almost any undergraduate run his hands all over me. Often faculty is invited, like your colleague Jack Saks. Often the chairman of the department's wife pops over and she runs her hands all over me too."

The effects of the beautiful joint I had smoked only an hour and a half ago were beginning to wane. I was getting a headache. I thought about the sweet little stash I kept in my lingerie drawer—all the grass I smoked at home tasted vaguely of sachet. I was longing to go upstairs where, underneath my socks, I had a little lump of African hash. I saw my future before me—a very depressing vision. I was fifty. Grown children. Going to the hairdresser to have my hair frosted. Doing some genteel work or other—I couldn't think what. Wearing a knit dress—the sort worn by the wife of the president of the college. Calling grimy boys from pay phones: "Hello, hello? Kenny? Steve? This is Mrs. Speizer calling. Do you have anything for me?"

There I would be in my proper hairdo. Facing change of life and still a total pothead. Locking the bathroom door behind me to toke up. By then Thorne would be the chairman of his department somewhere.

"That wife of mine," he would say—of course he only spoke this way in my fantasies—"does say the oddest things. Can't keep track of where that mind of hers is meandering to. Goes out at odd hours and what funny boys she gets to do the lawn work. I can't imagine where she gets them from."

In fact, this was the most depressing thought I had ever had. If you stay high enough you never wonder what will become of you. A large joint was waiting in my jacket pocket. How I longed to smoke it. Somewhere near me was adult life: I knew it. I could feel it breathing down my neck. Professor's wife smokes dope constantly must see shrink. Must grow up. Must find out why she cannot be straight. Why she refuses to enter the adult world. And so on. And Thorne—much sympathy for Thorne—for example, the chairman of the department's wife: "Dear Thorne, you poor thing! All alone in that house with a drug addict! When Ann has been sedated why don't you come over and have dinner with us and our lovely niece Allison and after Ann has been committed to a mental institution, you and Allison can establish a meaningful and truly adult relationship."

The thing that divides the children from the adults is that children know it's us against them—how right they are—and adults are children who grew up and are comfortable being them. Two terrible images flashed before me. One was that life was like an unruly horse that rears up and kicks you in the head. And the other was that my life was like a pane of glass being carried around by a nervous and incompetent person who was bound to let it slip and shatter into zillions of pieces on the pavement. My futureless life, besides being shattered and rearing up, unwound endlessly before me. What was around for me to be? There did not seem to be very much of anything. Suddenly I felt a rush of jaunty courage, the kind you feel when everything has bottomed out and just about everything old thing is lost.

"Thorne," I said. "I smoke marijuana unceasingly and always have. What do you think of that?"

"Incessantly," said Thorne.

"Thorne," I said. "I have been stoned from the first minute you laid eyes on me and I am stoned now."

He regarded me for a moment. "You mean, you came to my class high?" Thorne said. "And you're high now?"

"Yes," I said. "I was stoned in your class and I am stoned right now but not as stoned as I want to be. So I am going to take this great big gigantic reefer out of my pocket and light it up and I am going to share it with you."

He looked shocked.

"You can get in jail for smoking that stuff, Ann," he said in an awed voice.

"An interesting locution, Thorne," I said. He stopped looking awed and began to look rather keen and hungry. I realized with a sudden jolt of happiness that I could very well change my husband's life in one easy step.

"Take this and inhale it," I said.

"How can I when I don't smoke?" Thorne said.

"Make an effort. Try hard and be careful," I said. "Go slow and don't exhale for a long time."

"How long?" Thorne asked.

"Oh, a half an hour or so." He inhaled successfully several times. In a little while he was as high as a kite.

"My," he said, "this certainly is an interesting substance. I feel I've been standing here for a few centuries. My hands are cold and my mouth is dry. Are these symptoms?"

For an hour Thorne went from room to room having impressions. He was having a wonderful time. Finally, he sat down.

"Were you stoned on our wedding day?" he asked.

"I'm afraid so," I said.

"On our honeymoon?"

"I'm afraid so."

"I see," said Thorne. "In other words, you're like this all the time."

I said more or less, mostly more.

"In other words," said Thorne, "since you are like this all the time, you have no idea what it's like to be with me when you're not like this."

That seemed logical to me.

"In other words," Thorne said, "you have no idea what its like to be with me when you aren't like this."

I said that sounded very like his previous other words, and that such a thought had never occurred to me.

"This is terrible, Ann," said Thorne. "It isn't normal. Of course, this stuff is pretty interesting and all, but you can't be stoned all the time."

"I can," I said.

"Yes, but it must be wrong. There must be something terribly wrong, don't you think?"

"Actually, no," I said.

"But Ann, in other words, this is not normal reality. You have not been perceiving normal reality. How long has it been, Ann, since you actually perceived normal reality?"

"This is normal reality, silly," I said.

"Yes, well, but I mean I'm sure there is some reason why it's not right to be this way all the time."

"There may be, but I can't think of it. Besides," I added, "you seem to be having a swell old time."

"That cannot be gainsaid," said Thorne.

"Or cannot not be gainsaid."

"What does that mean, anyway?" said Thorne. "But never mind. The fact is that if you've been high all this time, we don't know each other at all, really."

"What," I said, thinking with sudden longing of the hashish upstairs, "is knowable?"

"An interesting point," said Thorne. "Maybe in the open knowableness of things their sheer knowableness is obscured. In other words, light darkening light, if you see what I mean."

I did see. I looked at my husband with great affection, realizing that he had possibilities I had not counted on.

"What about your affair with Lionel Browning?" Thorne said. "Is that knowable?"

"Yes," I said. "Lionel Browning is responsible only for the very substance that has put you in this state of mind, see?"

"I do see," Thorne said. "I see. In other words, you sit around and get high together."

"Often we stand up and get high together."

"And I as a professor can never join you since that would be undignified, right?"

"Right."

"Well, then, in honor of Lionel and in the interests of further study, let's have a little more of this stuff, okay?"

"A very good idea," I said.

"Yes," said Thorne, stretching out on the couch. "Let's carry this one step further."

"An interesting locution," I said. "I wonder how it works. In what way can a step be carried?"

Thorne sat up. He looked puzzled. "It must go like this: the step is the province of the foot, without which there can be no step. The foot is carried by the body, but the action of the step is carried by the foot. Therefore the step is to the foot as a baby is to its mother. And so it can be said that the foot is the mother of the step, or rather, the step is the potential baby of the foot."

I thought about that for a very long time.

"Say, Ann," Thorne said. "Where's the more we're supposed to have?"

"It's illegal, Thorne," I said. "We could get in jail for simply being in the same room with it."

"Get it if you have it," Thorne said.

I brought down a bag of Linnie's top quality and my lump of hash. This I scraped with our sharpest kitchen knife and sprinkled deftly on the unrolled reefer. I rolled wonderfully. Thorne was impressed, and he was intrigued by watching me do something I had obviously done millions of times but not in front of him.

"You're awfully good at that," he said.

"Years of practice," I said. "Now, Thorne, why have you never told me how much Lionel Browning looks like me?"

"Because he does *not* look like you," said Thorne. "You have the same loafers, that's all."

"We are virtually identical," I said.

"Ann, this mind-impairing substance has impaired your mind. Lionel Browning and you look nothing alike. Now are you going to roll those things all night or are you going to smoke them?"

THE THING ABOUT history is, most people just live through it. You never know what moment may turn out to be of profound historical significance. When you are meandering near the stream of current events, you do not know when you have dipped your toe into the waters of significance. I like to think that as I passed that joint to my husband, a new era opened. The decade was fairly new, and just about everything was about to happen. In what other era could a nice young thing pass a marijuana cigarette to her straight-laced husband?

In those days potheads liked to track down their fellow heads. Everyone had a list of suspects. William Blake was on everyone's list. On Linnie's list was Gerard Manley Hopkins. It amused him inexhaustibly to imagine the Jesuit father smoking dope and writing in sprung rhythm. I myself could not imagine any straight person writing those poems and as I watched a happy, glazed expression take possession of my husband's features, I had cause to think of my favorite Hopkins poem—"The Windhover"—which contains the line, "my heart in hiding/Stirred for a bird,—the achieve of, the mastery of the thing!"

I felt full of achievement and mastery—Thorne being the victim and beneficiary of both. Getting him stoned was a definite achievement of some sort or other.

I said to Thorne: "What do you think of it?"

"It produces a strange and extremely endearing form a cerebral energy," he said.

"Yes," I sighed in agreement. "Wonderful, isn't it?"

"It produces unhealthy mental excitement," Thorne said.

Suddenly I was full of optimism and hope for the future.

"Oh, Thorne," I said in a happy voice. "Isn't this fun?"

And as Thorne has frequently pointed out, that very well could have been the slogan for the years to come.

SIR ARTHUR CONAN DOYLE

❖

THE SIGN OF FOUR

SHERLOCK HOLMES TOOK his bottle from the corner of the mantelpiece, and his hypodermic syringe from its neat morocco case. With his long, white, nervous fingers he adjusted the delicate needle and rolled back his left shirtcuff. For some little time his eyes rested thoughtfully upon the sinewy forearm and wrist, all dotted and scarred with innumerable puncture-marks. Finally, he thrust the sharp point home, pressed down the tiny piston, and sank back into the velvet-lined armchair with a long sigh of satisfaction.

Three times a day for many months I had witnessed this performance, but custom had not reconciled my mind to it. On the contrary, from day to day I had become more irritable at the sight, and my conscience swelled nightly within me at the thought that I had lacked the courage to protest. Again and again I had registered a vow that I should deliver my soul upon the subject; but there was that in the cool, nonchalant air of my companion which made him the last man with whom one would care to take anything approaching to a liberty. His great powers, his masterly manner, and the experience which I had had of his many extraordinary qualities, all made me diffident and backward in crossing him.

Yet upon that afternoon, whether it was the Beaune which I had taken with my lunch or the additional exasperation produced by the extreme deliberation of his manner, I suddenly felt that I could hold out no longer.

"Which is it to-day," I asked, "morphine or cocaine?"

He raised his eyes languidly from the old black-letter volume which he had opened.

"It is cocaine," he said, "a seven-per-cent solution. Would you care to try it?"

"No, indeed," I answered brusquely. "My constitution has not got over the Afghan campaign yet. I cannot afford to throw any extra strain upon it."

He smiled at my vehemence. "Perhaps you are right, Watson," he said. "I suppose that its influence is physically a bad one. I find it, however, so transcendently stimulating and clarifying to the mind that its secondary action is a matter of small moment."

"But consider!" I said earnestly. "Count the cost! Your brain may, as you say, be roused and excited, but it is a pathological and morbid process which involves increased tissue-change and may at least leave a permanent weakness. You know, too, what a black reaction comes upon you. Surely the game is hardly worth the candle. Why should you, for a mere passing pleasure, risk the loss of those great powers with which you have been endowed? Remember that I speak not only as one comrade to another but as a medical man to one for whose constitution he is to some extent answerable."

He did not seem offended. On the contrary, he put his finger-tips together, and leaned his elbows on the arms of his chair, like one who has a relish for conversation.

"My mind," he said, "rebels at stagnation. Give me problems, give me work, give me the most abstruse cryptogram, or the most intricate analysis, and I am in my own proper atmosphere. I can dispense then with artificial stimulants. But I abhor the dull routine of existence. I crave for mental exaltation. That is why I have chosen my own particular profession, or rather created it, for I am the only one in the world."

"The only unofficial detective?" I said, raising my eyebrows.

"The only unofficial consulting detective," he answered. "I am the last and highest court of appeal in detection. When Gregson, or Lestrade, or Athelney Jones are out of their depths—which, by the way, is their normal state—the matter is laid before me. I examine the data, as an expert, and pronounce a specialist's opinion. I claim no credit in such cases. My name figures in no newspaper. The work itself, the pleasure of finding a field for my peculiar powers, is my highest reward. But you have yourself had some experience of my methods of work in the Jefferson Hope case."

"Yes, indeed," said I cordially. "I was never so struck by anything in my life. I even embodied it in a small brochure, with the somewhat fantastic title of 'A Study in Scarlet.'"

He shook his head sadly.

"I glanced over it," said he. "Honestly, I cannot congratulate you upon it. Detection is, or ought to be, an exact science and should be treated in the same cold and unemotional manner. You have attempted to tinge it with romanticism, which produces much the same effect as if you worked a love-story or an elopement into the fifth proposition of Euclid."

"But the romance was there," I remonstrated. "I could not tamper with the facts."

"Some facts should be suppressed, or, at least, a just sense of proportion should be observed in treating them. The only point in the case which deserved mention was the curious analytical reasoning from effects to causes, by which I succeeded in unravelling it."

I was annoyed at this criticism of a work which had been specially designed to please him. I confess, too, that I was irritated by the egotism which seemed to demand that every line of my pamphlet should be devoted to his own special doings. More than once during the years that I had lived with him in Baker Street I had observed that a small vanity underlay my companion's quiet and didactic manner. I made no remark, however, but sat nursing my wounded leg. I had had a Jezail bullet through it some time before, and though it did not prevent me from walking it ached wearily at every change of the weather.

"My practice has extended recently to the Continent," said Holmes after a white, filling up his old brier-root pipe. "I was consulted last week by François le Villard, who, as you probably know, has come rather to the front lately in the French detective service. He has all the Celtic power of quick intuition, but he is deficient in the wide range of exact knowledge which is essential to the higher developments of his art. The case was concerned with a will and possessed some features of interest. I was able to refer him to two parallel cases, the one at Riga in 1857, and the other at St. Louis in 1871, which have suggested to him the true solution. Here is the letter which I had this morning acknowledging my assistance."

He tossed over, as he spoke, a crumpled sheet of foreign notepaper. I glanced my eyes down it, catching a profusion of notes of admiration, with stray *magnifiques, coup-de-maîtres* and *tours-de-force,* all testifying to the ardent admiration of the Frenchman.

"He speaks as a pupil to his master," said I.

"Oh, he rates my assistance too highly," said Sherlock Holmes lightly. "He has considerable gifts himself. He possesses two out of the three qualities necessary for the ideal detective. He has the power of observation and that of deduction. He is only wanting in knowledge, and that may come in time. He is now translating my small works into French."

"Your works?"

"Oh, didn't you know?" he cried, laughing. "Yes, I have been guilty of several monographs. They are all upon technical subjects. Here, for example, is one 'Upon the Distinction between the Ashes of the Various Tobaccos.' In it I enumerate a hundred and forty forms of cigar, cigarette, and pipe tobacco, with coloured plates illustrating the difference in the ash. It is a point which is continually turning up in criminal trails, and which is sometimes of supreme importance as a clue. If you can say definitely, for example, that some murder had been done by a man who was smoking an Indian *lunkah,* it obviously narrows your field of search. To the trained eye there is as much difference between the black ash of a Trichinopoly and the white fluff of bird's-eye as there is between a cabbage and a potato."

"You have an extraordinary genius for minutiae," I remarked.

"I appreciate their importance. Here is my monograph upon the tracing of footsteps, with some remarks upon the uses of plaster of Paris as a preserver of impresses. Here, too, is a curious little work upon the influence of a trade upon the form of the hand, with lithotypes of the hands of slaters, sailors, cork-cutters, compositors, weavers, and diamond-polishers. That is a matter of great practical interest to the scientific detective—especially in cases of unclaimed bodies, or in discovering the antecedents of criminals. But I weary you with my hobby."

"Not at all," I answered earnestly. "It is of the greatest interest to me, especially since I have had the opportunity of observing your practical application of it. But you spoke just now of observation and deduction. Surely the one to some extent implies the other."

"Why, hardly," he answered, leaning back luxuriously in his armchair and sending up thick blue wreaths from his pipe. "For example, observation shows me that you have been to the Wigmore Street Post-Office this morning, but deduction lets me know that when there you dispatched a telegram."

"Right!" said I. "Right on both points! But I confess that I don't see how you arrived at it. It was a sudden impulse upon my part, and I have mentioned it to no one."

"It is simplicity itself," he remarked, chuckling at my surprise— "so absurdly simple that an explanation is superfluous; and yet it may serve to define the limits of observation and deduction. Observation tells me that you have a little reddish mould adhering to your instep. Just opposite the Wigmore Street Office they have taken up the pavement and thrown up some earth, which lies in such a way that it is difficult to avoid treading in it in entering. The earth is of this peculiar reddish tint which is found, as far as I know, nowhere else in the neighbourhood. So much is observation. The rest is deduction."

"How, then, did you deduce the telegram?"

"Why, of course I knew that you had not written a letter, since I sat opposite to you all morning. I see also in your open desk there that you have a sheet of stamps and a thick bundle of postcards. What could you go into the post-office for, then, but to send a wire? Eliminate all other factors, and the one which remains must be the truth."

"In this case it certainly is so," I replied after a little thought. "The thing, however, is, as you say, of the simplest. Would you think me impertinent if I were to put your theories to a more severe test?"

"On the contrary," he answered, "it would prevent me from taking a second dose of cocaine. I should be delighted to look into any problem which you might submit to me."

"I have heard you say it is difficult for a man to have any object in daily use without leaving the impress of his individuality upon it in such a way that a trained observer might read it. Now, I have here a watch which has recently come into my possession. Would you have the kindness to let me have an opinion upon the character or habits of the late owner?"

I handed him over the watch with some slight feeling of amusement in my heart, for the test was, as I thought, an impossible one, and I intended it as a lesson against the somewhat dogmatic tone which he occasionally assumed. He balanced the watch in his hand, gazed hard at the dial, opened the back, and examined the works, first with his naked eyes and then with a powerful convex lens. I could hardly keep from smiling at his crestfallen face when he finally snapped the case to and handed it back.

"There are hardly any data," he remarked. "The watch has been recently cleaned, which robs me of my most suggestive facts."

"You are right," I answered. "It was cleaned before being sent to me."

In my heart I accused my companion of putting forward a most lame and impotent excuse to cover his failure. What data could he expect from an uncleaned watch?

"Though unsatisfactory, my research has not been entirely barren," he observed, staring up at the ceiling with dreamy, lack-lustre eyes. "Subject to correction, I should judge that the watch belonged to your elder brother, who inherited it from your father."

"That you gather, no doubt, from the H. W. upon the back?"

"Quite so. The W. suggests your own name. The date of the watch is nearly fifty years back, and the initials are as old as the watch: so it was made for the last generation. Jewellery usually descends to the eldest son, and he is most likely to have the same name as the father. Your father has, if I remember right, been dead many years. It has, therefore, been in the hands of your eldest brother."

"Right, so far," said I. "Anything else?"

"He was a man of untidy habits—very untidy and careless. He was left with good prospects, but he threw away his chances, lived for some time in poverty with occasional short intervals of prosperity, and finally, taking to drink, he died. That is all I can gather."

I sprang from my chair and limped impatiently about the room with considerable bitterness in my heart.

"This is unworthy of you, Holmes," I said. "I could not have believed that you would have descended to this. You have made inquiries into the history of my unhappy brother, and you now pretend to deduce this knowledge in some fanciful way. You cannot expect me to believe that you have read all this from his old watch! It is unkind and, to speak plainly, has a touch of charlatanism in it."

"My dear doctor," said he kindly, "pray accept my apologies. Viewing the matter as an abstract problem, I had forgotten how personal and painful a thing it might be to you. I assure you, however, that I never even knew that you had a brother until you handed me the watch."

"Then how in the name of all that is wonderful did you get these facts? They are absolutely correct in every particular."

"Ah, that is good luck. I could only say what was the balance of probability. I did not at all expect to be so accurate."

"But it was not mere guesswork?"

"No, no: I never guess. It is a shocking habit—destructive to the logical faculty. What seems strange to you is only so because you do not follow my train of thought or observe the small facts upon which large inferences may depend. For example, I began by stating that your brother was careless. When you observe the lower part of that watch-case you notice that it is not only dinted in two places but it is cut and marked all over from the habit of keeping other hard objects, such as coins or keys, in the same pocket. Surely it is no great feat to assume that a man who treats a fifty-guinea watch so cavalierly must be a careless man. Neither is it a very far-fetched inference that a man who inherits one article of such value is pretty well provided for in other respects."

I nodded to show that I followed his reasoning.

"It is very customary for pawnbrokers in England, when they take a watch, to scratch the numbers of the ticket with a pin-point upon the inside of the case. It is more handy than a label as there is no risk of the number being lost or transposed. There are no less than four such numbers visible to my lens on the inside of this case. Inference—that your brother was often at low water. Secondary inference—that he had occasional bursts of prosperity, or he could not have redeemed the pledge. Finally, I ask you to look at the inner plate, which contains the keyhole. Look at the thousands of scratches all round the hole—marks where the key has slipped. What sober man's key could have scored those groves? But you will never see a drunkard's watch without them. He winds it at night, and leaves these traces of his unsteady hand. Where is the mystery in all this?"

"It is as clear as daylight," I answered. "I regret the injustice which I did you. I should have had more faith in your marvellous faculty. May I ask whether you have any professional inquiry on foot at present?"

"None. Hence the cocaine. I cannot live without brainwork. What else is there to live for? Stand at the window here. Was ever such a dreary, dismal, unprofitable world? See how the yellow fog swirls down the street and drifts across the dun-coloured houses. What could be more hopelessly prosaic and material? What is the use of having powers, Doctor, when one has no field upon which to exert them? Crime is commonplace, existence is commonplace, and no qualities save those which are commonplace have any function upon earth."

I had opened my mouth to reply to this tirade when, with a crisp knock, our landlady entered, bearing a card upon the brass salver.

"A young lady for you, sir," she said, addressing my companion.

"Miss Mary Morstan," he read. "Hum! I have no recollection of the name. Ask the young lady to step up, Mrs. Hudson. Don't go, Doctor. I should prefer that you remain."

PHILIP K. DICK

❖

THE THREE STIGMATA OF PALMER ELDRITCH

AT TEN IN the morning a terrific horn, familiar to him, hooted Sam Regan out of his sleep, and he cursed the UN ship upstairs; he knew the racket was deliberate. The ship, circling above the hovel Chicken Pox Prospects, wanted to be certain that colonists—and not merely indigenous animals—got the parcels that were to be dropped.

We'll get them, Sam Regan muttered to himself as he zipped his insulated overalls, put his feet into high boots, and then grumpily sauntered as slowly as possible toward the ramp.

"He's early today," Tod Morris complained. "and I'll bet it's all staples, sugar and food-basics like lard—nothing interesting such as, say, candy."

Putting his shoulders against the lid at the top of the ramp, Norman Schein pushed; bright cold sunlight spilled down on them and they blinked.

The UN ship sparkled overhead, set against the black sky as if hanging from an uneasy thread. Good pilot, this drop, Tod decided. Knows the Fineburg Crescent area. He waved at the UN ship and once more the huge horn burst out its din, making him clap his hands to his ears.

A projectile slid from the under part of the ship, extended stabilizers, and spiraled toward the ground.

"Sheeoot," Sam Regan said with disgust. "It is staples; they don't have the parachute." He turned away, not interested.

How miserable the upstairs looked today, he thought as he surveyed the landscape of Mars. Dreary. Why did we come here? Had to, were forced to.

Already the UN projectile had landed; its hull cracked open, torn by the impact, and the three colonists could see cannisters. It looked to be five hundred pounds of salt. Sam Regan felt even more despondent.

"Hey," Schein said, walking toward the projectile and peering. "I believe I see something we can use."

"Looks like radios in those boxes," Tod said. "Transistor radios." Thoughtfully he followed after Schein. "Maybe we can use them for something new in our layouts."

"Mine's already got a radio," Schein said.

"Well, build an electronic self-directing lawn mower with the parts," Tod said. "You don't have that, do you?" He knew the Scheins' Perky Pat layout fairly well; the two couples, he and his wife with Schein and his, had fused together a good deal, being compatible.

Sam Regan said, "Dibs on the radios, because I can use them." His layout lacked the automatic garage-door opener that both Schein and Tod had; he was considerably behind them. Of course all those items could be purchased. But he was out of skins. He had used his complete supply in the service of a need which he considered more pressing. He had, from a pusher, bought a fairly large quantity of Can-D; it was buried, hidden out of sight, in the earth under his sleep-compartment at the bottom level of their collective hovel.

He himself was a believer; he affirmed the miracle of translation—the near-sacred moment in which the miniature artifacts of the layout no longer merely represented Earth but *became* Earth. And he and the others, joined together in the fusion of doll-inhabitation by means of the Can-D, were transported outside of time and local space. Many of the colonists were as yet unbelievers; to them the layouts were merely symbols of a world which none of them could any longer experience. But, one by one, the unbelievers came around.

Even now, so early in the morning, he yearned to go back down below, chew a slice of Can-D from his hoard, and join with his fellows in the most solemn moment of which they were capable.

To Tod and Norman Schein he said, "Either of you care to seek transit?" That was the technical term they used for participation. "I'm going back below," he said. "We can use my Can-D; I'll share it with you."

An inducement like that could not be ignored; both Tod and Norm looked tempted. "So early?" Norm Schein said. "We just got out of bed. But I guess there's nothing to do anyhow." He kicked glumly at a huge semi-autonomic sand dredge; it had remained parked near the entrance of the hovel for days now. No one had the energy to come up to the surface and resume the clearing operations inaugurated earlier this month. "It seems wrong, though," he muttered. "We ought to be up here working in our gardens."

"And that's some garden you've got," Sam Regan said, with a grin. "What is that stuff you've got growing there? Got a name for it?"

Norm Schein, hands in the pockets of his coveralls, walked over the sandy, loose soil with its sparse vegetation to his once carefully maintained vegetable garden; he paused to look up and down the rows, hopeful that more of the specially prepared seeds had sprouted. None had.

"Swiss chard," Tod said encouragingly. "Right? Mutated as it is, I can still recognize the leaves."

Breaking off a leaf Norm chewed it, then spat it out; the leaf was bitter and coated with sand.

Now Helen Morris emerged from the hovel, shivering in the cold Martian sunlight. We have a question," she said to the three men. "I say that psychoanalysts back on Earth were charging Fifty dollars an hour and Fran says it was for only forty-five minutes." She explained, "We want to add an analyst to our layout and we want to get it right, because it's an authentic item, made on Earth and shipped here, if you remember that Bulero ship that came by last week—"

"We remember," Norm Schein said sourly. The prices that the Bulero salesman had wanted. And all the time in their satellite Allen and Charlotte Faine talked up the different items so, whetting everyone's appetite.

"Ask the Faines," Helen's husband Tod said. "Radio them the next time the satellite passes over." He glanced at his wristwatch. "In another hour. They have all the data on authentic items; in fact that particular datum should have been included with the item itself, right in the carton." It perturbed him because it had of course been his skins—his and Helen's together—that had gone to pay for the tiny figure of the human-type psychoanalyst, including the couch, desk, carpet, and bookcase of incredibly well-minned impressive books.

"You went to the analyst when you were still on Earth," Helen said to Norm Schein. "What was the charge?"

"Well, I mostly went to group therapy," Norm said. "At the Berkeley State Mental Hygiene Clinic, and they charged according to your ability to pay. And of course Perky Pat and her boyfriend go to a private analyst." He walked down the length of the garden solemnly deeded to him, between the rows of jagged leaves, all of which were to some extent shredded and devoured by microscopic native pests. If he could find one healthy plant, one untouched—it would be enough to restore his spirits. Insecticides from Earth simply had not done the job, here; the native pests thrived. They had been waiting ten thousand years, biding their time, for someone to appear and make an attempt to raise crops.

Tod said, "You better do some watering."

"Yeah," Norm Schein agreed. He meandered gloomily in the direction of Chicken Pox Prospects' hydro-pumping system; it was attached to their now partially sand-filled irrigation network which served all the gardens of their hovel. Before watering came sand-removal, he realized. If they didn't get the big Class-A dredge started up soon they wouldn't be able to water even if they wanted to. But he did not particularly want to.

And yet he could not, like Sam Regan, simply turn his back on the scene up there, return below to fiddle with his layout, build or insert new items, make improvements . . . or, as Sam proposed, actually get out a quantity of the carefully hidden Can-D and begin the communication. We have responsibilities, he realized.

To Helen he said, "Ask my wife to come up here." She could direct him as he operated the dredge; Fran had a good eye.

"I'll get her," Sam Regan agreed, starting back down below. "No one wants to come along?"

No one followed him; Tod and Helen Morris had gone over to inspect their own garden, now, and Norm Schein was busy pulling the protective wrapper from the dredge, preparatory to starting it up.

Back below, Sam Regan hunted up Fran Schein; he found her crouched at the Perky Pat layout which the Morrises and the Scheins maintained together, intent on what she was doing.

Without looking up, Fran said, "We've got Perky Pat all the way downtown in her new Ford hardtop convert and parked and a dime in the meter and she's shopped and now she's in the analyst's office reading *Fortune*. But what does she pay?" She glanced up, smoothed back her long dark hair, and smiled at him. Beyond a doubt Fran was the handsomest and most dramatic person in their collective hovel; he observed this now, and not for anything like the first time.

He said, "How can you fuss with that layout and not chew—" He glanced around; the two of them appeared to be alone. Bending down he said softly to her, "Come on and we'll chew some first-rate Can-D. Like you and I did before. Okay?" His heart labored as he waited for her to answer; recollections of the last time the two of them had been translated in unison made him feel weak.

"Helen Morris will be—"

"No, they're cranking up the dredge, above. They won't be back down for an hour." He took hold of Fran by the hand, led her to her feet. "What arrives in a plain brown wrapper," he said as he steered her from the compartment out into the corridor, "should be used, not just buried. It gets old and stale. Loses its potency." And we pay a lot for that potency, he thought morbidly. Too much to let it go to waste. Although some—not in this hovel—claimed that the power to insure translation did not come from the Can-D but from the accuracy of the layout. To him this was a nonsensical view, and yet it had its adherents.

As they hurriedly entered Sam Regan's compartment Fran said, "I'll chew in unison with you, Sam, but let's not do anything while we're there on Terra that—you know. We wouldn't do here. I mean, just because we're Pat and Walt and not ourselves that doesn't give us license." She gave him a warning frown, reproving him for his former conduct and for leading her to that yet unasked.

"Then you admit we really go to Earth." They had argued this point—and it was cardinal—many times in the past. Fran tended to take the position that the translation was one of appearance only, of what the colonists called *accidents*—the mere outward manifestation of the places and objects involved, not the essences.

"I believe," Fran said slowly, as she disengaged her fingers from his and stood by the hall door of the compartment, "that whether it's a play of imagination, or drug-induced hallucination, or an actual translation from Mars to Earth-as-it-was by an agency we know nothing of—" Again she eyed him sternly. "I think we should abstain. In order not to contaminate the experience of communication." As she watched him carefully remove the metal bed from the wall and reach, with an elongated hook, into the cavity revealed, she said, "It should be a purifying experience. We lose our fleshy bodies, our corporeality, as they say. And put on imperishable bodies instead, for a time anyhow. Or forever, if you believe as some do that it's outside of time and space, that it's eternal. Don't you agree, Sam?" She sighed. "I know you don't."

"Spirituality," he said with disgust as he fished up the packet of Can-D from its cavity beneath the compartment. "A denial of reality, and what do you get instead? Nothing."

"I admit," Fran said as she came closer to watch him open the packet, "that I can't *prove* you get anything better back, due to abstention. But I do know this. What you and other sensualists among us don't realize is that when we chew Can-D and leave our bodies *we die.* And by dying we lose the weight of—" She hesitated.

"Say it," Sam said as he opened the packet; with a knife he cut a strip from the mass of brown, tough, plant-like fibers.

Fran said, "Sin."

Sam Regan howled with laughter. "Okay—at least you're orthodox." Because most colonists would agree with Fran. "But," he said, redepositing the packet back in its safe place, "that's not why I chew it; I don't want to lose anything . . . I want to gain something." He shut the door of the compartment, then swiftly got out his own Perky Pat layout, spread it on the floor, and put each object in place, working at eager speed. "Something to which we're not normally entitled," he added, as if Fran didn't know.

Her husband—or his wife or both of them or everyone in the entire hovel—could show up while he and Fran were in the state of translation. And their two bodies would be seated at proper distance one from the other; no wrong-doing could be observed, however prurient the observers were. Legally this had been ruled on; no cohabitation could be proved, and legal experts among the ruling UN authorities on Mars and the other colonies had tried—and failed. While translated one could commit incest, murder, anything, and it remained from a juridical standpoint a mere fantasy, an impotent wish only.

This highly interesting fact had long inured him to the use of Can-D; for him life on Mars had few blessings.

"I think," Fran said, "you're tempting me to do wrong." As she seated herself she looked sad; her eyes, large and dark, fixed futilely on a spot at the center of the layout, near Perky Pat's enormous wardrobe. Absently, Fran began to fool with a mink sable coat, not speaking.

He handed her half of a strip of Can-D, then popped his own portion into his mouth and chewed greedily.

Still looking mournful, Fran also chewed.

He was Walt. He owned a Jaguar XXB sports ship with a flatout velocity of fifteen thousand miles an hour. His shirts came from Italy and his shoes were made in England. As he opened his eyes he looked for the little G.E. clock TV set by his bed; it would be on automatically, tuned to the morning show of the great newsclown Jim Briskin. In his flaming red wig Briskin was already forming on the screen. Walt sat up, touched a button which swung his bed, altered to support him in a sitting position, and lay back to watch for a moment the program in progress.

"I'm standing here at the corner of Van Ness and Market in downtown San Francisco," Briskin said pleasantly, "and we're just about to view the opening of the exciting new subsurface conapt building Sir Francis Drake, the first to be *entirely underground.* With us, to dedicate the building, standing right by me is that enchanting female of ballad and—"

Walt shut off the TV, rose, and walked barefoot to the window; he drew the shades, saw out then onto the warm sparkling early-morning San Francisco street, the hills and white houses. This was Saturday morning and he did not have to go to his job down in Palo Alto at Ampex Corporation; instead—and this rang nicely in his mind—he had a date with his girl, Pat Christensen, who had a modern little apt over on Potrero Hill.

It was always Saturday.

In the bathroom he splashed his face with water, then squirted on shave cream, and began to shave. And, while he shaved, staring into the mirror at his familiar features, he saw a note tacked up, and in his own hand.

THIS IS AN ILLUSION. YOU ARE SAM REGAN, A COLONIST ON MARS. MAKE USE OF YOUR TIME OF TRANSLATION, BUDDY BOY. CALL UP PAT PRONTO!

And the note was signed Sam Regan.

An illusion, he thought, pausing in his shaving. In what way? He tried to think back; Sam Regan and Mars, a dreary colonists' hovel . . . yes, he could dimly make the image out, but it seemed remote and vitiated and not convincing. Shrugging, he resumed shaving, puzzled, now, and a little depressed. All right, suppose the note was correct; maybe he did remember that other world, that gloomy quasi-life of involuntary expatriation in an unnatural environment. So what? Why did he have to wreck this? Reaching, he yanked down the note, crumpled it and dropped it into the bathroom disposal chute.

As soon as he had finished shaving he vidphoned Pat.

"Listen," she said at once, cool and crisp; on the screen her blonde hair shimmered: she had been drying it. "I don't want to see you, Walt. Please. Because I know what you have in mind and I'm just not interested; do you understand?" Her blue-gray eyes were cold.

"Hmmm," he said, shaken, trying to think of an answer. "But it's a terrific day—we ought to get outdoors. Visit Golden Gate Park, maybe."

"It's going to be too hot to go outdoors."

"No," he disagreed, nettled. "That's later. Hey, we could walk along the beach, splash around in the waves. Okay?"

She wavered, visibly. "But that conversation we had just before—"

"There was no conversation. I haven't seen you in a week, not since last Saturday." He made his tone as firm and full of conviction as possible. "I'll drop by your place in half an hour and pick you up. Wear your swimsuit, you know, the yellow one. The Spanish one that has a halter."

"Oh," she said disdainfully, "that's completely out of fash now. I have a new one from Sweden; you haven't seen it. I'll wear that, if it's permitted. The girl at A & F wasn't sure."

"It's a deal," he said, and rang off.

A half hour later in his Jaguar he landed on the elevated field of her conapt building.

Pat wore a sweater and slacks; the swimsuit, she explained, was on underneath. Carrying a picnic basket, she followed him up the ramp to his parked ship. Eager and pretty, she hurried ahead of him, pattering along in her sandals. It was all working out as he had hoped; this was going to be a swell day after all, after his initial trepidations had evaporated . . . as thank God they had.

"Wait until you see this swimsuit," she said as she slid into the parked ship, the basket on her lap. "It's really daring; it hardly exists: actually you sort of have to have faith to believe in it." As he got in beside her she leaned against him. "I've been thinking over that conversation we had—let me finish." She put her fingers against his lips, silencing him. "I *know* it took place, Walt. But in a way you're right; in fact basically you have the proper attitude. We should try to obtain as much from this as possible. Our time is short enough as it is . . . at least so it seems to me." She smiled wanly. "So drive as fast as you can; I want to get to the ocean."

Almost at once they were setting down in the parking lot at the edge of the beach.

"It's going to be hotter," Pat said soberly. "Every day. Isn't it? Until finally it's unbearable." She tugged off her sweater, then shifted about on the seat of the ship, managed to struggle out of her slacks. "But we won't live that long . . . it'll be another fifty years before no one can go out at noon. Like they say, become mad dogs and Englishmen; we're not that yet." She opened the door and stepped out in her swimsuit. And she had been correct; it took faith in things unseen to make the suit out at all. It was perfectly satisfactory, to both of them.

Together, he and she plodded along the wet, hard-packed sand, examining jelly fish, shells, and pebbles, the debris tossed up by the waves.

"What year is this?" Pat asked him suddenly, halting. The wind blew her untied hair back; it lifted in a mass of cloudlike yellow, clear and bright and utterly clean, each strand separate.

He said, "Well, I guess it's—" And then he could not recall; it eluded him. "Damn," he said crossly.

"Well, it doesn't matter." Linking arms with him she trudged on. "Look, there's that little secluded spot ahead, past those rocks." She increased her tempo of motion; her body rippled as her strong, taut muscles strained against the wind and the sand and the old, familiar gravity of a world lost long ago. "Am I what's-her-name—Fran?" she asked suddenly. She stepped past the rocks, foam and water rolled over her feet, her ankles; laughing, she leaped, shivered from the sudden chill. "Or am I Patricia Christensen?" With both hands she smoothed her hair. "This is blonde, so I must be Pat. Perky Pat." She disappeared beyond the rocks; he quickly followed, scrambling after her. "I used to be Fran," she said over her shoulder, "but that doesn't matter now. I could have been anyone before, Fran or Helen or Mary, and it wouldn't matter now. Right?"

"No," he disagreed, catching up with her. Panting, he said, "It's important that you're Fran. In essence."

" 'In essence.' " She threw herself down on the sand, lay resting on her elbow, drawing by means of a sharp black rock in savage swipes which left deeply gouged lines; almost at once she tossed the rock away, and sat around to face the ocean. "But the accidents . . . they're Pat." She put her hands beneath her breasts, then, languidly lifting them, a puzzled expression on her face. "These," she said, "are Pat's. Not mine. Mine are smaller; I remember."

He seated himself beside her, saying nothing.

"We're here," she said presently, "to do what we can't do back at the hovel. Back where we've left our corruptible bodies. As long as we keep our layouts in repair this—" She gestured at the ocean, then once more touched herself, unbelievingly. "It can't decay, can it? We've put on immortality." All at once she lay back, flat against the sand, and shut her eyes, one arm over her face. "And since we're here, and we can do things denied us at the hovel, then your theory is we *ought* to do those things. We ought to take advantage of the opportunity."

He leaned over her, bent and kissed her on the mouth.

Inside his mind a voice thought, "But I can do this any time." And, in the limbs of his body, an alien mastery asserted itself; he sat back, away from the girl. "After all," Norm Schein thought, "I'm married to her." He laughed, then.

"Who said you could use my layout?" Sam Regan thought angrily. "Get out of my compartment. And I bet it's my Can-D, too."

"You offered it to us," the co-inhabitant of his mind-body answered. "So I decided to take you up on it."

"I'm here, too," Tod Morris thought. "And if you want my opinion—"

"Nobody asked you for yours," Norm Schein thought angrily. "In fact nobody asked you to come along; why don't you go back up and mess with that rundown no-good garden of yours, where you ought to be?"

Tod Morris thought calmly, "I'm with Sam. I don't get a chance to do this, except here." The power of his will combined with Sam's; once more Walt bent over the reclining girl; once again he kissed her on the mouth, and this time heavily, with increased agitation.

Without opening her eyes Pat said in a low voice, "I'm here, too. This is Helen." She added, "And also Mary. But we're not using your supply of Can-D, Sam; we brought some we had already." She put her arms around him as the three inhabitants of Perky Pat joined in unison in one endeavor. Taken by surprise, Sam Regan broke contact with Tod Morris; he joined the effort of Norm Schein, and Walt sat back away from Perky Pat.

The waves of the ocean lapped at the two of them as they silently reclined together on the beach, two figures comprising the essences of six persons. Two in six, Sam Regan thought. The mystery repeated; how is it accomplished? The old question again. But all I care about, he thought, is whether they're using up my Can-D. And I bet they are; I don't care what they say: I don't believe them.

Rising to her feet Perky Pat said, "Well, I can see I might just as well go for a swim; nothing's doing here." She padded into the water, splashed away from them as they sat in their body, watching her go.

"We missed our chance," Tod Morris thought wryly.

"My fault," Sam admitted. By joining, he and Tod managed to stand; they walked a few steps after the girl and then, ankle-deep in the water, halted.

Already Sam Regan could feel the power of the drug wearing off; he felt weak and afraid and bitterly sickened at the realization. So goddam soon, he said to himself. All over; back to the hovel, to the pit in which we twist and cringe like worms in a paper bag, huddled away from the daylight. Pale and white and awful. He shuddered.

—Shuddered, and saw, once more, his compartment with its tinny bed, washstand, desk, kitchen stove . . . and, in slumped, inert heaps, the empty husks of Tod and Helen Morris, Fran and Norm Schein, his own wife Mary; their eyes stared emptily and he looked away, appalled.

On the floor between them was his layout; he looked down and saw the dolls, Walt and Pat, placed at the edge of the ocean, near the parked Jaguar. Sure enough, Perky Pat had on the near-invisible Swedish swimsuit, and next to them reposed a tiny picnic basket.

And, by the layout, a plain brown wrapper that had contained Can-D; the five of them had chewed it out of existence, and even now as he looked—against his will—he saw a thin trickle of shiny brown syrup emerge from each of their slack, will-less mouths.

Across from him Fran Schein stirred, opened her eyes, moaned; she focused on him, then wearily sighed.

"They got to us," he said.

"We took too long." She rose unsteadily, stumbled, and almost fell; at once he was up, too, catching hold of her. "You were right; we should have done it right away if we intended to. But—" She let him hold her, briefly. "I like the preliminaries. Walking along the beach, showing you the swimsuit that is no swimsuit." She smiled a little.

Sam said, "They'll be out for a few more minutes, I bet."

Wide-eyed, Fran said, "Yes, you're right." She skipped away from him, to the door; tugging it open, she disappeared out into the hall. "In our compartment," she called back. "Hurry!"

Pleased, he followed. It was too amusing; he was convulsed with laughter. Ahead of him the girl scampered up the ramp to her level of the hovel; he gained on her, caught hold of her as they reached her compartment. Together they tumbled in, rolled giggling and struggling across the hard metal floor to bump against the far wall.

We won after all, he thought as he deftly unhooked her bra, began to unbutton her shirt, unzipped her skirt, and removed her laceless slipperlike shoes in one swift operation; he was busy everywhere and Fran sighed, this time not wearily.

"I better lock the door." He rose, hurried to the door and shut it, fastening it securely. Fran, meanwhile, struggled out of her undone clothes.

"Come back," she urged. "Don't just watch." She piled them in a hasty heap, shoes on top like two paperweights.

He descended back to her side and her swift, clever fingers began on him; dark eyes alit she worked away, to his delight.

And right here in their dreary abode on Mars. And yet—they had still managed it in the old way, the sole way: through the drug brought in by the furtive pushers. Can-D had made this possible; they continued to require it. In no way were they free.

As Fran's knees clasped his bare sides he thought, And in no way do we want to be. In fact just the opposite. As his hands traveled down her flat, quaking stomach he thought, We could even use a little more.

RIG VEDA

SOMA

IT IS DRUNK by the sick man as medicine at sunrise; partaking of it strengthens the limbs, preserves the legs from breaking, wards off all disease and lengthens life. Then need and trouble vanish away, pinching want is driven off and flees when the inspiring one lays hold of the mortal; the poor man, in the intoxication of the Soma, feels himself rich; the draught impels the singer to lift his voice and inspires him for song; it gives the poet supernatural power, so that he feels himself immortal. On account of this inspiring power of the drink, there arose even in the Indo-Iranian period a personification of the sap as the god Soma, and ascription to him of almost all the deeds of other gods, the strength of the gods even being increased by this draught. Like Agni, Soma causes his radiance to shine cheeringly in the waters; like Vayu, he drives on with his steeds; like the Acvins, he comes in haste with aid when summoned; like Pusan, he excites reverence, watches over the herds, and leads by the shortest roads to success. Like Indra, as the sought-for ally, he overcomes all enemies, near and far, frees from the evil intentions of the envious, from danger and want, brings goodly riches from heaven, from earth and the air. Soma, too, makes the sun rise in the heavens, restores what has been lost, has a thousand ways and means of help, heals all, blind and lame, chases away the black skin [aborigines], and gives everything into the possession of the pious Arya. In his, the world-ruler's, ordinances these lands stand; he, the bearer of heaven and the prop of earth, holds all people in his hand. Bright shining as Mitra, awe-compelling as Aryaman, he exults and gleams like Surya; Varuna's commands are his commands; he, too, measures the earth's spaces, and built the vault of the heavens; like him, he, too, full of wisdom, guards the community,

watches over men even in hidden places, knows the most secret things.
. . . He will lengthen the life of the devout endlessly, and after death
make him immortal in the place of the blessed, in the highest heaven.

MILES DAVIS

FERRARI

I DID SOME weird shit back in those days, too many weird things to describe. But I'll tell you a couple. I remember one day when I was really paranoid from snorting and staying up all the time. I was driving my Ferrari up West End Avenue and I passed these policemen sitting in a patrol car. They knew me—all of them knew me in my neighborhood—so they spoke to me. When I got about two blocks away from them, I became paranoid and thought that there was a conspiracy to get me, bust me for some drugs. I look down in the compartment on the door and see this white powder. I never took coke out of the house with me. It's winter and snowing and some snow got inside the car. But I didn't realize that; I thought it was some coke that someone had planted in the car just so I could get busted. I panicked, stopped the car in the middle of the street, ran into a building on West End Avenue, looked for the doorman, but he wasn't there. I ran to the elevator and got on and went up to the seventh floor and hid in the trash room. I stayed up there for hours with my Ferrari parked in the middle of West End Avenue with the keys in it. After a while I came to my senses. The car was still sitting where I had left it.

I did that another time just like that and a woman was on the elevator. I thought that I was still in my Ferrari, so I told her, "Bitch, what are you doing in my goddamn car!" And then I slapped her and ran out of the building. That's the kind of weird sick shit that a lot of drugs will make you do. She called the police and they arrested me and put me in the nut ward at Roosevelt Hospital for a few days before letting me out.

Another time, I had a white woman dealer and sometimes— when nobody was at my house—I would run over to her place to pick up some coke. One time I didn't have no money, so I asked her if I could give it to her later. I had always paid her and I was buying a lot of shit from her, but she told me, "No money, no cocaine, Miles." I tried to talk her into it, but she wasn't budging. Then the doorman calls upstairs and tells her her boyfriend is on his way up. So I ask her one more time, but she won't do it. So I just lay down on her bed, and started to take off my clothes. I know her boyfriend knows I got a reputation for being big with the ladies, so what's he going to think when he sees me on her bed like that? So now she's begging me to leave, right? But I'm just laying there with my dick in one hand and my other hand held out for the dope, and I'm grinning, too, because I know she's going to give it to me and she does. She cursed me like a motherfucker on my way out, and when the elevator opened and her boyfriend passed me, he kind of looked at me funny, you know, like, "Has this nigger been with my old lady?" I never went back by there after that.

ALDOUS HUXLEY

❖

THE DOORS OF PERCEPTION

FROM WHAT I had read of the mescalin experience I was convinced in advance that the drug would admit me, at least for a few hours, into the kind of inner world described by Blake and Æ. But what I had expected did not happen. I had expected to lie with my eyes shut, looking at visions of many-colored geometries, of animated architectures, rich with gems and fabulously lovely, of landscapes with heroic figures, of symbolic dramas trembling perpetually on the verge of the ultimate revelation. But I had not reckoned, it was evident, with the idiosyncrasies of my mental make-up, the facts of my temperament, training and habits.

I am and, for as long as I can remember, I have always been a poor visualizer. Words, even the pregnant words of poets, do not evoke pictures in my mind. No hypnagogic visions greet me on the verge of sleep. When I recall something, the memory does not present itself to me as a vividly seen event or object. By an effort of the will, I can evoke a not very vivid image of what happened yesterday afternoon, of how the Lungarno used to look before the bridges were destroyed, of the Bayswater Road when the only buses were green and tiny and drawn by aged horses at three and a half miles an hour. But such images have little substance and absolutely no autonomous life of their own. They stand to real, perceived objects in the same relation as Homer's ghosts stood to the men of flesh and blood, who came to visit them in the shades. Only when I have a high temperature do my mental images come to independent life. To those in whom the faculty of visualization is strong my inner world must seem curiously drab, limited and uninteresting. This was the world—a poor thing but my own—which I expected to see transformed into something completely unlike itself.

The change which actually took place in that world was in no sense revolutionary. Half an hour after swallowing the drug I became aware of a slow dance of golden lights. A little later there were sumptuous red surfaces swelling and expanding from bright nodes of energy that vibrated with a continuously changing, patterned life. At another time the closing of my eyes revealed a complex of gray structures, within which pale bluish spheres kept emerging into intense solidity and, having emerged, would slide noiselessly upwards, out of sight. But at no time were there faces or forms of men or animals. I saw no landscapes, no enormous spaces, no magical growth and metamorphosis of buildings, nothing remotely like a drama or a parable. The other world to which mescalin admitted me was not the world of visions; it existed out there, in what I could see with my eyes open. The great change was in the realm of objective fact. What had happened to my subjective universe was relatively unimportant.

I took my pill at eleven. An hour and a half later, I was sitting in my study, looking intently at a small glass vase. The vase contained only three flowers—a full-blown Belle of Portugal rose, shell pink with a hint at every petal's base of a hotter, flamier hue; a large magenta and cream-colored carnation; and, pale purple at the end of its broken stalk, the bold heraldic blossom of an iris. Fortuitous and provisional, the little nosegay broke all the rules of traditional good taste. At breakfast that morning I had been struck by the lively dissonance of its colors. But that was no longer the point. I was not looking now at an unusual flower arrangement. I was seeing what Adam had seen on the morning of his creation—the miracle, moment by moment, of naked existence.

"Is it agreeable?" somebody asked. (During this part of the experiment, all conversations were recorded on a dictating machine, and it has been possible for me to refresh my memory of what was said.)

"Neither agreeable nor disagreeable," I answered. "It just *is*."

Istigkeit—wasn't that the word Meister Eckhart liked to use? "Is-ness." The Being of Platonic philosophy—except that Plato seems to have made the enormous, the grotesque mistake of separating Being from becoming and identifying it with the mathematical abstraction of the Idea. He could never, poor fellow, have seen a bunch of flowers shining with their own inner light and all but quivering under the pressure of the significance with which they were charged; could never have perceived that what rose and iris and carnation so intensely signified was nothing more, and nothing less, than what they were—a transience that was yet eternal life, a perpetual perishing that was at the same time pure Being, a bundle of minute, unique particulars in which, by some unspeakable and yet self-evident paradox, was to be seen the divine source of all existence.

I continued to look at the flowers, and in their living light I seemed to detect the qualitative equivalent of breathing—but of a breathing without returns to a starting point, with no recurrent ebbs but only a repeated flow from beauty to heightened beauty, from deeper to ever deeper meaning. Words like "grace" and "transfiguration" came to mind, and this, of course, was what, among other things, they stood for. My eyes traveled from the rose to the carnation, and from that feathery incandescence to the smooth scrolls of sentient amethyst which were the iris. The Beatific Vision, Sat Chit Ananda, Being-Awareness-Bliss— for the first time I understood, not on the verbal level, not by inchoate hints or at a distance, but precisely and completely what those prodigious syllables referred to. And then I remembered a passage I had read in one of Suzuki's essays. "What is the Dharma-Body of the Buddha?" ("The Dharma-Body of the Buddha" is another way of saying Mind, Suchness, the Void, the Godhead.) The question is asked in a Zen monastery by an earnest and bewildered novice. And with the prompt irrelevance of one of the Marx Brothers, the Master answers, "The hedge at the bottom of the garden." "And the man who realizes this truth," the novice dubiously inquires, "what, may I ask, is he?" Groucho gives him a whack over the shoulders with his staff and answers, "A golden-haired lion."

It had been, when I read it, only a vaguely pregnant piece of nonsense. Now it was all as clear as day, as evident as Euclid. Of course the Dharma-Body of the Buddha was the hedge at the bottom of the garden. At the same time, and no less obviously, it was these flowers, it was anything that I—or rather the blessed Not-I, released for a moment from my throttling embrace—cared to look at. The books, for example, with which my study walls were lined. Like the flowers, they glowed, when I looked at them, with brighter colors, a profounder significance. Red books, like rubies; emerald books; books bound in white jade; books of agate; of aquamarine, of yellow topaz; lapis lazuli books whose color was so intense, so intrinsically meaningful, that they seemed to be on the point of leaving the shelves to thrust themselves more insistently on my attention.

"What about spatial relationships?" the investigator inquired, as I was looking at the books.

It was difficult to answer. True, the perspective looked rather odd, and the walls of the room no longer seemed to meet in right angles. But these were not the really important facts. The really important facts were that spatial relationships had ceased to matter very much and that my mind was perceiving the world in terms of other than spatial categories. At ordinary times the eye concerns itself with such problems as *Where?—How far?—How situated in relation to what?* In the mescalin experience the implied questions to which the eye responds are of another order. Place and distance cease to be of much interest. The mind does its perceiving in terms of intensity of existence, profundity of significance, relationships within a pattern. I saw the books, but was not at all concerned with their positions in space. What I noticed, what impressed itself upon my mind was the fact that all of them glowed with living light and that in some the glory was more manifest than in others. In this context position and the three dimensions were beside the point. Not, of course, that the category of space had been abolished. When I got up and walked about, I could do so quite normally, without misjudging the whereabouts of objects. Space was still there; but it had lost its predominance. The mind was primarily concerned, not with measures and locations, but with being and meaning.

And along with indifference to space there went an even more complete indifference to time.

"There seems to be plenty of it," was all I would answer, when the investigator asked me to say what I felt about time.

Plenty of it, but exactly how much was entirely irrelevant. I could, of course, have looked at my watch; but my watch, I knew, was in another universe. My actual experience had been, was still, of an indefinite duration or alternatively of a perpetual present made up of one continually changing apocalypse.

From the books the investigator directed my attention to the furniture. A small typing table stood in the center of the room; beyond it, from my point of view, was a wicker chair and beyond that a desk. The three pieces formed an intricate pattern of horizontals, uprights and diagonals—a pattern all the more interesting for not being interpreted in terms of spatial relationships. Table, chair and desk came together in a composition that was like something by Braque or Juan Gris, a still life recognizably related to the objective world, but rendered without depth, without any attempt at photographic realism. I was looking at my furniture, not as the utilitarian who has to sit on chairs, to write at desks and tables, and not as the cameraman or scientific recorder, but as the pure aesthete whose concern is only with forms and their relationships within the field of vision or the picture space. But as I looked, this purely aesthetic, Cubist's-eye view gave place to what I can only describe as the sacramental vision of reality. I was back where I had been when I was looking at the flowers—back in a world where everything shone with the Inner Light, and was infinite in its significance. The legs, for example, of that chair—how miraculous their tubularity, how supernatural their polished smoothness! I spent several minutes—or was it several centuries?—not merely gazing at those bamboo legs, but actually *being* them—or rather being myself in them; or, to be still more accurate (for "I" was not involved in the case, nor in a certain sense were "they") being my Not-self in the Not-self which was the chair.

Reflecting on my experience, I find myself agreeing with the eminent Cambridge philosopher, Dr. C. D. Broad, "that we should do well to consider much more seriously than we have hitherto been inclined to do the type of theory which Bergson put forward in connection with memory and sense perception. The suggestion is that the function of the brain and nervous system and sense organs is in the main *eliminative* and not productive. Each person is at each moment capable of remembering all that has ever happened to him and of perceiving everything that is happening everywhere in the universe. The function of the brain and nervous system is to protect us from being overwhelmed and confused by this mass of largely useless and irrelevant knowledge, by shutting out most of what we should otherwise perceive or remember at any moment, and leaving only that very small and special selection which is likely to be practically useful. According to such a theory, each one of us is potentially Mind at Large. But in so far as we are animals, our business is at all costs to survive. To make biological survival possible, Mind at Large has to be funnelled through the reducing valve of the brain and nervous system. What comes out at the other end is a measly trickle of the kind of consciousness which will help us to stay alive on the surface of this particular planet. To formulate and express the contents of this reduced awareness, man has invented and endlessly elaborated those symbol-systems and implicit philosophies which we call languages. Every individual is at once the beneficiary and the victim of the linguistic tradition into which he has been born—the beneficiary inasmuch as language gives access to the accumulated records of other people's experience, the victim in so far as it confirms him in the belief that reduced awareness is the only awareness and as it bedevils his sense of reality, so that he is all too apt to take his concepts for data, his words for actual things. That which, in the language of religion, is called "this world" is the universe of reduced awareness, expressed, and, as it were, petrified by language. The various "other worlds," with which human beings erratically make contact are so many elements in the totality of the awareness belonging to Mind at Large. Most people, most of the time, know only what comes through the reducing valve and is consecrated as genuinely real by the local language. Certain persons, however, seem to be born with a kind of by-pass that circumvents the reducing valve. In others temporary by-passes may be acquired either spontaneously, or as the result of deliberate "spiritual exercises," or through hypnosis, or by means of drugs. Through these permanent or temporary by-passes there flows, not indeed the perception "of everything that is happening everywhere in the universe" (for the by-pass does not abolish the reducing valve, which still excludes the total content of Mind at Large), but something more than, and above all something different from, the carefully selected utilitarian material which our narrowed, individual minds regard as a complete, or at least sufficient, picture of reality.

The brain is provided with a number of enzyme systems which serve to coordinate its workings. Some of these enzymes regulate the supply of glucose to the brain. Mescalin inhibits the production of these enzymes and thus lowers the amount of glucose available to an organ that is in constant need of sugar. When mescalin reduces the brain's normal ration of sugar what happens? Too few cases have been observed, and therefore a comprehensive answer cannot yet be given. But what happens to the majority of the few who have taken mescalin under supervision can be summarized as follows.

(1) The ability to remember and to "think straight" is little if at all reduced. (Listening to the recordings of my conversation under the influence of the drug, I cannot discover that I was then any stupider than I am at ordinary times.)

(2) Visual impressions are greatly intensified and the eye recovers some of the perceptual innocence of childhood, when the sensum was not immediately and automatically subordinated to the concept. Interest in space is diminished and interest in time falls almost to zero.

(3) Though the intellect remains unimpaired and though perception is enormously improved, the will suffers a profound change for the worse. The mescalin taker sees no reason for doing anything in particular and finds most of the causes for which, at ordinary times, he was prepared to act and suffer, profoundly uninteresting. He can't be bothered with them, for the good reason that he has better things to think about.

(4) These better things may be experienced (as I experienced them) "out there," or "in here," or in both worlds, the inner and the outer, simultaneously or successively. That they *are* better seems to be self-evident to all mescalin takers who come to the drug with a sound liver and an untroubled mind.

These effects of mescalin are the sort of effects you could expect to follow the administration of a drug having the power to impair the efficiency of the cerebral reducing valve. When the brain runs out of sugar, the undernourished ego grows weak, can't be bothered to undertake the necessary chores, and loses all interest in those spatial and temporal relationships which mean so much to an organism bent on getting on in the world. As Mind at Large seeps past the no longer watertight valve, all kinds of biologically useless things start to happen. In some cases there may be extra-sensory perceptions. Other persons discover a world of visionary beauty. To others again is revealed the glory, the infinite value and meaningfulness of naked existence, of the given, unconceptualized event. In the final stage of egolessness there is an "obscure knowledge" that All is in all—that All is actually each. This is as near, I take it, as a finite mind can ever come to "perceiving everything that is happening everywhere in the universe."

THE AFRICAN FANG LEGENDS

❊

EBOKA

ZAME YE MEBEGE (the last of the creator gods) gave us *eboka*. He saw the misery in which blackman was living. He thought how to help him. One day he looked down and saw a blackman, the Pygmy Bitumu, high in an Atanga tree, gathering its fruit. He made him fall. He died and Zame brought his spirit to him. Zame cut off the little fingers and the little toes of the cadaver of the Pygmy and planted them in various parts of the forest. They grew into the *eboka* bush.

THE VISION (NDEM EBOKA) OF NDONG ASSEKO
(Age 22; clan Essabam; unmarried)

WHEN I ATE *eboka* I found myself taken by it up a long road in a deep forest until I came to a barrier of black iron. At that barrier, unable to pass, I saw a crowd of black persons also unable to pass. In the distance beyond the barrier it was very bright. I could see many colors in the air but the crowd of black people could not pass. Suddenly my father descended from above in the form of a bird. He gave to me then my *eboka* name, Onwan Misengue, and enabled me to fly up after him over the barrier of iron. As we proceeded the bird who was my father changed from black to white—first his tail feathers, then all his plumage. We came then to a river the color of blood in the midst of which was a great snake of three colors—blue, black, and red. It closed its gaping mouth so that we were able to pass over it. On the other side there was a crowd of people all in white. We passed through them and they shouted at us words of recognition until we arrived at another river—all white. This we crossed by means of a giant chain of gold. On the other side there were no trees but only a grassy upland. On the top of the hill was a round house made entirely of glass and built upon one post only. Within I saw a man, the hair on his head piled up in the form of a Bishop's hat. He had a star on his breast but on coming closer I saw that it was his heart in his chest beating. We moved around him and on the back of his neck there was a red cross tattooed. He had a long beard. Just then I looked up and saw a woman in the moon—a bayonet was piercing her heart from which a bright white fire was pouring forth. Then I felt a pain on my shoulder. My father told me to return to earth. I had gone far enough. If I went further I would not return.

The Vision of Eman Ela

(Age 30; clan Essamenyang; married with one wife)

When I ate *eboka* very quickly my grandfather came to me. First he had black skin. Then he returned and he had white skin. It was he that gave me my *eboka* name. My grandmother then appeared in the same way. Because my grandfather was dead before I was born he asked me if I knew how I recognized him. It was through *eboka*. He then seized me by the hand and we found ourselves embarked on a grand route. I didn't have the sense of walking but just of floating along. We came to a table in that road. There we sat and my grandfather asked me all the reasons I had eaten *eboka*. He gave me others. Then my grandfather disappeared and suddenly a white spirit appeared before me. He grasped me by the arm and we floated along. Then we came to a crossroads. The road on which we were traveling was red. The other two routes were black and white. We passed over. Finally we arrived at a large house on a hill. It was built on one post. Within I found the wife of my mother's father. She gave me my *eboka* name a second time and also gave me the talent to play the *ngombi* harp. We passed on and finally arrived after passing over more crossroads at a great desert.

There I saw descend from the sky—from the moon—a giant circle which came down and encircled the earth, as a rainbow of three colors—blue, red, and white. I began playing the *ngombi* under the rainbow and I heard the applause of men. I returned. All the *banzie* thought I had gone too far and was dead. Since then I have seen nothing in *eboka*. But each time I take it I hear the spirits who give the power to play the *ngombi*. I play what I hear from them. Only if I come into the chapel in a bad heart does *eboka* fail me.

CHARLES BAUDELAIRE

❀

THE DOUBLE ROOM

A BEDROOM THAT resembles a dream, a truly *spiritual* room, where the stagnant atmosphere is slightly tinted pink and blue.

The soul is bathed here in idleness, perfumed by regret and desire. The feeling is one of twilight, of pinkness and blueness: a voluptuous dream during an eclipse.

The furniture is elongated, prostrate, languid. The furniture seems to be dreaming; you'd think it was endowed with a sleepwalking life, like vegetables and minerals. The fabrics speak a mute language, like flowers, like skies, like setting suns.

There are no artistic abominations on the walls. Compared to the pure dream, to the unanalyzed impression, definite art, precise art is blasphemous. Here, everything has the abundant clarity and delicious obscurity of harmony.

An infinitesimal aroma of the most exquisite choice, mingled with a very slight damp, swims in the air, where the dozing spirit is lulled by hothouse sensations.

Muslin rains down abundantly before the windows and before the bed; it pours out in snowy waterfalls. On this bed lies the Idol, the sovereign of dreams. How did she get here? Who brought her? What magical power has installed her on this throne of dream and sensuality? What does it matter! Here she is: I recognize her.

These are the eyes whose flame pierces twilight; these subtle and terrible eyes, which I recognize by their terrifying malice. They attract, they subjugate, they devour any imprudent gaze that dares contemplate them. I have often studied them, these black stars so demanding of curiosity and admiration.

To what benevolent demon do I owe my surroundings, so

mysterious, silent, peaceful and perfumed? Oh, beatitude! What we ordinarily call life, even at its happiest, has nothing in common with this supreme life that I now know and that I savor, minute by minute, second by second!

No. There are no more minutes, no more seconds. Time has disappeared. Eternity reigns: an eternity of delights.

But then a terrible loud blow resounded on the door, and as in a nightmare, I felt a pickaxe strike me in the belly.

And then a Specter entered: A bailiff come to torture me in the name of the law; or an unspeakable concubine come to cry poverty and add the trivialities of her life to the pain of mine; or else the peon of some newspaper editor come to demand his manuscript.

The chamber of paradise, the idol, the queen of dreams, the *Sylphide* as René would have said: all this magic disappeared with the Specter's brutal knock.

Appalling! I remember! I remember! Yes, this squalid hovel, this room of eternal boredom, is mine. These are my sticks of furniture, stupid, dusty, ramshackle; the fireplace, unwarmed by flames or embers, soiled with spit; the dismal windows, where rain has stained the dust; the manuscripts, crossed out or half-finished; the calendar, where a pencil has marked off every dreary day.

And that otherworldly perfume that so exhilarated my perfect sensibilities: alas, it is replaced by the fetid odor of tobacco mixed with an unidentifiable, nauseating mold. Now we inhale the rancid odor of desolation.

In this narrow world, so filled with disgust, only one familiar object smiles at me: the vial of laudanum, an old and terrible lover: and like all lovers, alas, fecund in caresses and betrayals.

Oh yes: Time has reappeared; Time is the sovereign now, and with that hideous old man has returned his whole demonic retinue of Memories, Regrets, Spasms, Fears, Worries, Nightmares, Anger and Neuroses.

Now you can be sure that the seconds are strongly, solemnly accentuated, and each one, bursting from the clock, says, "I am Life, intolerable, relentless Life!"

In human life, there is only one Second whose mission it is to announce good news, the *good news* that is so inexplicably terrifying to us all.

Yes, Time reigns: its brutal dictatorship is back. And it drives me like an ox, with its double goad — "Giddup, nag! Sweat, slave! *Live,* you who are damned!"

TERENCE McKENNA

❖

KATHMANDU INTERLUDE

I WAS GOING to take LSD the night of the solstice and sit up all night on my roof, smoking hashish and star-gazing. I mentioned my plan to my two English friends, who expressed a desire to join me. This was fine with me, but there was a problem; there was not enough reliable LSD to go around. My own tiny supply had arrived in Kathmandu, prophetically hidden inside a small ceramic mushroom mailed from Aspen.

Almost as a joke, I suggested that they substitute the seed of the Himalayan Datura, *Datura metel*, for the LSD. Daturas are annual bushes and the source of a number of tropane alkaloids—scopalamine, hylosciamine, and so on—compounds that produce a pseudo-hallucinogenic effect. They give an impression of flying or of confronting vague and fleeting visions, but all in a realm hard to keep control of and hard to recollect later. The seeds of *Datura metel* are used in Nepal by *saddhus* (wandering hermits and holy men), so their use was known in the area. Nevertheless my suggestion was made facetiously, since the difficulty of controlling Datura is legendary. To my surprise, my friends agreed that this was something they wanted to do, so we arranged that they would arrive at my home at six p.m. on the appointed day to make the experiment.

When the evening finally came, I moved my blankets and pipes up to the roof of the building. From there I could command a fine view of the surrounding village with its enormous *Stupa*, a conical temple with staring Buddha eyes painted on its higher portion in gold leaf. The upper golden levels of the Stupa were at that time encased in scaffolding, where repairs necessitated by a lightning strike suffered some months previously were under way. The white-domed bulk of the Stupa gave the whitewashed adobe mud village of Boudanath a saucerian and unearthly quality. Farther away, rising up many thousands of feet, I could see the great Annapurna Range; in the middle distance, the land was a patchwork of emerald paddies.

Six o'clock came and went, and my friends had not arrived. At seven they still had not been seen, and so I took my treasured tab of Orange Sunshine and settled down to wait. Ten minutes later, they arrived. I could already feel myself going, so I gestured to the two piles of Datura seeds that I had prepared. They took them downstairs to my room and ground them with a mortar and pestle before washing them down with some tea. By the time they had returned to the roof and gotten comfortably settled, I was surging through mental space.

Hours seemed to pass. When they seated themselves, I was too distant to be aware of them. She was seated directly across from me, and he farther back and to one side, in the shadows. He played his flute. I passed the hash pipe. The moon rose full and high in the sky. I fell into long hallucinatory reveries that each lasted many minutes but felt like whole lifetimes. When I had emerged from a particularly long spell of visions, I found that my friend had stopped playing and had gone away, leaving me with his lady.

I had promised them both that I would let them try some DMT during the evening. My glass pipe and tiny stash of waxy orange DMT were before me. Slowly, and with the fluid movements of a dream, I filled the pipe and gave it to her. The stars, hard and glittering, stared down from a mighty distance on all of this. She held the pipe and took two deep inhalations, sufficient for a person so frail, then the pipe was returned to me, and I followed her into it with four huge inhalations, the fourth of which I held onto until I had broken through. For me it was an enormous amount of DMT, and I immediately had a sense of entering a high vacuum. I heard a high-pitched whine and the sound of cellophane ripping as I was transformed into the ultra-high-frequency orgasmic goblin that is a human being in DMT ecstasy. I was surrounded by the chattering of elf machines and the more-than-Arabian vaulted spaces that would shame a Bibiena. Manifestations of a power both alien and bizarrely beautiful raged around me.

At the point where I would normally have expected the visions to fade, the pretreatment with LSD synergized my state to a higher level. The cavorting hoards of DMT elf machines faded to a mere howling as the elfin mob moved on. I suddenly found myself flying hundreds of miles above the earth and in the company of silvery disks. I could not tell how many. I was fixated on the spectacle of the earth below and realized that I was moving south, apparently in polar orbit, over Siberia. Ahead of me I could see the Great Plain of Shang and the mass of the Himalayas rising up in front of the red-yellow waste of India. The sun would rise in about two hours. In a series of telescoping leaps, I went from orbit to a point where I could specifically pick out the circular depression that is the Kathmandu Valley. Then, in the next leap, the valley filled my field of vision. I seemed to be approaching it at great speed. I could see the Hindu temple and the houses of Kathmandu, the Temple of Svayambhunath to the west of the city and the Stupa at Boudanath, gleaming white and a few miles to the east. Then Boudanath was a mandala of houses and circular streets filling my vision. Among the several hundred roof tops I found my own. In the next moment I slammed into my body and was refocused on the roof top and the woman in front of me.

Incongruously, she had come to the event wearing a silver satin, full-length evening dress—an heirloom—the sort of thing one could find in an antique clothing store in Notting Hill Gate. I fell forward and thought that my hand was covered by some cool, white liquid. It was the fabric of the dress. Until that moment neither of us had considered the other a potential lover. Our relationship had functioned on quite a different level. But suddenly all the normal sets of relations were obviated. We reached out toward each other, and I had the distinct impression of passing through her, of physically reaching beyond her. She pulled her dress over her head in a single gesture. I did the same with my shirt, which ripped to pieces in my hands as I took it off over my head. I heard buttons fly, and somewhere my glasses landed and shattered.

Then we made love. Or rather we had an experience that vaguely related to making love but was a thing unto itself. We were both howling and singing in the glossolalia of DMT, rolling over the ground with everything awash in crawling, geometric hallucinations. She was transformed; words exist to describe what she became—pure anima, Kali, Leucothea, something erotic but not human, something addressed to the species and not to the individual, glittering with the possibility of cannibalism, madness, space, and extinction. She seemed on the edge of devouring me.

Reality was shattered. This kind of fucking occurs at the very limit of what is possible. Everything had been transformed into orgasm and visible, chattering oceans of elf language. Then I saw that where our bodies were glued together there was flowing, out of her, over me, over the floor of the roof, flowing everywhere, some sort of obsidian liquid, something dark and glittering, with color and lights within it. After the DMT flash, after the seizures of orgasms, after all that, this new thing shocked me to the core. What was this fluid and what was going on? I looked at it. I looked right into it, and it was the surface of my own mind reflected in front of me. Was it translinguistic matter, the living opalescent excrescence of the alchemical abyss of hyperspace, something generated by the sex act performed under such crazy conditions? I looked into it again and now saw in it the lama who taught me Tibetan, who would have been asleep a mile away. In the fluid I saw him, in the company of a monk I had never seen; they were looking into a mirrored plate. Then I realized that they were watching me! I could not understand it. I looked away from the fluid and away from my companion, so intense was her aura of strangeness.

Then I realized that we had been singing and yodeling and uttering wild orgasmic howls for what must have been several minutes on my roof! It meant everyone in Boudanath would have been awakened and was about to open their doors and windows and demand to know what was going on. And what *was* going on? My grandfather's favorite expostulation seemed appropriate: "Great God! said the woodcock when the hawk struck him." This grotesquely inappropriate recollection brought uncontrollable laughter.

Then the thought of discovery sobered me enough to realize that we must get away from this exposed place. Both of us were completely naked, and the scene around us was one of total, unexplainable chaos. She was lying down, unable to rise, so I picked her up and made my way down the narrow staircase, past the grain storage bins and into my room. The whole time I remember saying over and over to her and to myself: "I am a human being. I am a human being." I had to reassure myself, for I was not at that moment sure.

We waited in my room many minutes. Slowly we realized that by some miracle no less strange than everything else that had occurred, no one was awake demanding to know what was going on. No one seemed even to have heard! To calm us, I made tea and, as I did this, I was able to assess my companion's state of mind. She seemed quite delirious, quite unable to discuss with me what had happened only a few moments before on the roof. It is an effect typical of Datura that whatever one experiences is very difficult, indeed usually impossible, to recollect later. It seemed that while what had transpired had involved the most intimate of acts between two people, I was nevertheless the only witness who could remember anything at all of what happened.

Pondering all of this, I crept back to the roof and collected my glasses. Incredibly, they were unbroken, although I had distinctly heard them shatter. Obsidian liquids, the ectoplasmic excrescences of tantric hanky-2, were nowhere to be seen. With my glasses and our clothes, I returned to my room where my companion was sleeping. I smoked a little hashish and then climbed into the mosquito net and lay down beside her. In spite of all the excitement and the stimulation of my system, I immediately went to sleep.

I have no idea how long I slept. When I awoke it was with a start and from a deep slumber. It was still dark. And there was no sign of my friend. I felt a stab of alarm; if she was delirious then it would be dangerous for her to be wandering alone around the village at night. I jumped up and threw on my *jalaba* and began to search. She was not on the roof, nor near the grain storage bins.

I found her on the ground floor of my building. She was sitting on the earthen floor staring at her reflection in the gas tank of a motorcycle, which belonged to the miller's son-in-law. Still disoriented in the way that is typical of Datura, she was hallucinating persons not present and mistaking one person for another. "Are you my tailor?" she asked me several times as I led her back to my room. "Are you my tailor?"

When we were once again upstairs in my quarters, I took off my *jalaba*, and we both discovered that I was wearing what she delicately described as her "knickers." They were too small on me and neither of us knew how they had come to be there. This little cross-dressing episode capped an amazing evening, and I roared with laughter. I returned her knickers and we went to bed, puzzled, reassured, exhausted, and amused.

As this experience passed behind us, the girl and I became even closer friends. We never made love again; it was not really the relationship that suited us. She remembered nothing of the events on the roof. About a week after all this was over, I told her my impression of what had happened. She was amazed but accepting. I did not know what had happened. I christened the obsidian fluid we had generated "luv," something more than love, something less than love, perhaps not love at all, but some kind of unplumbed potential human experience very little is known about.

L E W I S C A R R O L L

❧

D O W N   T H E   R A B B I T - H O L E

ALICE WAS BEGINNING to get very tired of sitting by her sister on the bank and of having nothing to do: once or twice she had peeped into the book her sister was reading, but it had no pictures or conversations in it, "and what is the use of a book," thought Alice, "without pictures or conversations?"

So she was considering, in her own mind (as well as she could, for the hot day made her feel very sleepy and stupid), whether the pleasure of making a daisy-chain would be worth the trouble of getting up and picking the daisies, when suddenly a White Rabbit with pink eyes ran close by her.

There was nothing so *very* remarkable in that; nor did Alice think it so *very* much out of the way to hear the Rabbit say to itself "Oh dear! Oh dear! I shall be too late!" (when she thought it over afterwards it occurred to her that she ought to have wondered at this, but at the time it all seemed quite natural); but, when the Rabbit actually *took a watch out of its waistcoat-pocket*, and looked at it, and then hurried on, Alice started to her feet, for it flashed across her mind that she had never before seen a rabbit with either a waistcoat-pocket, or a watch to take out of it, and burning with curiosity, she ran across the field after it, and was just in time to see it pop down a large rabbit-hole under the hedge.

In another moment down went Alice after it, never once considering how in the world she was to get out again.

The rabbit-hole went straight on like a tunnel for some way, and then dipped suddenly down, so suddenly that Alice had not a moment to think about stopping herself before she found herself falling down what seemed to be a very deep well.

Either the well was very deep, or she fell very slowly, for she had plenty of time as she went down to look about her, and to wonder what was going to happen next. First, she tried to look down and make out what she was coming to, but it was too dark to see anything; then she looked at the sides of the well, and noticed that they were filled with cupboards and book-shelves: here and there she saw maps and pictures hung upon pegs. She took down a jar from one of the shelves as she passed: it was labeled "ORANGE MARMALADE" but to her great disappointment it was empty: she did not like to drop the jar, for fear of killing somebody underneath, so she managed to put it into one of the cupboards as she fell past it.

"Well!" thought Alice to herself. "After such a fall as this, I shall think nothing of tumbling down-stairs! How brave they'll think me at home! Why, I wouldn't say anything about it, even if I fell off the top of the house! (Which was very likely true.)

Down, down, down. Would the fall *never* come to an end? "I wonder how many miles I've fallen by this time?" she said aloud. "I must be getting somewhere near the centre of the earth. Let me see: that would be four thousand miles down, I think—" (for, you see, Alice had learnt several things of this sort in her lessons in the school-room, and though this was not a *very* good opportunity for showing off her knowledge, as there was no one to listen to her, still it was good practice to say it over) "—yes, that's about the right distance—but then I wonder what Latitude or Longitude I've got to?" (Alice had not the slightest idea what Latitude was, or Longitude either, but she thought they were nice grand words to say.)

Presently she began again. "I wonder if I shall fall right *through* the earth! How funny it'll seem to come out among the people that walk with their heads downwards! The antipathies, I think—" (she was rather glad there *was* no one listening, this time, as it didn't sound at all the right word) "—but I shall have to ask them what the name of the country is, you know. Please, Ma'am, is this New Zealand? Or

Australia?" (and she tried to curtsey as she spoke—fancy, *curtseying* as
you're falling through the air! Do you think she could manage it?) "and
what an ignorant little girl she'll think me for asking! No, it'll never do
to ask: perhaps I shall see it written up somewhere."

Down, down, down. There was nothing else to do, so Alice
soon began talking again. "Dinah'll miss me very much to-night, I
should think!" (Dinah was the cat.) "I hope they'll remember her
saucer of milk at tea-time, Dinah, my dear! I wish you were down here
with me! There are no mice in the air, I'm afraid, but you might catch a
bat, and that's very like a mouse, you know. But do cats eat bats, I
wonder?" And here Alice began to get rather sleepy, and went on
saying to herself, in a dreamy sort of way, "Do cats eat bats? Do cats eat
bats?" and sometimes "Do bats eat cats?" for, you see, as she couldn't
answer either question, it didn't much matter which way she put it. She
felt that she was dozing off, and had just begun to dream that she was
walking hand in hand with Dinah, and was saying to her, very
earnestly, "Now, Dinah, tell me the truth: did you ever eat a bat?" when
suddenly, thump! thump! down she came upon a heap of sticks and dry
leaves, and the fall was over.

Alice was not a bit hurt, and she jumped up onto her feet in a
moment: she looked up, but it was all dark overhead: before her was
another long passage, and the White Rabbit was still in sight, hurrying
down it. There was not a moment to be lost: away went Alice like the
wind, and was just in time to hear it say, as it turned a corner, "Oh my
ears and whiskers, how late it's getting!" She was close behind it when
she turned the corner, but the Rabbit was no longer to be seen: she
found herself in a long, low hall, which was lit up by a row of lamps
hanging from the roof.

There were doors all round the hall, but they were all locked;
and when Alice had been all the way down one side and up the other,
trying every door, she walked sadly down the middle, wondering how
she was ever to get out again.

Suddenly she came upon a little three-legged table, all made of solid glass: there was nothing on it but a tiny golden key, and Alice's first idea was that this might belong to one of the doors of the hall; but, alas! either the locks were too large, or the key was too small, but at any rate it would not open any of them. However, on the second time round, she came upon a low curtain she had not noticed before, and behind it was a little door about fifteen inches high: she tried the little golden key in the lock, and to her great delight it fitted!

Alice opened the door and found that it led into a small passage, not much larger than a rathole: she knelt down and looked along the passage into the loveliest garden you ever saw. How she longed to get out of that dark hall, and wander about among those beds of bright flowers and those cool fountains, but she could not even get her head through the doorway; "and even if my head *would* go through," thought poor Alice, "it would be of very little use without my shoulders. Oh, how I wish I could shut up like a telescope! I think I could, if I only knew how to begin." For, you see, so many out-of-the-way things had happened lately, that Alice had begun to think that very few things indeed were really impossible.

There seemed to be no use in waiting by the little door, so she went back to the table, half hoping she might find another key on it, or at any rate a book of rules for shutting people up like telescopes: this time she found a little bottle on it ("which certainly was not here before," said Alice), and tied round the neck of the bottle was a paper label, with the words "DRINK ME" beautifully printed on it in large letters.

It was all very well to say "Drink me," but the wise little Alice was not going to do that in a hurry; "No, I'll look first," she said, "and see whether it's marked 'poison' or not"; for she had read several nice little stories about children who had got burnt, and eaten up by wild beasts, and other unpleasant things, all because they would not remember the simple rules their friends had taught them: such as, that a red-hot poker will burn you if you hold it too long: and that, if you cut your finger *very* deeply with a knife, it usually bleeds; and she had never forgotten that, if you drink much from a bottle marked "poison," it is almost certain to disagree with you, sooner or later.

However, this bottle was *not* marked "poison," so Alice ventured to taste it, and, finding it very nice (it had, in fact, a sort of mixed flavour of cherry-tart, custard, pine-apple, roast turkey, toffy, and hot buttered toast), she very soon finished it off.

"WHAT A CURIOUS feeling!" said Alice. "I must be shutting up like a telescope!"

And so it was indeed: she was now only ten inches high, and her face brightened up at the thought that she was now the right size for going through the little door into that lovely garden. First, however, she waited for a few minutes to see if she was going to shrink any further: she felt a little nervous about this; "for it might end, you know," said Alice to herself, "in my going out altogether, like a candle. I wonder what I should be like then?" And she tried to fancy what the flame of a candle looks like after the candle is blown out, for she could not remember ever having seen such a thing.

After a while, finding that nothing more happened, she decided on going into the garden at once; but, alas for poor Alice! when she got to the door, she found she had forgotten the little golden key, and when she went back to the table for it, she found she could not possibly reach it: she could see it quite plainly through the glass, and she tried her best to climb up one of the legs of the table, but it was too slippery; and when she had tired herself out with trying, the poor little thing sat down and cried.

"Come, there's no use in crying like that!" said Alice to herself rather sharply. "I advise you to leave off this minute!" She generally gave herself very good advice (though she very seldom followed it), and sometimes she scolded herself so severely as to bring tears into her eyes; and once she remembered trying to box her own ears for having cheated herself in a game of croquet she was playing against herself, for this curious child was very fond of pretending to be two people. "But it's no use now," thought poor Alice, "to pretend to be two people! Why, there's hardly enough of me left to make *one* respectable person!"

Soon her eye fell on a little glass box that was lying under the table: she opened it, and found in it a very small cake, on which the words "EAT ME" were beautifully marked in currants. "Well, I'll eat it," said Alice, "and if it makes me grow larger, I can reach the key; and if it makes me grow smaller, I can creep under the door: so either way I'll get into the garden, and I don't care which happens!"

She ate a little bit, and said anxiously to herself "Which way? Which way?", holding her hand on the top of her head to feel which way it was growing; and she was quite surprised to find that she remained the same size. To be sure, this is what generally happens when one eats cake; but Alice had got so much into the way of expecting nothing but out-of-the-way things to happen, that it seemed quite dull and stupid for life to go on in the common way.

So she set to work, and very soon finished off the cake.

HUNTER S. THOMPSON

❖

WHEN THE GOING GETS WEIRD, THE WEIRD TURN PRO

WE WERE SOMEWHERE around Barstow on the edge of the desert when the drugs began to take hold. I remember saying something like "I feel a bit lightheaded; maybe you should drive. . . ." And suddenly there was a terrible roar all around us and the sky was full of what looked like huge bats, all swooping and screeching and diving around the car, which was going about a hundred miles an hour with the top down to Las Vegas. And a voice was screaming: "Holy Jesus! What are these goddamn animals?"

Then it was quiet again. My attorney had taken his shirt off and was pouring beer on his chest, to facilitate the tanning process. "What the hell are you yelling about?" he muttered, staring up at the sun with his eyes closed and covered with wraparound Spanish sunglasses. "Never mind," I said. "It's your turn to drive." I hit the brakes and aimed the Great Red Shark toward the shoulder of the highway. No point mentioning those bats, I thought. The poor bastard will see them soon enough.

It was almost noon, and we still had more than a hundred miles to go. They would be tough miles. Very soon, I knew, we would both be completely twisted. But there was no going back, and no time to rest. We would have to ride it out. Press registration for the fabulous Mint 400 was already underway, and we had to get there by four to claim our sound-proof suite. A fashionable sporting magazine in New York had taken care of the reservations, along with this huge red Chevy convertible we'd just rented off a lot on the Sunset strip . . . and I was, after all, a professional journalist; so I had an obligation to *cover the story*, for good or ill.

The sporting editors had also given me $300 in cash, most of which was already spent on extremely dangerous drugs. The trunk of the car looked like a mobile police narcotics lab. We had two bags of grass, seventy-five pellets of mescaline, five sheets of high-powered blotter acid, a salt shaker half full of cocaine, and a whole galaxy of multi-colored uppers, downers, screamers, laughers . . . and also a quart of tequila, a quart of rum, a case of Budweiser, a pint of raw ether and two dozen amyls.

All this had been rounded up the night before, in a frenzy of high-speed driving all over Los Angeles County—from Topanga to Watts, we picked up everything we could get our hands on. Not that we *needed* all that for the trip, but once you locked into a serious drug connection, the tendency is to push it as far as you can.

The only thing that really worried me was the ether. There is nothing in the world more helpless and irresponsible and depraved than a man in the depths of an ether binge. And I knew we'd get into that rotten stuff pretty soon. Probably at the next gas station. We had sampled almost everything else, and now—yes, it was time for a long snort of ether. And then do the next hundred miles in a horrible, slobbering sort of spastic stupor. The only way to keep alert on ether is to do up a lot of amyls—not all at once, but steadily, just enough to maintain the focus at ninety miles an hours through Barstow.

"Man, this is the way to travel," said my attorney. He leaned over to turn the volume up on the radio, humming along with the rhythm section and kind of moaning the words: "One toke over the line, Sweet Jesus . . . One toke over the line . . ."

One toke? You poor fool! Wait till you see those goddamn bats. I could barely hear the radio . . . slumped over on the far side of the seat, grappling with a tape recorder turned all the way up on "Sympathy for the Devil." That was the only tape we had, so we played it constantly, over and over, as a kind of demented counterpoint to the radio. And also to maintain our rhythm on the road. A constant speed is good for gas mileage—and for some reason that seemed important at the time. Indeed. On a trip like this one *must* be careful about gas consumption. Avoid those quick bursts of acceleration that drag blood to the back of the brain.

BAYARD TAYLOR

❀

HASHEESH

THE SENSE OF limitation—of the confinement of our senses within the bounds of our own flesh and blood—instantly fell away. The walls of my frame were burst outward and tumbled into ruin; and, without thinking what form I wore—losing sight even of all idea of form—I felt that I existed throughout a vast extent of space . . . the spirit (demon shall I rather say?) of Hasheesh had entire possession of me. I was cast upon the flood of his illusions, and drifted helplessly withersoever they might choose to bear me. The thrills which ran through my nervous system became more rapid and fierce, accompanied with sensations that steeped my whole being in unutterable rapture. I was encompassed by a sea of light, through which played the pure, harmonious colors that are born of light. While endeavoring, in broken expression, to describe my feelings to my friends, who sat looking upon me incredulously—not yet having been affected by the drug—I suddenly found myself at the foot of the great Pyramid of Cheops. The tapering courses of yellow limestone gleamed like gold in the sun, and the pile rose so high that it seemed to lean for support upon the blue arch of the sky. I wished to ascend it, and the wish alone placed me immediately upon its apex, lifted thousands of feet above the wheat-fields and palm-groves of Egypt. I cast my eyes downward, and, to my astonishment, saw that it was built, not of limestone, but of huge square plugs of Cavendish tobacco! Words cannot paint the overwhelming sense of the ludicrous which I then experienced. I writhed on my chair in an agony of laughter, which was only relieved by the vision melting away like a dissolving view; till, out of my confusion of indistinct images and fragments of images, another and more wonderful vision arose.

The more vividly I recall the scene which followed, the more carefully I restore its different features, and separate the many threads of sensation which it wove into one gorgeous web, the more I despair of representing its exceeding glory. I was moving over the Desert, not upon the rocking dromedary, but seated in a barque made of mother-of pearl, and studded with jewels of surpassing lustre. The sand was of grains of gold, and my keel slid through them without jar or sound. The air was radiant with excess of light, though no sun was to be seen. I inhaled the most delicious perfumes; and harmonies, such as Beethoven may have heard in dreams, but never wrote, floated around me. The atmosphere itself was light, odor, music; and each and all sublimated beyond anything the sober senses are capable of receiving. Before me—for a thousand leagues, as it seemed—stretched a vista of rainbows, whose colors gleamed with the splendor of gems—arches of living amethyst, sapphire, emerald, topaz, and ruby. By thousands and tens of thousands, they flew past me, as my dazzling barge sped down the magnificent arcade; yet the vista still stretched as far as ever before me. I revelled in a sensuous elysium, which was perfect, because no sense was left ungratified. But beyond all, my mind was filled with a boundless feeling of triumph.

PAUL BOWLES

❖

THE TAKING OF MAJOUN

THERE I MADE inquiries about *majoun* and was directed to a barbershop behind the Zaouia of Moulay Idriss where there were always four or five tins of it in a drawer along with the clippers. I felt that I had come upon a fantastic secret: to change worlds, I had only to spread a bit of jam on a biscuit and eat it. I began a series of experiments with the still-unfamiliar substance in order to determine my own set of optimum conditions regarding the quantity to be ingested, the time of day for the dose, the accompanying diet, and the general physical and psychological ambiances most conducive to pleasure during the experience. Large quantities of hot tea were essential. Twilight was the best hour for taking the dose; the effect came on slowly after an hour and a half or even two hours had passed, preferably at the moment of sitting down to dinner. A clear soup followed by a small steak and salad seemed to interfere the least with the *majoun*'s swift circulation. It was imperative to be unmitigatedly content with all the facets of existence beforehand. The most minimal preoccupation, the merest speck of cloud on the emotional horizon, had a way of italicizing itself during the alteration of consciousness and assuming gigantic proportions, thus completely ruining the inner journey. It is a delicate operation, the taking of *majoun*. Since its success or failure can be measured only in purely subjective terms, it is also a supremely egotistical pastime. Above all, there must be no interruptions, no surprises; everything must come about according to the timetable furnished by the substance itself.

ARTHUR RIMBAUD

❖

COMEDY OF THIRST

COME, THE WINES go to the Beaches,

And the waves by the millions!

See the wild Bitter

Rolling from the top of the mountains!

Let us, wise pilgrims, reach

The Absinthe with the green pillars . . .

MARIE CORELLI

❈

WORMWOOD

"NEVER TASTED IT!" exclaimed Gessonex amazedly. "Mon dieu! You a born and bred Parisian, have never tasted absinthe?"

I smiled at his excitement.

"Never! I have seen others drinking it often—but I have not liked the look of it somehow. A repulsive color to me, that medicinal green!"

He laughed a trifle nervously, and his hand trembled. But he gave no immediate reply, for at that moment the waiter placed a flacon of the drink in question on the table, together with the usual supply of water and tumblers. Carefully preparing and stirring the opaline mixture, Gessonex filled the glasses to the brim, and pushed one across to me. I made a faint sign of rejection. He laughed again in apparent amusement at my hesitation.

"By Venus and Cupid, and all the dear old heathen deities who are so remarkably convenient myths to take one's oath upon," he said. "I hope you will not compel me to consider you a fool, Beauvais! What an idea that is of yours—'medicinal green!' Think of melted emeralds instead! There, beside you, you have the most marvelous cordial in all the world—drink and you will find your sorrows transmuted—yourself transformed! Even if no better result be obtained than escaping the chill you have incurred in this night's heavy drenching, that is surely enough! Life without absinthe! I cannot imagine it! For me it would be impossible! I should hang, drown or shoot myself into infinitude, out of sheer rage at the continued cruelty and injustice of the world—but with this divine nectar of Olympus I can defy misfortune and laugh at poverty, as though they were the merest bagatelles! Come!—to your health, mon brave! Drink with me!"

He raised his glass glimmering pallidly in the light,—his words, his manner, fascinated me, and a curious thrill ran through my brains. There was something spectral in his expression too, as though the skeleton of the man had become suddenly visible beneath its fleshly covering, as though Death had for a moment peered through the veil of Life . . .

T O M   W O L F E

❖

P S Y C H O - D E L I C

LSD; HOW CAN—now that those big fat letters are babbling out on coated stock from every newsstand . . . But this was late 1959, early 1960, a full two years before Mom&Dad&Buddy&Sis heard of the dread letters and clucked because Drs. Timothy Leary and Richard Alpert were french-frying the brains of Harvard boys with it. It was even before Dr. Humphry Osmond had invented the term "psychodelic," which was later amended to "psychedelic" to get rid of the nuthouse connotation of "psycho" . . . LSD! It was quite a little secret to have stumbled onto, a hulking supersecret, in fact—the triumph of the guinea pigs! In a short time he and Lovell had tried the whole range of the drugs, LSD, psilocybin, mescaline, peyote, IT-290 the superamphetamine, Ditran the bummer, morning-glory seeds. They were onto a discovery that the Menlo Park clinicians themselves never—mighty fine irony here: the White Smocks were supposedly using *them.* Instead the White Smocks had handed them the very key itself. *And you don't even know, bub . . . with these drugs your perception is altered enough that you find yourself looking out of completely strange eyeholes. All of us have a great deal of our minds locked shut. We're shut off from our own world. And these drugs seem to be the key to open these locked doors.* How many?—many two dozen people in the world were on to this incredible secret! One was Aldous Huxley, who had taken mescaline and written about it in *The Doors of Perception*. He compared the brain to a "reducing valve." In ordinary perception, the senses send an overwhelming flood of information to the brain, which the brain then filters down to a trickle it can manage for the purpose of survival in a highly competitive world. Man has become so rational, so utilitarian, that the trickle becomes most pale and thin. It is efficient, for mere survival, but it screens out the most wondrous part of man's potential experience without his even knowing it. *We're shut off from our own world.* Primitive man once experienced the rich and sparkling flood of the senses fully. Children experience it for a few months—until "normal" training, conditioning, close the doors on this other world, usually for good. Somehow, Huxley had said, the drugs opened these ancient doors. And through them modern man may at last go, and rediscover his divine birthright—

But these are *words*, man! *And you couldn't put it into words.* The White Smocks liked to put it into words, like *hallucination* and *dissociative phenomena.* They could understand the visual skyrockets. Give them a good case of an ashtray turning into a Venus flytrap or eyelid movies of crystal cathedrals, and they could groove on that, *Kluver, op cit., p. 43n.* That was swell. *But don't you see?*—the visual stuff was just the décor with LSD. In fact, you might go through the whole experience without any true hallucination. The whole thing was . . . *the experience* . . . this certain indescribable *feeling* . . . Indescribable, because words can only jog the memory, and if there is no memory of . . . The *experience* of the barrier between the subjective and the objective, the personal and the impersonal, the *I* and the *not-I* disappearing . . . that *feeling!* . . . Or can you remember when you were a child watching someone put a pencil to a sheet of paper for the first time, to draw a picture . . . and the line begins to grow—into a nose! and it is not just a pattern of graphite line on a sheet of paper but the very miracle of creation itself and your own dreams flowed into that magical . . . growing . . . line, and it was not a picture but a *miracle* . . . an *experience* . . . and now that you're soaring on LSD that *feeling* is coming on again—only now the creation is of the entire universe—

TIMOTHY LEARY,
RALPH METZNER,
AND RICHARD ALPERT

❖

PSYCHEDELIC SESSIONS

IN PLANNING A session, the first question to be decided is "what is the goal?" Classic Hinduism suggests four possibilities:

(1) For increased personal power, intellectual understanding, sharpened insight into self and culture, improvement of life situation, accelerated learning, professional growth.

(2) For duty, help of others, providing care, rehabilitation, rebirth for fellow men.

(3) For fun, sensuous enjoyment, aesthetic pleasure, interpersonal closeness, pure experience.

(4) For transcendence, liberation from ego and space-time limits; attainment of mystical union.

This manual aims primarily at the latter goal—that of liberation-enlightenment. This emphasis does not preclude attainment of the other goals—in fact, it guarantees their attainment because illumination requires that the person be able to step out beyond game problems of personality, role, and professional status. The initiate can decide beforehand to devote the psychedelic experience to any of the four goals. The manual will be of assistance in any event.

If there are several people having a session together they should either agree collaboratively on a goal, or at least be aware of each other's goals. If the session is to be "programmed" then the participants should either agree on or design a program collaboratively, or they should agree to let one member of the group do the programming. Unexpected or undesired manipulations by one of the participants can easily "trap" the other voyagers into paranoid Third Bardo delusions.

The voyager, especially in an individual session, may also wish to have either an extroverted or an introverted experience. In the *extroverted* transcendent experience, the self is ecstatically fused with external objects (e.g. flowers, or other people). In the *introverted* state, the self is ecstatically fused with internal life processes (lights, energy-waves, bodily events, biological forms, etc.). Of course, either the extroverted or the introverted state may be negative rather than positive, depending on the attitude of the voyager. Also it may be primarily conceptual or primarily emotional. The eight types of experience thus derived (four positive and four negative) have been described more fully in Visions 2 to 5 of the Second Bardo.

For the extroverted mystic experience one would bring to the session objects or symbols to guide the awareness in the desired direction. Candles, pictures, books, incense, music or recorded passages. An introverted mystic experience requires the elimination of all stimulation; no light, no sound, no smell, no movement.

The *mode of communication* with the other participants should also be agreed on beforehand. You may agree on certain signals, silently indicating companionship. You may arrange for physical contact—clasping hands, embracing. These means of communication should be pre-arranged to avoid game-misinterpretations that may develop during the heightened sensitivity of ego-transcendence.

Drugs and Dosages

A WIDE VARIETY of chemicals and plants have psychedelic ("mind-manifesting") effects. The most widely used substances are listed here together with dosages adequate for a normal adult of average size. The dosage to be taken depends, of course, on the goal of the session. Two figures are therefore given. The first column indicates a dosage which should be sufficient for an inexperienced person to enter the transcendental worlds described in this manual. The second column gives a smaller dosage figure, which may be used by more experienced persons or by participants in a group session.

	A	B
LSD-25 (lysergic acid diethylamide)	200–500µg	100–200µg
Mescaline	600–800 mg	300–500mg
Psilocybin	40–60 mg	20–30 mg

The time of onset, when the drugs are taken orally on an empty stomach, is approximately 20–30 minutes for LSD and psilocybin, and one to two hours for mescaline. The duration of the session is usually eight to ten hours for LSD and mescaline, and five to six hours for psilocybin. DMT (dimethyltryptamine), when injected intramuscularly in dosages of 50–60 mg, gives an experience approximately equivalent to 500 µg of LSD, but which lasts only 30 minutes.

Some persons have found it useful to take other drugs before the session. A very anxious person, for example, may take 30 to 40 mg of Librium about one hour earlier, to calm and relax himself. Methedrine has also been used to induce a pleasant, euphoric mood prior to the session. Sometimes, with excessively nervous persons, it is advisable to stagger the drug-administration: for example, 200 µg of LSD may be taken initially, and a "booster" of another 200 µg may be taken after the person has become familiar with some of the effects of the psychedelic state.

Nausea may sometimes occur. Usually this is a mental symptom, indicating fear, and should be regarded as such. Sometimes, however, particularly with the use of morning-glory seeds and peyote, the nausea can have a physiological cause. Anti-nauseant drugs such as Marezine, Bonamine, Dramamine, or Tigan, may be taken beforehand to prevent this.

If a person becomes trapped in a repetitive game-routine during a session, it is sometimes possible to "break the set" by administering 50 mg of DMT, or even 25 mg of Dexedrine or Methedrine. Such additional dosages, of course, should only be given with the person's own knowledge and consent.

Should external emergencies call for it, Thorazine (100-200 mg, i.m.) or other phenothiazine-type tranquilizers will terminate the effects of psychedelic drugs. Antidotes should not be used simply because the voyager or the guide is frightened. Instead, the appropriate sections of the Third Bardo should be read.

Preparation

Psychedelic chemicals are not drugs in the usual sense of the word. There is no specific reaction, no expected sequence of events, somatic or psychological.

The specific reaction has little to do with the chemical and is chiefly a function of *set* and *setting:* preparation and environment. The better the preparation, the more ecstatic and revelatory the session. In initial sessions and with unprepared persons, setting—particularly the actions of others—is most important. With persons who have prepared thoughtfully and seriously, the setting is less important.

There are two aspects of set: long-range and immediate.

Long-range set refers to the personal history, the enduring personality. The kind of person you are—your fears, desires, conflicts, guilts, secret passions—determines how you interpret and manage any situation you enter, including a psychedelic session. Perhaps more important are the reflex mechanisms used when dealing with anxiety— the defenses, the protective maneuvers typically employed. Flexibility, basic trust, religious faith, human openness, courage, interpersonal warmth, creativity, are characteristics which allow for fun and easy learning. Rigidity, desire to control, distrust, cynicism, narrowness, cowardice, coldness, are characteristics which make any new situation threatening. Most important is insight. No matter how many cracks in the record, the person who has some understanding of his own recording machinery, who can recognize when he is not functioning as he would wish, is better able to adapt to any challenge—even the sudden collapse of his ego.

The most careful preparation would include some discussion of the personality characteristics and some planning with the guide as to how to handle expected emotional reactions when they occur.

Immediate set refers to the expectations about the session itself. Session preparation is of critical importance in determining how the experience unfolds. People tend naturally to impose their personal and social game perspectives on any new situation. Careful thought should precede the session to prevent narrow sets being imposed.

Medical expectations. Some ill-prepared subjects unconsciously impose a medical model on the experience. They look for symptoms, interpret each new sensation in terms of sickness/health, place the guide in a doctor-role, and, if anxiety develops, demand chemical rebirth—i.e., tranquilizers. Occasionally one hears of casual, ill-planned, non-guided sessions which end in the subject demanding to be hospitalized, etc. It is even more problem-provoking if the guide employs a medical model, watches for symptoms, and keeps hospitalization in mind to fall back on, as protection for himself.

Rebellion against convention may be the motive of some people who take the drug. The idea of doing something "far out" or vaguely naughty is a naive set which can color the experience.

Intellectual expectations are appropriate when subjects have had much psychedelic experience. Indeed, LSD offers vast possibilities for accelerated learning and scientific-scholarly research. But for initial sessions, intellectual reactions can become traps. The Tibetan Manual never tires of warning about the dangers of rationalization. "Turn your mind off" is the best advice for novitiates. Control of your consciousness is like flight instruction. After you have learned how to move your consciousness around—into ego-loss and back, at will—then intellectual exercises can be incorporated into the psychedelic experience. The last stage of the session is the best time to examine concepts. The objective of this particular manual is to free you from your verbal mind for as long as possible.

Religious expectations invite the same advice as intellectual set. Again, the subject in early sessions is best advised to float with the stream, stay "up" as long as possible, and postpone theological interpretations until the end of the session, or to later sessions.

Recreational and aesthetic expectations are natural. The psychedelic experience, without question, provides ecstatic moments which dwarf any personal or cultural game. Pure sensation can capture awareness. Interpersonal intimacy reaches Himalayan heights. Aesthetic delights—musical, artistic, botanical, natural—are raised to the millionth power. But all of these reactions can be Third Bardo ego games: "*I* am having this ecstasy. How lucky *I* am." Such reactions can become tender traps, preventing the subject from reaching pure ego-loss (First Bardo) or the glories of Second Bardo creativity.

Planned expectations. This manual prepares the person for a mystical experience according to the Tibetan model. The Sages of the Snowy Ranges have developed a most sophisticated and precise understanding of human psychology, and the student who studies this manual will become oriented for a voyage which is much richer in scope and meaning than any Western psychological theory. We remain aware, however, that the *Bardo Thödol* model of consciousness is a human artifact, a Second Bardo hallucination, however grand its scope.

Some practical recommendations. The subject should set aside at least three days for his experience; a day before, the session day, and a follow-up day. This scheduling guarantees a reduction in external pressure and a more sober commitment to the voyage.

Talking to others who have taken the voyage is excellent preparation, although the Second Bardo hallucinatory quality of all descriptions should be recognized. Observing a session is another valuable preliminary. The opportunity to see others during and after a session shapes expectations.

Reading books about mystical experience is a standard orientation procedure. Reading the accounts of others' experience is another possibility (Aldous Huxley, Alan Watts, and Gordon Wasson have written powerful accounts).

Meditation is probably the best preparation for a psychedelic session. Those who have spent time in the solitary attempt to manage the mind, to eliminate thought and to reach higher stages of concentration, are the best candidates for a psychedelic session. When the ego-loss state occurs, they are ready. They recognize the process as an end eagerly awaited, rather than a strange event ill-understood.

THE SETTING

THE FIRST AND most important thing to remember, in the preparation for a psychedelic session, is to provide a setting which is removed from one's usual social and interpersonal games and which is as free as possible from unforeseen distractions and intrusions. The voyager should make sure that he will not be disturbed by visitors or telephone calls, since these will often jar him into hallucinatory activity. Trust in the surroundings and privacy are necessary.

A period of time (usually at least three days) should be set aside in which the experience will run its natural course and there will be sufficient time for reflection and meditation. It is important to keep schedules open for three days and to make these arrangements beforehand. A too-hasty return to game-involvements will blur the clarity of the vision and reduce the potential for learning. If the experience was with a group, it is very useful to stay together after the session in order to share and exchange experiences.

There are differences between night sessions and day sessions. Many people report that they are more comfortable in the evening and consequently that their experiences are deeper and richer. The person should chose the time of day that seems right according to his own temperament at first. Later, he may wish to experience the difference between night and day sessions.

Similarly, there are differences between sessions out-of-doors and indoors. Natural settings such as gardens, beaches, forests, and open country have specific influences which one may or may not wish to incur. The essential thing is to feel as comfortable as possible in the surroundings, whether in one's living room or under the night sky. A familiarity with the surroundings may help one to feel confident in hallucinatory periods. If the session is held indoors, one must consider the arrangement of the room and the specific objects one may wish to see and hear during the experience. Music, lighting, the availability of food and drink, should be considered beforehand. Most people report no desire for food during the height of the experience, and then, later on, prefer to have simple, ancient foods like bread, cheese, wine, and fresh fruit. Hunger is usually not the issue. The senses are wide open, and the taste and smell of a fresh orange are unforgettable.

In group sessions, the arrangement of the room is quite important. People usually will not feel like walking or moving very much for a long period, and either beds or mattresses should be provided. The arrangement of the beds or mattresses can vary. One suggestion is to place the heads of the beds together to form a star pattern. Perhaps one may want to place a few beds together and keep one or two some distance apart for anyone who wishes to remain aside for some time. Often, the availability of an extra room is desirable for someone who wishes to be in seclusion for a period.

If it is desired to listen to music or to reflect on paintings or religious objects, one should arrange these so that everyone in the group feels comfortable with what they are hearing or seeing. In a group session, all decisions about goals, setting, etc. should be made with collaboration and openness.

The Psychedelic Guide

For initial sessions, the attitude and behavior of the guide are critical factors. He possesses enormous power to shape the experience. With the cognitive mind suspended, the subject is in a heightened state of suggestibility. The guide can move consciousness with the slightest gesture or reaction.

The key issue here is the guide's ability to turn off his own ego and social games—in particular, to muffle his own power needs and fears. To be there relaxed, solid, accepting, secure. The Tao wisdom of creative quietism. To sense all and do nothing except to let the subject know your wise presence.

A psychedelic session lasts up to twelve hours and produces moments of intense, *intense*, INTENSE reactivity. The guide must never be bored, talkative, intellectualizing. He must remain calm during long periods of swirling mindlessness.

He is the ground control in the airport tower. Always there to receive messages and queries from high-flying aircraft. Always ready to help navigate their course, to help them reach their destination. An airport-tower-operator who imposes his own personality, his own games upon the pilot is unheard of. The pilots have their own flight plan, their own goals, and ground control is there, ever waiting to be of service.

The pilot is reassured to know that an expert who has guided thousands of flights is down there, available for help. But suppose the flier has reason to suspect that ground control is harboring his own motives and might be manipulating the plane towards selfish goals. The bond of security and confidence would crumble.

It goes without saying, then, that the guide should have had considerable experience in psychedelic sessions himself and in guiding others. To administer psychedelics without personal experience is unethical and dangerous.

The greatest problem faced by human beings in general, and the psychedelic guide in particular, is *fear.* Fear of the unknown. Fear of losing control. Fear of trusting the genetic process and your companions. From our own research studies and our investigations into sessions run by others—serious professionals or adventurous bohemians—we have been led to the conclusion that almost every negative LSD reaction has been caused by fear on the part of the guide which has augmented the transient fear of the subject. When the guide acts to protect himself, he communicates his concern to the subject.

The guide must remain passively sensitive and intuitively relaxed for several hours. This is a difficult assignment for most Westerners. For this reason, we have sought ways to assist the guide in maintaining a state of alert quietism in which he is poised with ready flexibility. The most certain way to achieve this state is for the guide to take a low dose of the psychedelic with the subject. Routine procedure is to have one trained person participate in the experience and one staff member present in ground control without psychedelic aid.

The knowledge that one experienced guide is "up" and keeping the subject company, is of inestimable value; intimacy and communication; cosmic companionship; the security of having a trained pilot flying at your wing tip; the scuba diver's security in the presence of an expert comrade in the deep.

It is not recommended that guides take large doses during sessions for new subjects. The less experienced he is, the more likely will the subject impose Second and Third Bardo hallucinations. These intense games affect the experienced guide, who is likely to be in a state of mindless void. The guide is then pulled into the hallucinatory field of the subject, and may have difficulty orienting himself. During the First Bardo there are no familiar fixed landmarks, no place to put your foot, no solid concept upon which to base your thinking. All is flux. Decisive Second Bardo action on the part of the subject can structure the guide's flow if he has taken a heavy dose.

The role of the psychedelic guide is perhaps the most exciting and inspiring role in society. He is literally a liberator, one who provides illumination, one who frees men from their life-long internal bondage. To be present at the moment of awakening, to share the ecstatic revelation when the voyager discovers the wonder and awe of the divine life-process, is for many the most gratifying part to play in the evolutionary drama. The role of the psychedelic guide has a built-in protection against professionalism and didactic oneupmanship. The psychedelic liberation is so powerful that it far outstrips earthly game ambitions. Awe and gratitude—rather than pride—are the rewards of this new profession.

THOMAS DE QUINCEY

❖

CONFESSIONS OF AN ENGLISH OPIUM-EATER

I HAVE OFTEN been asked—how it was, and through what series of steps, that I became an opium-eater. Was it gradually, tentatively, mistrustingly, as one goes down a shelving beach into a deepening sea, and with a knowledge from the first of the dangers lying on that path; half-courting those dangers, in fact, whilst seeming to defy them? Or was it, secondly, in pure ignorance of such dangers, under the misleadings of mercenary fraud? since oftentimes lozenges, for the relief of pulmonary affections, found their efficacy upon the opium which they contain, upon this, and this only, though clamorously disavowing so suspicious an alliance: and under such treacherous disguises multitudes are seduced into a dependency which they had not foreseen upon a drug which they had not known; not known even by name or by sight: and thus the case is not rare—that the chain of abject slavery is first detected when it has inextricably wound itself about the constitutional system. Thirdly, and lastly, was it [*Yes*, by passionate anticipation, I answer, before the question is finished]— was it on a sudden, overmastering impulse derived from bodily anguish? Loudly I repeat *Yes*; loudly and indignantly—as in answer to a willful calumny. Simply as an anodyne it was, under the mere coercion of pain the severest, that I first resorted to opium; and precisely that same torment it is, or some similar medicine, taken three times a-week, would more certainly than opium have delivered me from that terrific curse. In this ignorance, however, which misled me into making war upon toothache when ripened and manifesting itself in effects of pain, rather than upon its germs and gathering causes, I did but follow the rest of the world. To intercept the evil whilst yet in elementary stages of formation, was the true policy; whereas I in my blindness sought only for some mitigation to the evil when already formed, and past all reach of interception. In this stage of the suffering, formed and perfect, I was thrown passively upon chance advice, and therefore, by a natural consequence, upon opium—that being the one sole anodyne that is almost notoriously such, and which in that great function is universally appreciated.

But from this I now pass to what is the main subject of these latter Confessions—to the history and journal of what took place in my dreams; for these were the immediate and proximate cause of shadowy terrors that settled and brooded over my whole waking life.

The first notice I had of any important change going on in this part of my physical economy, was from the re-awaking of a state of eye oftentimes incident to childhood. I know not whether my reader is aware that many children have a power of painting, as it were, upon the darkness all sorts of phantoms; in some that power is simply a mechanic affection of the eye; others have a voluntary or semi-voluntary power to dismiss or summon such phantoms; or, as a child once said to me, when I questioned him on this matter, "I can tell them to go, and they go; but sometimes they come when I don't tell them to come." He had by one-half as unlimited a command over apparitions as a Roman centurion over his soldiers. In the middle of 1817 this faculty became increasingly distressing to me: at night, when I lay awake in bed, vast processions moved along continually in mournful pomp; friezes of never-ending stories, that to my feelings were as sad and solemn as stories drawn from times before Oedipus or Priam, before Tyre, before Memphis. And, concurrently with this, a corresponding change took place in my dreams; a theatre seemed suddenly opened and lighted up within my brain, which presented nightly spectacles of more than earthly splendour. And the four following facts may be mentioned, as noticeable at this time:—

1. That, as the creative state of the eye increased, a sympathy seemed to arise between the waking and the dreaming states of the brain in one point—that whatsoever I happened to call up and to trace by a voluntary act upon the darkness was very apt to transfer itself to my dreams; and at length I feared to exercise this faculty; for, as Midas turned all things to gold that yet baffled his hopes and defrauded his human desires, so whatsoever things capable of being visually represented I did but think of in the darkness, immediately shaped themselves into phantoms for the eye; and, by a process apparently no less inevitable, when thus once traced in faint and visionary colours, like writings in sympathetic ink, they were drawn out, by the fierce chemistry of my dreams, into insufferable splendour that fretted my heart.

2. This and all other changes in my dreams were accompanied by deep-seated anxiety and funereal melancholy, such as are wholly incommunicable by words. I seemed every night to descend—not metaphorically, but literally to descend—into chasms and sunless abysses, depths below depths, from which it seemed hopeless that I would ever re-ascend. Nor did I, by waking, feel that I had re-ascended. Why should I dwell upon this? For indeed the state of gloom which attended these gorgeous spectacles, amounting at last to utter darkness, as of some suicidal despondency, cannot be approached by words.

3. The sense of space, and in the end the sense of time, were both powerfully affected. Buildings, landscapes, etc., were exhibited in proportions so vast as the bodily eye is not fitted to receive. Space swelled, and was amplified to an extent of unutterable and self-repeating infinity. This disturbed me very much less than the vast expansion of time. Sometimes I seemed to have lived for seventy or a hundred years in one night; nay, sometimes had feelings representative of a duration far beyond the limits of any human experience.

4. The minutest incidents of childhood, or forgotten scenes of later years, were often revived. I could not be said to recollect them; for,

if I had been told of them when waking, I should not have been able to acknowledge them as parts of my past experience. But placed as they were before me, in dreams like intuitions, and clothed in all their evanescent circumstances and accompanying feelings, I recognised them instantaneously. I was once told by a near relative of mine, that having in her childhood fallen into a river, and being on the very verge of death but for the assistance which reached her at the last critical moment, she saw in a moment her whole life, clothe in its forgotten incidents, arrayed before her as in a mirror, not successively, but simultaneously; and she had a faculty developed as suddenly for comprehending the whole and every part. This, from some opium experiences, I can believe; I have, indeed, seen the same thing asserted twice in modern books, and accompanied by a remark which probably is true—viz., that the dread book of account, which the Scriptures speak of, is, in fact, the mind itself of each individual. Of this, at least, I feel assured, that there is no such thing as ultimate *forgetting;* traces once impressed upon the memory are indestructible; a thousand accidents may and will interpose a veil between our present consciousness and the secret inscriptions on the mind. Accidents of the same sort will also rend away this veil. But alike, whether veiled or unveiled, the inscription remains forever; just as the stars seem to withdraw before the common light of day, whereas, in fact, we all know that it is the light which is drawn over them as a veil; and that they are waiting to be revealed, whenever the obscuring daylight itself shall have withdrawn.

Having noticed these four facts as memorably distinguishing my dreams from those of health, I shall now cite a few illustrative cases; and shall then cite such others as I remember, in any order that may give them most effect as pictures to the reader.

I had been in youth, and ever since, for occasional amusement, a great reader of Livy, whom I confess that I prefer, both for style and matter, to any other of the roman historians; and I had often felt as solemn and appalling sounds, emphatically representative of Roman majesty, the two words so often occurring in Livy, *Consul Romanus;* especially when the consul is introduced in his military character. I mean to say, that the words king, sultan, regent, etc., or any other titles of those who embody in their own persons the collective majesty of a great people, had less power over my reverential feelings. I had also, though no great reader of history, made myself critically familiar with one period of English history—viz., the period of the Parliamentary War—having been attracted by the moral grandeur of some who figured in that day, and by the interesting memoirs which survive those unquiet times. Both these parts of my lighter reading, have furnished me often with matter of reflection, now furnished me with matter for my dreams. Often I used to see, after painting upon the blank darkness a sort of rehearsal whilst waking, a crowd of ladies, and perhaps a festival and dances. And I heard it said, or I said to myself, "These are English ladies from the unhappy times of Charles I. These are the wives and daughters of those who met in peace, and sat at the same tables, and were allied by marriage or blood; and yet, after a certain day in August 1642, never smiled upon each other again, nor met but in the field of battle; and at Marston Moor, at Newbury, or at Naseby, cut asunder all ties of love by the cruel sabre, and washed away in blood the memory of ancient friendship." The ladies danced, and looked as lovely as at the court of George IV. Yet even in my dream I knew that they had been in the grave for nearly two centuries. This pageant would suddenly dissolve; and, at a clapping of hands, would be heard the heart-shaking sound of *Consul Romanus;* and immediately came "sweeping by," in gorgeous paludaments, Paullus or Marius, girt around by a company of centurions, with the crimson tunic hoisted on a spear, and followed by the *alalagmos* of the Roman legions.

Many years ago, when I was looking over Piranesi's *Antiquities of Rome*, Coleridge, then standing by, described to me a set of plates from that artist, called his *Dreams*, and which record the scenery of his own visions during the delirium of a fever. Some of these (I describe only from memory of Coleridge's account) represented vast Gothic halls; on the floor of which stood mighty engines and machinery, wheels, cables, catapults, etc., expressive of enormous power put forth, or resistance overcome. Creeping along the sides of the walls, you perceived a staircase; and upon this, groping his way upwards, was Piranesi himself. Follow the stairs a little farther, and you perceive them reaching an abrupt termination, without any balustrade, and allowing no step onwards to him who should reach the extremity, except into the depths below. Whatever is to become of poor Piranesi, at least you suppose that his labours must now in some way terminate. But raise your eyes, and behold a second flight of stairs still higher, on which again Piranesi is perceived, by this time standing on the very brink of the abyss. Once again elevate your eye, and a still more aërial flight is descried; and there, again, is the delirious Piranesi, busy on his aspiring labours: and so on, until the unfinished stairs and the hopeless Piranesi both are lost in the upper gloom of the hall. With the same power of endless growth and self-reproduction did my architecture proceed in dreams. In the early stage of the malady, the splendours of my dreams were indeed chiefly architectural; and I beheld such pomp of cities and palaces as never yet was beheld by the waking eye, unless in the clouds. From a great modern poet I cite the part of a passage which describes, as an appearance actually beheld in the clouds, what in many of its circumstances I saw frequently in sleep:—

> The appearance, instantaneously disclosed,
> Was of a mighty city—boldly say
> A wilderness of building, sinking far
> And self-withdrawn into a wondrous depth,
> Far sinking into splendour without end!
> Fabric it seem'd of diamond and of gold,
> With alabaster domes and silver spires,
> And blazing terrace upon terrace, high

Uplifted; here, serene pavilions bright,
In avenues disposed; there towers begirt
With battlements that on their restless fronts
Bore stars—illumination of all gems!
By earthly nature had the effect been wrought
Upon the dark materials of the storm
Now pacified; on them, and on the coves,
And mountain-steeps and summits, whereunto
The vapours had receded—taking there
Their station under a cerulean sky.

The sublime circumstance—"that on their restless fronts bore stars"—might have been copied from my own architectural dreams, so often did it occur. We hear it reported of Dryden, and in later times of Fuseli, that they ate raw meat for the sake of obtaining splendid dreams: how much better, for such a purpose, to have eaten opium, which yet I do not remember that any poet is recorded to have done, except the dramatist Shadwell; and in ancient days, Homer is, I think, rightly reputed to have known the virtues of opium . . . as an anodyne.

To my architecture succeeded dreams of lakes and silvery expanses of water: these haunted me so much, that I feared lest some dropsical state or tendency of the brain might thus be making itself (to use a metaphysical word) *objective;* and that the sentient organ might be projecting itself as its own object. For two months I suffered greatly in my head—a part of my bodily structure which had hitherto been so clear from all touch or taint of weakness (physically, I mean), that I used to say of it, as the last Lord Oxford said of his stomach, that it seemed likely to survive the rest of my person. Till now, I had never felt a headache even, or any the slightest pain, except rheumatic pains caused by my own folly.

The waters gradually changed their character—from translucent lakes, shining like mirrors, they became seas and oceans.

And now came a tremendous change, which, unfolding itself slowly like a scroll, through many months, promised an abiding torment; and, in fact, it never left me, though recurring more or less intermittingly. Hitherto the human face had often mixed in my dreams, but not despotically, nor with any special power of tormenting. But now that affection, which I have called the tyranny of the human face, began to unfold itself. Perhaps some part of my London life (the searching for Ann amongst fluctuating crowds) might be answerable for this. Be that as it may, now it was that upon the rocking waters of the ocean the human face began to reveal itself; the sea appeared paved with innumerable faces, upturned to the heavens; faces, imploring, wrathful, despairing; faces that surged upwards by thousands, by myriads, by generations: infinite was my agitation; my mind tossed as it seemed, upon the billowy ocean, and weltered upon the weltering waves.

THEN SUDDENLY WOULD come a dream of far different character—a tumultuous dream—commencing with a music such as now I often heard in sleep—music of preparation and of awakening suspense. The undulations of fast-gathering tumults were like the opening of the Coronation Anthem; and, like *that*, gave the feeling of a multitudinous movement, of infinite cavalcades filing off, and the tread of innumerable armies. The morning was come of a mighty day—a day of crisis and of ultimate hope for human nature, then suffering mysterious eclipse, and labouring in some dread extremity. Somewhere, but I knew not where—somehow, but I knew not how—by some beings, but I knew not by whom—a battle, a strife, an agony, was travelling through all its stages—was evolving itself, like the catastrophe of some mighty drama, with which my sympathy was the more insupportable, from deepening confusion as to its local scene, its cause, its nature, and its undecipherable issue. I (as is usual in dreams where, of necessity, we make ourselves central to every movement) had the power, and yet had not the power, to decide it. I had the power, if I could raise myself to will it; and yet again had not the power, for the weight of twenty Atlantics was upon me, or the oppression of inexpiable guilt. "Deeper than ever plummet sounded," I lay inactive. Then, like a chorus, the passion deepened. Some greater interest was at stake, some mightier cause, then ever yet the sword had pleaded, or trumpet had proclaimed. Then came sudden alarms; hurryings to and fro; trepidations of innumerable fugitives, I knew not whether from the good cause or the bad; darkness and lights; tempest and human faces; and at last, with the sense that all was lost, female forms, and the features that were worth all the world to me; and but a moment allowed—and clasped hands, with heart-breaking partings, and then—everlasting farewells! and, with a sigh such as the caves of hell sighed when the incestuous mother uttered the abhorred name of Death, the sound was reverberated— everlasting farewells! and again, and yet again reverberated— everlasting farewells!

And I awoke in struggles, and cried aloud, "I will sleep no more!"

Now, at last, I had become awestruck at the approach of sleep, under the condition of visions so afflicting, and so intensely life-like as those which persecuted my phantom-haunted brain. More and more also I felt violent palpitations in some internal region, such as are commonly but erroneously, called palpitations of the heart—being, as I suppose, referable exclusively to derangements in the stomach. These were evidently increasing rapidly in frequency and in strength. Naturally, therefore, on considering how important my life had become to others beside myself, I became alarmed; and I paused seasonably; but with a difficulty that is past all description. Either way it seemed as though death had, in military language, "thrown himself astride of my path." Nothing short of mortal anguish, in a physical sense, it seemed, to wean myself from opium; yet, on the other hand, death through overwhelming nervous terrors—death by brain fever or by lunacy—seemed too certainly to besiege the alternative course. Fortunately I had still so much of firmness left as to face that choice, which, with most of instant suffering, showed in the far distance a possibility of final escape.

This possibility was realised: I *did* accomplish my escape. And the issue of that particular stage in my opium experiences (for such it was—simply a provisional stage, that paved the way subsequently for many milder stages, to which gradually my constitutional system accommodated itself) was, pretty nearly in the following words, communicated to my readers in the earliest edition of these Confessions:—

I triumphed. But infer not, reader, from this word *"triumphed,"* a condition of joy or exultation. Think of me as of one, even when four months had passed, still agitated, writhing, throbbing, palpitating, shattered; and much, perhaps, in the situation of him who has been racked, as I collect the torments of that state from the affecting account of them left by a most innocent sufferer (in the time of James I.). Meantime, I derived no benefit from any medicine whatever, except ammoniated tincture of valerian. The moral of the narrative is addressed to the opium-eater; and therefore, of necessity, limited in its application. If he is taught to fear and tremble, enough has been effected. But he may say that the issue of my case is at least a proof that opium, after an eighteen years' use, and an eight years' abuse of its powers, may still be renounced; and that he may chance to bring to the task greater energy than I did, or that, with a stronger constitution, he may obtain the same results with less. This may be true; I would not presume to measure the efforts of other men by my own. Heartily I wish him more resolution; heartily I wish him an equal success. Nevertheless, I had motives external to myself which he may unfortunately want; and these supplied me with conscientious supports, such as merely selfish interests might fail in supplying to a mind debilitated by opium.

Lord Bacon conjectures that it may be as painful to be born as to die. That seems probable; and, during the whole period of diminishing the opium, I had the torments of a man passing out of one mode of existence into another, and liable to the mixed or the alternate pains of birth and death. The issue was not death, but a sort of physical regeneration; and I may add, that ever since, at intervals, I have had a restoration of more than youthful spirits.

One memorial of my former condition nevertheless remains: my dreams are not calm; the dread swell and agitation of the storm have not wholly subsided; the legions that encamped in them are drawing off, but not departed; my sleep is still tumultuous; and, like the gates of Paradise to our first parents when looking back from afar, it is still (in the tremendous line of Milton)—

With dreadful faces thronged and fiery arms.

ROGER GILBERT-LECOMTE

❖

MISTER MORPHEUS

I N T H E I M P U R E night of mud and blood where humanity drags behind it its miserable life like a flayed man drags his skin—eaten up with suffering, second by second, a mountain made of the discarded wings of insects; in the impure night of mud and lava where no-one can recognize even himself—I, Morpheus the Ghost; I, Morpheus the Vampire; I reign, tutelary, sarcastic, over my cursed subjects, like a king condor pirouetting in the clouds above a pack of hares ridden by a quiver of fear across an arid, immense steppe, smooth as the geographical representation of the roundness of the earthly globe.

And, leaving aside Maldoror—the beacon of evil, awake across the night of the earth—all the human hares, fascinated by the concentric circles of my Morphean gaze, fall backwards, their faces peeled away from those of their doubles, into the subterranean torrents of sleep that will cast them into the lake of death. But for a few privileged ones, disseminated across all of time and space, I multiply a *little* death and perfect its image until it approaches the most authentic death; I give them the starry dust that covers my wings, the stinging insects that travel on them, the wind my wings raise, and, for pipes, the quills of my feathers. *(Translator's note: The references here are to the dust of cocaine; the insect-like injections of morphine; the vapors of ether and the long, quill-like pipes of opium.)*

But these elected beings of nocturnal malediction *(note: drug-takers)* are and will always remain relatively rare. My empire, alas, is subject to biological laws. Statistics can easily demonstrate that—with the exception of a few, superior people, so evolved they can escape most social strictures—my subjects, the Morpheans, become a majority, legion, unanimous, only in races facing their own decline: aging tribes, dying peoples. Think of the alcoholism of the Indians of North America. Among peoples living through the conquering phase of their expansion, Morpheans are, in fact, the monstrous exception. And, under any circumstances, miserable laws of prohibition will never prevent these gigantic and fatal ethnic reactions.

In your moribund European cities, where all races and all phases of history rub against each other in final contact, you may observe, shoulder to shoulder, all my subjects—the victims of ethnic phenomena, and the victims of individual dramas . . . Of course, a majority of individuals escape from my clutches: those who harbor a true, invincible repulsion for drugs, reinforced to some degree by moral scruples. These are beings in whom organic youth—which has nothing to do with age, but passes like age—conquers the instinct for self-destruction of which we never dare to speak, and which nonetheless does, in most human consciousnesses, hold an equal share.

But, against these so-called healthy men—for whom their nightly sleep, even reduced to its strict minimum, remains a heavy charge from which they wish only to free themselves, the better to consecrate themselves to action—there are the others: lovers of long, dreamless sleeps, those harassed by an unknown evil, those for whom happiness is Death-In-Life. And everywhere, heavy and merciless, in the closed field of the dark body, take place great battles between the immortal enemies, Will-to-life and Non-action . . .

There exist a certain number of acutely sensitive beings who have a consciousness of alternately opposed states, intensely exalting and painful. And the signs of such crises are exaggerated in a few, predestined people, who are monstrous by the sole fact that they carry deep within themselves, like their own death-sentence, a super-human element that overtakes and contradicts their era: gigantic flashes of the spirit or of physical energy. Such elements are sufficient to magnificently unbalance a human life—above all by their anti-social character: they provoke actions indomitable to the universal judgment of common mortals, who take revenge by tracing around the cursed one a magic circle of hateful incomprehension, constructing constraints, which force him to the bitterness of solitude, which we also call madness.

Now, admit this principle, which is the only justification for the taste for the narcotic: what drug-users are looking for in their drugs, consciously or unconsciously, is not those ambiguous carnal pleasures, that hyper-acute sensual sensitivity, that excitement and all those other trivialities that people who are ignorant of the 'artificial paradises' dream of. It is solely, simply, a change in their state—a new climate where their consciousnesses will be less painful . . .

If one observes the regular and progressive use of drugs from the point of view of the states of consciousness they provoke, one can see intoxication being substituted, little by little, in the predisposed individual, with states of Death-In-Life; in other words, preeminently, a disinterest in those actions necessary for the maintenance of life; and we quickly come to consider this, not just only from a physiological point of view, but also from a psychological point of view, as a method of suicide. Because it is no longer a bet, a choice between life and an unknown state different from life and which we call death, but a slow, irreversible evolution of the whole being—leading, by the ruin of the organism and by forgetfulness and the progressive distaste for all that characterizes human life, towards the cessation of that disfigured life, softly, distantly, forgotten, in favor of an authentic, anticipated experience of death, throughout states of deep dreaming more or less similar to death.

I wish these rapid and incomplete considerations to bring to a few minds this conclusion: for a certain number of individuals, drugs are inescapable necessities. Certain beings can only survive by destroying themselves. Laws will never be able to stop this in any way. Take away their alcohol, and they will drink gasoline; their ether, and they will suffocate themselves with benzene, or insecticide; their mutilating knives, and they will make swords of their gazes.

Muzzled in vain by your society's laws, there sleep among you destructive energies capable of blowing up the world. By their fire-lighting eyes, I recognize them in the deserted construction yards: Attila, Genghis Khan, Tamburlane. The intoxication of alcohol is for these working men their most noble protest against the sordid life that is their lot. In anticipation of the death, at last, of Western thought, I, Morpheus, shape the hordes to come with my rough discipline. As we await the hour, I force them to practice on themselves their capacity for destruction. And the voluntary mutilations, the terrible alcoholic poisonings that take the heaving, gasping being to the edge of death, the pounding of heads against the wall, all the self-inflicted sufferings— these are the only criteria that can assure me of men physically desperate enough, dead enough to their own individuality, to display on their faces the impassive sarcasm of their disinterest in life which is the sole guarantor of every super-human act."

And as Morpheus the Vampire, frenzied, devoured his own flesh and disappeared, the faithful cried out:

"Make it strong, bite to the death."

SIGMUND FREUD

❀

COCA

I HAVE CARRIED out experiments and studied, in myself and others, the effect of coca on the healthy human body; my findings agree fundamentally with Mantegazza's description of the effects of coca leaves.

The first time I took 0.05g. of *cocaïnum muriaticum* in a 1% water solution was when I was feeling slightly out of sorts from fatigue. This solution was rather viscous, somewhat opalescent, and has a strange aromatic smell. At first it has a bitter taste, which yields afterwards to a series of very pleasant aromatic flavors. Dry cocaine salt has the same smell and taste, but to a more concentrated degree.

A few minutes after taking cocaine, one experiences a sudden exhilaration and feeling of lightness. One feels a certain furriness on the lips and palate, followed by a feeling of warmth in the same areas; if one now drinks cold water, it feels warm on the lips and cold in the throat. On other occasions the predominant feeling is a rather pleasant coolness in the mouth and throat.

During this first trial I experienced a short period of toxic effects, which did not recur in subsequent experiments. Breathing became slower and deeper and I felt tired and sleepy; I yawned frequently and felt somewhat dull. After a few minutes the actual cocaine euphoria began, introduced by repeated cooling eructation. Immediately after taking the cocaine I noticed a slight slackening of the pulse and a later moderate increase.

I have observed the same physical signs of the effect of cocaine in others, mostly people my own age. The most constant symptom proved to be the repeated cooling eructation. This is often accompanied by a rumbling which must originate from high up in the intestine; two of the people I observed, who said they were able to recognize movements of their stomachs, declared emphatically that they had repeatedly detected such movements. Often, at the outset of the cocaine effect, the subjects alleged that they experienced an intense feeling of heat in the head. I noticed this in myself as well in the course of some later experiments, but on other occasions it was absent. In only two cases did coca give rise to dizziness. On the whole the toxic effects of coca are of short duration, and much less intense than those produced by effective doses of quinine or salicylate of soda; they seem to become even weaker after repeated use of cocaine.

Mantegazza refers to the following occasional effects of coca: temporary erythema, an increase in the quantity of urine, dryness of the conjunctiva and nasal mucous membranes. Dryness of the mucous membrane of the mouth and of the throat is a regular symptom which lasts for hours. Some observers (Marvaud, Collan) report a slight cathartic effect. Urine and feces are said to take on the smell of coca. Different observers give very different accounts of the effect on the pulse rate. According to Mantegazza, coca quickly produces a considerably increased pulse rate which becomes even higher with higher doses; Collin, too, noted an acceleration of the pulse after coca was taken, while Rossier, Demarle, and Marvaud experienced, after the initial acceleration, a longer lasting retardation of the pulse rate. Christison noticed in himself, after using coca, that physical exertion caused a smaller increase in the pulse rate than otherwise; Reiss disputes any effect on the pulse rate. I do not find any difficulty in accounting for this lack of agreement; it is partly owing to the variety of the preparations used (warm infusion of the leaves, cold cocaine solution, etc.), and the way in which they are applied, and partly to the varying reactions of individuals. With coca this latter factor, as Mantegazza has already reported, is in general of very great significance. There are said to be people who cannot tolerate coca at all; on the other hand, I have found not a few who remained unaffected by 5cg, which for me and others is an effective dose.

The psychic effect of *cocaïnum muriaticum* in doses of 0.05–0.10g consists of exhilaration and lasting euphoria, which does not differ in any way from the normal euphoria of a healthy person. The feeling of excitement which accompanies stimulus by alcohol is completely lacking; the characteristic urge for immediate activity which alcohol produces is also absent. One senses an increase of self-control and feels more vigorous and more capable of work; on the other hand, if one works, one misses that heightening of the mental powers which alcohol, tea, or coffee induce. One is simply normal, and soon finds it difficult to believe that one is under the influence of any drug at all.

This gives the impression that the mood induced by coca in such doses is due not so much to direct stimulation as to the disappearance of elements in one's general state of well-being which cause depression. One may perhaps assume that the euphoria resulting from good health is also nothing more than the normal condition of a well-nourished cerebral cortex which "is not conscious" of the organs of the body to which it belongs.

During this stage of the cocaine condition, which is not otherwise distinguished, appear those symptoms which have been described as the wonderful stimulating effect of coca. Long-lasting, intensive mental or physical work can be performed without fatigue; it is as though the need for food and sleep, which otherwise makes itself felt peremptorily at certain times of the day, were completely banished. While the effects of cocaine last one can, if urged to do so, eat copiously and without revulsion; but one has the clear feeling that the meal was superfluous. Similarly, as the effect of coca declines it is possible to sleep on going to bed, but sleep can just as easily be omitted with no unpleasant consequences. During the first hours of the coca effect one cannot sleep, but this sleeplessness is in no way distressing.

I have tested this effect of coca, which wards off hunger, sleep, and fatigue and steels one to intellectual effort, some dozen times on myself; I had no opportunity to engage in physical work.

A very busy colleague gave me an opportunity to observe a striking example of the manner in which cocaine dispels extreme fatigue and a well justified feeling of hunger; at 6:00 p.m. this colleague, who had not eaten since the early morning and who had worked exceedingly hard during the day, took 0.05g of *cocaïnum muriaticum.* A few minutes later he declared that he felt as though he had just eaten an ample meal, that he had no desire for an evening meal, and that he felt strong enough to undertake a long walk.

This stimulative effect of coca is vouched for beyond any doubt by a series of reliable reports, some of which are quite recent.

By way of an experiment, Sir Robert Christison—who is seventy-eight years old—tired himself to the point of exhaustion by walking fifteen miles without partaking of food. After several days he repeated the procedure with the same result; during the third experiment he chewed 2 drams of coca leaves and was able to complete the walk without the exhaustion experienced on the earlier occasions; when he arrived home, despite the fact that he had been for nine hours without food or drink, he experienced no hunger or thirst, and woke the next morning without feeling tired at all. On yet another occasion he climbed a 3000-foot mountain and arrived completely exhausted at the summit; he made the descent upon the influence of coca, with youthful vigor and no feeling of fatigue.

Clemens and J. Collan have had similar experiences—the latter after walking for several hours over snow; Mason calls coca "an excellent thing for a long walk"; Aschenbrandt reported recently how Bavarian soldiers, weary as a result of hardships and debilitating illnesses, were nevertheless capable, after taking coca, of participating in maneuvers and marches. Moréno y Maïz was able to stay awake whole nights with the aid of coca; Mantegazza remained for forty hours without food. We are, therefore, justified in assuming that the effect of coca on Europeans is the same as that which the coca leaves have on the Indians of South America.

The effect of a moderate dose of coca fades away so gradually that, in normal circumstances, it is difficult to define its duration. If one works intensively while under the influence of coca, after from three to five hours there is a decline in the feeling of well-being, and a further dose of coca is necessary in order to ward off fatigue. The effect of coca seems to last longer if no heavy muscular work is undertaken. Opinion is unanimous that the euphoria induced by coca is not followed by any feeling of lassitude or other state of depression. I should be inclined to think that after moderate doses (0.05–0.10g) a part at least of the coca effect lasts for over twenty-four hours. In my own case, at any rate, I have noticed that even on the day after taking coca my condition compares favorably with the norm. I should be inclined to explain the possibility of a lasting gain in strength, such as has often been claimed for coca by the totality of such effects.

It seems probable, in the light of reports which I shall refer to later, that coca, if used protractedly but in moderation, is not detrimental to the body. Von Anrep treated animals for thirty days with moderate doses of cocaine and detected no detrimental effects on their bodily functions. It seems to me noteworthy—and I discovered this in myself and in other observers who were capable of judging such things—that a first dose or even repeated doses of coca produce no compulsive desire to use the stimulant further; on the contrary, one feels a certain unmotivated aversion to the substance. This circumstance may be partly responsible for the fact that coca, despite some warm recommendations, has not established itself in Europe as a stimulant.

The effect of large doses of coca was investigated by Mantegazza in experiments on himself. He succeeded in achieving a state of greatly increased happiness accompanied by a desire for complete immobility; this was interrupted occasionally, however, by the most violent urge to move. The analogy with the results of the animal experiments performed by von Anrep is unmistakable. When he increased the dose still further he remained in a *sopore beato:* His pulse rate was extremely high and there was a moderate rise in body temperature; he found that his speech was impeded and his handwriting unsteady; and eventually he experienced the most splendid and colorful hallucinations, the tenor of which was frightening for a short time, but invariably cheerful thereafter. This coca intoxication, too, failed to produce any state of depression, and left no sign whatsoever that the experimenter had passed through a period of intoxication. Moréno y Maïz also experienced a similar powerful compulsion to move after taking fairly large doses of coca. Even after using 18 drams of coca leaves Mantegazza experienced no impairment of full consciousness. A chemist who attempted to poison himself by taking 1.5g of cocaine became sick and showed symptoms of gastroenteritis, but there was no dulling of the consciousness.

The Therapeutic Uses of Coca

It was inevitable that a plant which had achieved such a reputation for marvelous effects in its country of origin should have been used to treat the most varied disorders and illnesses of the human body. The first Europeans who became aware of this treasure of the native population were similarly unreserved in their recommendation of coca. On the basis of wide medical experience, Mantegazza later drew up a list of the therapeutic properties of coca, which one by one received the acknowledgment of other doctors. In the following section I have tried to collate the recommendations concerning coca, and, in doing so, to distinguish between recommendations based on successful treatment of illnesses and those which relate to the psychological effects of the stimulant. In general the latter outweigh the former. At present there seems to be some promise of widespread recognition and use of coca preparations in North America, while in Europe doctors scarcely know them by name. The failure of coca to take hold in Europe, which in my opinion is unmerited, can perhaps be attributed to reports of unfavorable consequences attendant upon its use, which appeared shortly after its introduction into Europe; or to the doubtful quality of the preparations, their relative scarcity and consequent high price. Some of the evidence which can be found in favor of the use of coca has been proved valid beyond any doubt, whereas some warrants at least an unprejudiced investigation. Merk's [sic] cocaine and its salts are, as has been proved, preparations which have the full or at least the essential effects of coca leaves.

a) *Coca as a stimulant.* The main use of coca will undoubtedly remain that which the Indians have made of it for centuries: it is of value in all cases where the primary aim is to increase the physical capacity of the body for a given short period of time and to hold strength in reserve to meet further demands—especially when outward circumstances exclude the possibility of obtaining the rest and nourishment normally necessary for great exertion. Such situations arise in wartime, on journeys, during mountain climbing and other expeditions, etc.—indeed, they are situations in which the alcoholic stimulants are also generally recognized as being of value. Coca is a far more potent and far less harmful stimulant than alcohol, and its widespread utilization is hindered at present only by its high cost. Bearing in mind the effect of coca on the natives of South America, a medical authority as early as Pedro Crespo (Lima, 1793) recommended its use by European navies; Neudörfer (1870), Clemens (1867) and Surgeon-Major E. Charles recommended that it should be adopted by the armies of Europe as well; and Aschenbrandt's experiences should not fail to draw the attention of army administrators to coca. If cocaine is given as a stimulant, it is better that it should be given in small effective doses (0.05–0.10g) and repeated so often that the effects of the doses overlap. Apparently cocaine is not stored in the body; I have already stressed the fact that there is no state of depression when the effects of coca have worn off.

At present it is impossible to assess with any certainty to what extent coca can be expected to increase human mental powers. I have the impression that protracted use of coca can lead to a lasting improvement if the inhibitions manifested before it is taken are due only to physical causes or to exhaustion. To be sure, the instantaneous effect of a dose of coca cannot be compared with that of a morphine injection; but, on the good side of the ledger, there is no danger of general damage to the body as is the case with the chronic use of morphine.

Many doctors felt that coca would play an important role by filling a gap in the medicine chest of the psychiatrists. It is a well-known fact that psychiatrists have an ample supply of drugs at their disposal for reducing the excitation of nerve centers, but none which would serve to increase the reduced functioning of the nerve centers. Coca has consequently been prescribed for the most diverse kinds of psychic debility—hysteria, hypochondria, melancholic inhibition, stupor, and similar maladies. Some successes have been reported: for instance, the Jesuit, Antonio Julian (Lima, 1787) tells of a learned missionary who was freed from severe hypochondria; Mantegazza praises coca as being almost universally effective in improving those functional disorders which we now group together under the name of neurasthenia; Fliessburg reports excellent results from the use of coca in cases of "nervous prostration"; and according to Caldwell, it is the best tonic for hysteria.

E. Morselli and G. Buccola carried out experiments involving the systematic dispensation of cocaine, over a period of months, to melancholics. They gave a preparation of cocaine, as prescribed by Trommsdorf, in subcutaneous injections, in doses ranging from 0.0025–0.10g per dose. After one or two months they confirmed a slight improvement in the condition of their patients, who became happier, took nourishment, and enjoyed regular digestion.

On the whole, the efficacy of coca in cases of nervous and psychic debility needs further investigation, which will probably lead to partially favorable conclusions. According to Mantegazza coca is of no use, and is sometimes even dangerous, in cases of organic change and inflammation of the nervous system.

b) *The use of coca for digestive disorders of the stomach.* This is the oldest and most firmly founded use of coca, and at the same time it is the most comprehensible to us. According to the unanimous assertions of the oldest as well as the most recent authorities (Julian, Martius, Unanuè, Mantegazza, Bingel, Scrivener, Frankl, and others) coca in its most various forms banishes dyspeptic complaints and the disorders and debility associated therewith, and after protracted use results in a permanent cure. I have myself made a series of such observations.

Like Mantegazza and Frankl, I have experienced personally how the painful symptoms attendant upon large meals—viz, a feeling of pressure and fullness in the stomach, discomfort and a disinclination to work—disappear with eructation following small doses of cocaine (0.025–0.05). Time and again I have brought such relief to my colleagues; and twice I observed how the nausea resulting from gastronomic excesses responded in a short time to the effects of cocaine, and gave way to a normal desire to eat and a feeling of bodily well-being. I have also learned to spare myself stomach troubles by adding a small amount of cocaine to salicylate of soda.

My colleague, Dr. Josef Pollak, has given me the following account of an astonishing effect of cocaine, which shows that it can be used to treat not merely local discomfort in the stomach but also serious reflex reactions; one must therefore assume that cocaine has a powerful effect on the mucous membrane and the muscular system of this organ.

"A forty-two-year-old, robust man, whom the doctor knew very well, was forced to adhere most strictly to a certain diet and to prescribed mealtimes; otherwise he could not avoid the attacks about to be described. When traveling or under the influence of any emotional strain he was particularly susceptible. The attacks followed a regular pattern: They began in the evening with a feeling of discomfort in the epigastrium, followed by flushing of the face, tears in the eyes, throbbing in the temples and violent pain in the forehead, accompanied by a feeling of great depression and apathy. He could not sleep during the night; toward morning there were long painful spasms of vomiting which lasted for hours. Round about midday he experienced some relief, and on drinking a few spoonfuls of soup had a feeling 'as though the stomach would at last eject a bullet which had lain in it for a long time.' This was followed by rancid eructation, until, toward evening, his condition returned to normal. The patient was incapable of work throughout the day and had to keep to his bed.

"At 8:00 p.m. on the tenth of June the usual symptoms of an attack began. At ten o'clock, after the violent headache had developed, the patient was given 0.075g *cocaïnum muriaticum*. Shortly thereafter he experienced a feeling of warmth and eructation, which seemed to him to be 'still too little.' At 10:30 a second dose of 0.075g of cocaine was given; the eructations increased; the patient felt some relief and was able to write a long letter. He alleged that he felt intensive movement in the stomach; at twelve o'clock, apart from a slight headache, he was normal, even cheerful, and walked for an hour. He could not sleep until 3:00 a.m., but that did not distress him. He awoke the next morning healthy, ready for work, and with a good appetite."

The effect of cocaine on the stomach—Mantegazza assumes this as well—is two-fold: stimulation of movement and reduction of the organ's sensitivity. The latter would seem probable not only because of the local sensations in the stomach after cocaine has been taken but because of the analogous effect of cocaine on other mucous membranes. Mantegazza claims to have achieved the most brilliant successes in treatments of gastralgia and enteralgia, and all painful and cramping afflictions of the stomach and intestines, which he attributes to the anesthetizing properties of coca. On this point I cannot confirm Mantegazza's experiences; only once, in connection with a case of gastric catarrh, did I see the sensitivity of the stomach to pressure disappear after the administration of coca. On other occasions I have observed myself, and also heard from other doctors, that patients suspected of having ulcers or scars in the stomach complained of increased pain after using coca; this can be explained by the increased movement of the stomach.

Accordingly, I should say that the use of coca is definitely indicated in cases of atonic digestive weakness and the so-called nervous stomach disorders; in such cases it is possible to achieve not merely a relief of the symptoms but a lasting improvement.

c) *Coca in cachexia*. Long-term use of coca is further strongly recommended—and allegedly has been tried with success—in all diseases which involve degeneration of the tissues, such as severe anemia, phthisis, long-lasting febrile diseases, etc.; and also during recovery from such diseases. Thus McBean noted a steady improvement in cases of typhoid fever treated with coca. In the case of phthisis, coca is said to have a limiting effect on the fever and sweating. Peckham reports with regard to a case of definitely diagnosed phthisis that after fluid extract of coca had been used for seven months there was a marked improvement in the patient's condition. Hole gives an account of another rather serious case in which chronic lack of appetite had led to an advanced condition of emaciation and exhaustion; here, too, the use of coca restored the patient to health. R. Bartholow observed, in general, that coca proved useful in treating phthisis and other "consumptive processes." Mantegazza and a number of other authorities attribute to coca the same invaluable therapeutic quality: that of limiting degeneration of the body and increasing strength in the cases of cachexia.

One might wish to attribute such successes partly to the undoubted favorable effect of coca on the digestion, but one must bear in mind that a good many of the authors who have written on coca regard it as a "source of savings"; i.e., they are of the opinion that a system which has absorbed even an extremely small amount of cocaine is capable, as a result of the reaction of the body to coca, of amassing a greater store of vital energy which can be converted into work than would have been possible without coca. If we take the amount of work as being constant, the body which has absorbed cocaine should be able to manage with a lower metabolism, which in turn means a smaller intake of food.

This assumption was obviously made to account for the, according to von Voit, unexplained effect of coca on the Indians. It does not even necessarily involve a contradiction of the law of conservation of energy. For labor which draws upon food or tissue components involves a certain loss, either in the utilization of assimilated food or in the conversion of energy into work; this loss could perhaps be reduced if certain appropriate steps were taken. It has not been proved that such a process takes place, however. Experiments designed to determine the amount of urine eliminated with and without the use of coca have not been altogether conclusive; indeed, these experiments have not always been conducted in such conditions that they could furnish conclusive results. Moreover, they seem to have been carried out on the assumption that the elimination of urine—which is known not to be effected by labor—would provide a measure of metabolism in general. Thus Christison noted a slight reduction in the solid components of his urine during the walks on which he took coca; Lippmann, Demarle, Marvaud, and more recently Mason similarly concluded from their experiments that the consumption of coca reduces the amount of urine elimination. Gazeau, on the other hand, established an *increase* of urine elimination of 11–24% under the influence of coca. A better availability of materials already stored in the body explains, in his opinion, the body's increased working power and ability to do without food when under the influence of coca. No experiments have been carried out with regard to the elimination of carbon dioxide.

Voit proved that coffee, which also rated as a "source of savings," had no influence on the breakdown of albumen in the body. We must regard the conception of coca as a "source of savings" as disproven after certain experiments in which animals were starved, both with and without cocaine, and the reduction of their body weight and the length of time they were able to withstand inanition were observed. Such experiments were carried out by Cl. Bernard, Moréno y Maïz, Demarle, Gazeau, and von Anrep. The result was that the animals to which cocaine had been administered succumbed to inanition just as soon—perhaps even sooner—than those which had received no cocaine. The starvation of La Paz—an experiment carried out by history itself, and reported by Unanuè—seems to contradict this conclusion, however, for the inhabitants who had partaken of coca are said to have escaped death by starvation. In this connection one might recall the fact that the human nervous system has an undoubted, if somewhat obscure, influence on the nourishment of tissues; psychological factors can, after all, cause a healthy man to lose weight.

The therapeutic quality of coca which we took as our argument at the outset does not, therefore, deserve to be rejected out of hand. The excitation of nerve centers by cocaine can have a favorable influence on the nourishment of the body afflicted by a consumptive condition, even though that influence might well not take the form of a slowing down of metabolism.

I should add here that coca has been warmly praised in connection with the treatment of syphilis. R. W. Taylor claims that a patient's tolerance of mercury is increased and the mercury cachexia kept in check when coca is administered at the same time. J. Collan recommends it as the best remedy for *stomatitus mercurialis* and reports that Pagvalin always prescribes it in conjunction with preparations of mercury.

d) *Coca in the treatment of morphine and alcohol addiction.* In America the important discovery has recently been made that coca preparations possess the power to suppress the craving for morphine in habitual addicts, and also to reduce to negligible proportions the serious symptoms of collapse which appear while the patient is being weaned away from the morphine habit. According to my information (which is largely from the *Detroit Therapeutic Gazette*), it was W. H. Bentley who announced, in May 1878, that he had substituted coca for the customary alkaloid in the case of a female morphine addict. Two years later, Palmer, in an article in the *Louisville Medical News,* seems to have aroused the greatest general interest in this treatment of morphine addiction; for the next two years "*Erythroxylon coca* in the opium habit" was a regular heading in the reports of the *Therapeutic Gazette*. From then on information regarding successful cures became rarer: whether because the treatment became established as a recognized cure, or because it was abandoned, I do not know. Judging by the advertisements of drug dealers in the most recent issues of American papers, I should rather conclude that the former was the case.

There are some sixteen reports of cases in which the patient has been successfully cured of addiction; in only one instance is there a report of failure of coca to alleviate morphine addiction, and in this case the doctor wondered why there had been so many warm recommendations for the use of coca in cases of morphine addiction. The successful cases vary in their conclusiveness. Some of them involve large doses of opium or morphine and addictions of long standing. There is not much information on the subject or relapses, as most cases were reported within a very short time of the cure having been effected. Symptoms which appear during abstention are not always reported in detail. There is especial value in those reports which contain the observation that the patients were able to dispense with coca after a few weeks without experiencing any further desire for morphine. Special attention is repeatedly called to the fact that morphine cachexia gave way to excellent health, so that the patients were scarcely recognizable after their cure. Concerning the method of withdrawal, it should be made clear that in the majority of cases a gradual reduction of the habitual dose of the drug, accompanied by a gradual increase of the coca dose, was the method chosen; however, sudden discontinuation of the drug was also tried. In the latter case Palmer describes that a certain dose of coca should be repeated as often during the day as the desire for morphine recurs. The daily dose of coca is lessened gradually until it is possible to dispense with the antidote altogether. From the very beginning the attacks experienced during abstinence were either slight or else became milder after a few days. In almost every case the cure was effected by the patient himself, whereas the cure of morphine addiction without the help of coca, as practiced in Europe, requires surveillance of the patient in a hospital.

I once had occasion to observe the case of a man who was subjected to the type of cure involving sudden withdrawal of morphine, assisted by the use of coca; the same patient had suffered severe symptoms as a result of abstinence in the course of a previous cure. This time his condition was tolerable; in particular there was no sign of depression or nausea as long as the effects of coca lasted; chills and diarrhea were now the only permanent symptoms of his abstinence. The patient was not bedridden, and could function normally. During the first days of the cure he consumed 3dg of *cocaïnum muriaticum* daily, and after ten days he was able to dispense with the coca treatment altogether.

The treatment of morphine addiction with coca does not, therefore, result merely in the exchange of one kind of addiction for another—it does not turn the morphine addict into a *coquero;* the use of coca is only temporary. Moreover, I do not think that it is the general toughening effect of coca which enables the system weakened by morphine to withstand, at the cost of only insignificant symptoms, the withdrawal of morphine. I am rather inclined to assume that coca has a directly antagonistic effect on morphine, and in support of my view I quote the following observations of Dr. Josef Pollak on a case in point:

"A thirty-three-year-old woman has been suffering for years from severe menstrual migraine which can be alleviated only by morphia injections. Although the lady in question never takes morphia or experiences any desire to do so when she is free of migraine, during the attacks she behaves like a morphine addict. A few hours after the injection she suffers intense depression, biliousness, attacks of vomitting, which are stopped by a second morphine injection; thereupon, the symptoms of intolerance recur, with the result that an attack of migraine, along with all its consequences, keeps the patient in bed for three days in a most wretched condition. Cocaine was then tried to combat the migraine, but the treatment proved unsuccessful. It was necessary to resort to morphine injections. But as soon as the symptoms of morphine intolerance appeared, they were quickly relieved by 1 dg of cocaine, with the result that the patient recovered from her attack in a far shorter time and consumed much less morphine in the process."

Coca was tried in America for the treatment of chronic alcoholism at about the same time as it was introduced in connection with morphine addiction, and most reports dealt with the two uses conjointly. In the treatment of alcoholism, too, there were cases of undoubted success, in which the irresistible compulsion to drink was either banished or alleviated, and the dyspeptic complaints of the drinkers were relieved. In general, however, the suppression of the alcohol craving through the use of coca proved to be more difficult than the suppression of morphomania; in one case reported by Bentley the drinker became a *coquero*. One need only suggest the immense economic significance which coca would acquire as a "source of savings" in another sense, if its effectiveness in combating alcoholism were confirmed.

e) *Coca and asthma.* Tschudi and Markham report that by chewing coca leaves they were spared the usual symptoms of the so-called mountain sickness while climbing in the Andes; this complex of symptoms includes shortness of breath, pounding of the heart, dizziness, etc. Poizat reports that the asthmatic attacks of a patient were arrested in every case by coca. I mention this property of coca because it appears to admit of a physiological explanation. Von Anrep's experiments on animals resulted in early paralysis of certain branches of the vagus; and altitude asthma, as well as the attacks characteristic of chronic bronchitis, may be interpreted in terms of a reflex excitation originating in the pulmonary branches of the vagus. The use of coca should be considered for the treatment of other vagus neuroses.

f) *Coca as an aphrodisiac.* The natives of South America, who represent their goddess of love with coca leaves in her hand, did not doubt the stimulative effect of coca on the genitalia. Mantegazza confirms that the *coqueros* sustain a high degree of potency right into old age; he even reports cases of the restoration of potency and the disappearance of functional weaknesses following the use of coca, although he does not believe that coca would produce such an effect in all individuals. Marvaud emphatically supports the view that coca has a stimulative effect; other writers strongly recommend coca as a remedy for occasional functional weaknesses and temporary exhaustion; and Bentley reports on a case of this type in which coca was responsible for the cure.

Among the person to whom I have given coca, three reported violent sexual excitement which they unhesitatingly attributed to the coca. A young writer, who was enabled by treatment with coca to resume his work after a longish illness, gave up using the drug because of the undesirable secondary effect which it had on him.

g) *Local application of coca.* Cocaine and its salts have a marked anesthetizing effect when brought in contact with the skin and mucous membrane in concentrated solution; this property suggests its occasional use as a local anesthetic, especially in connection with affections of the mucous membrane. According to Collin, Ch. Fauvel strongly recommends cocaine for treating diseases of the pharynx, describing it as *"le tenseur par excellence des chordes vocales."* Indeed, the anesthetizing properties of cocaine should make it suitable for a good many further applications.

CARRIE FISHER

❧

POSTCARDS FROM THE EDGE

. . . THAT'S IT, I'VE quit. This time I've really quit. I'm not doing cocaine anymore. If someone came up and *offered* me cocaine I wouldn't do it. I doubt that anyone will offer it to me, though. No one offers cocaine anymore. It used to be a way that people got friendly, sharing a few toots, but now everyone *hoards* their cocaine.

My first party without drugs. Interesting. I mean, when I was a little kid I always went to birthday parties straight, but that was a while ago.

I wonder if anyone here even *has* any cocaine. That guy Steve looks like he might, he usually has some. I *loathe* that guy, but he always has great cocaine . . .

No, I promised myself I would not do any cocaine, because that last time was such a *nightmare* and . . . But it was fun in the beginning. Sometimes it's fun. I don't know, Freud took it, so how bad could it be?

But this is the new me. I'm totally on a health kick. I have not taken any cocaine in *four days*. I don't even like it anymore. I never really *did* like it, I just did it 'cause it was *around*. And I don't think I was really heavy into it, not like Steve over there. Steve is really, really into cocaine. I would say *he's* got a problem. He can't stop. Well, sometimes he stops for a while, but he can't stay stopped. I really think *I* can. I think I have willpower, I just haven't used it in a while. I've been kind of on a willpower break, but now I feel it's coming back. I really think I can stay with this commitment of not doing cocaine.

Besides, this healthy life is great. I really love this being straight. You know, you see people jogging and you think, *"Yuuucccchh,"* but I'm getting on. I'm in my late twenties, and I think taking drugs was all part of being young. I don't think I had a *problem*, I think I was just *young*. And that by definition isn't a problem it's just a point in your life when it seems *okay* to take a lot of cocaine. And then that point passes.

I don't know, I think it was the bad relationship I was in that really determined my drug intake. And now Joan's left me, and I really feel good about myself. I mean I *want* to. And I went to that juice bar today and bought chlorophyll juice, that green drink. It gave me diarrhea, but I feel really good tonight. And I feel like it's a beginning. You go to a place like that and you buy the chlorophyll juice and the carrot juice, and you're making a statement. And I bought some new sneakers, I'm gonna start running . . . I actually got up at nine thirty this morning and moved my exercise bike right next to my bed, so tomorrow morning I *know* I'm just gonna hop on that cycle. Ten minutes is enough for aerobics, I guess. And then maybe I'll go to that Canyon Ranch health spa. Maybe then I could meet a really great girl. I think if I meet someone who doesn't do drugs, then we won't do them together, obviously, and that'll really help me. I think all of these choices reflect where you're at with *you*.

The only thing that bothers me is the idea of giving it up *completely*. I should be able to celebrate every now and again. Like if I stay straight for a while, I should be able to celebrate by getting loaded. I don't see what's wrong with that. Steve does that, but Steve has a *problem*. I think that once I get this under control, I'll be able to do it. And I really feel like I've made a strong beginning. God, my stomach is upset from that juice, though. I wonder if everything good for you tastes awful. I hope not, because I'm really gonna get into it.

Steve looks kind of loaded now. That looks so awful. You see people and they're loaded and . . . Look how dumb it looks. It looks so *stupid*. I can't believe I ever did it. I feel so good about being on the other side of it now. It really erodes your self-esteem to make a decision like not taking drugs and then taking them. The thing is, I also think you can take a little bit, and not do it to excess. Not *everybody* can—

obviously there are some personality types who can't do *anything* a little bit—but I'm not one of those. There are certain areas of my life where I do a *very* little bit, and I think if I practice, one of those areas could be cocaine.

Well, maybe not cocaine, but maybe I could take a speed pill every so often. I love what speed and coke do to my weight. It's unnatural, I know. I *could* just exercise . . .

God, there's that great feeling right at the beginning. If you get some *good* coke. From now on, I'm just gonna do *good* coke. When I do it, I'm gonna make sure. I'll *never* go to the dealer in Brentwood again. *Never.* I think *that* was the problem. His coke hurts your face, it becomes a *chore* to do it. I'll just do pharmaceutical, that's not hard on the membrane, and I really want to take care of my body. I think I'm unusual, because even during all those years when I was doing drugs, I still sometimes went to the gym. Joan accused me of trying to maintain my body so I could destroy it with chemicals, but I think that's a little harsh. And even if I did, I'm certainly better off than someone like *Steve*, who's just frying himself *and* eating burgers and sugar. I eat no carcinogenic food, I'm drinking some juices now . . . I went overboard today, but . . .

I'm *tired.* Who's that girl? She's attractive . . . Aauuggh, I don't want to get into another relationship thing again. God, I'm so *tired.* I shouldn't be drinking. I shouldn't have started drinking, 'cause I associate the two, alcohol and cocaine. I'm just gonna *not drink* now. Oh, he sees me, he's coming over. I should ignore him so he gets that I'm not interested in doing any—

"Hi Steve, how ya doin'? Yeah, yeah. I'm fine. No, I feel okay. I don't look *that* bad. I have a stomach thing today. How are you? You seem very *up*. No, I'm . . . I'm not doing any right now. I've quit. Yeah, No, I feel great. No, I'm serious. What do you mean, that's not a great line reading? *I feel great.* I'm absolutely committed to this. No, I don't mean it like a judgment on you. I think it's fine that some people still do coke, you know? I don't think it's weak . . .

"No, I don't think I had a *problem*. It's just that my nose started . . . I don't know. I'll probably end up still doing a little bit every so often, you know. Not right now. Maybe . . . well, like, maybe . . . I don't know, let me just . . . Is there food at this party? All right, maybe like a hit, but *that's*—who is that girl over there?—*that's* it, though. I'm gonna do . . . No, this is . . . I'm not . . . All right, give me one hit. But don't give me any more even if I ask you to. This is good coke, right? It's not from Brentwood? All right, one hit.

"(sniff) Mmmmmmmhh! (sniff) Ooohhh, fantastic. Oh, *great*. Shit, that's great! Mmmmhhhh! It just burns a little bit. There's not much cut in it, right? Yeah? It's good. No, I really don't need any more. I mean, I can *handle* it, I just think that was it. You know, people come to a party and they do one hit to break the tension, and I think I can really master that now. I can do a little bit.

"God, I feel so . . . I really feel *good* about my commitment to not doing drugs. I mean, just doing a little bit of drugs. Feel my arm. I feel really good. Well, I *know* I don't look that great, but I didn't sleep that much and I drank this bad juice.

"Let's go over and talk to that girl. I wanna go over and talk to that girl. Who is that girl? Lisa what? What is she, an actress or something? I *loathe* actresses. She looks smart, though. Smart people always wear black. Who's the guy she's talking to? *Craig?* I wanna go talk to her. God, he's such a *loser*. I should talk to her, I'm like a real guy. I have to go talk to her. Give me another hit of that stuff, maybe I'll go talk to her. I *know* what I said, I know what I said. Just give me one more hit. What are you, stingy with the blow now? I'll help pay for it. I'm just gonna do it . . . Like, I'm gonna celebrate not doing it by doing a little bit. (sniff) Mmmmmhh! (sniff) *Yeessss!*

"I wish there was something like holistic blow, you know what I mean? That there would be some way in nature you could take blow and it would be *good* for you. I wish my doctor would make me take it for some weird ailment I have. This is *good* coke, though. This is really good.

How much did you pay for this? Not bad. That is *not bad*. And who did you get it from? Oh, yeah, I had some once from him that was so great. Remember the night we . . . Give me another hit. Give me one more hit.

"(sniff) Aaaahhh! (sniff) Ooooww! No, it's not the coke, it's me. I had this cold last week. Actually, I think it was more my sinuses. I have a sinus problem, or I seem to more in the last couple of years. I don't know, I have to go to a doctor at some point.

"Nah, I don't want to talk to that girl anyway. I wanna talk to *you*. I've missed you. I really feel like I can talk to you, I really feel we have a lot in common. I know we don't see each other much socially, but I've gottta say every time that we've spent time together, I've enjoyed it. Remember the night in Vegas when we met? You weren't actually dealing then, were you? Someone said you were a dealer once, I nearly punched the guy out. You're like a really good guy, man. I really like you.

"Think we can get any more of this stuff? 'Cause, I mean, I'm quitting after tonight anyway because, I don't know, I should start taking care of myself. Whew, my heart is really palpitating. You think if I took one more hit it might calm me down a little bit? I know that sounds like a dumb cocaine question, but I think if you do a certain amount and then taper off, you can *hit* that peak and *really* be buzzing, you know, when you feel like the world is lined up just *exactly right*. God, I sure love life. Can I have another hit?

"I think this is good for me—to test my resistance. I mean, I think it's wimpy to give up cocaine. Master the drug, *that's* the key—the total key to the whole thing. I mean, people who actually have to go and give it up—it just shows they're weak. They go to groups like Cocaine Anonymous and those people, they always fuckin' talk about drugs. You know? It's like all they do is not do drugs. Well, man, I'd rather *do* drugs. Do you have another hit?

"Man, this party's a drag. I don't know, I feel so agitated and, you know, itchy to . . . Can we go to your place? Hey, come over to mine.

Well, let's just go outside then, let's walk around. There's nobody here that I like. God, look, they're *eating*. Uuggh, look at that shit, it looks awful. Come on, let's go outside and talk.

"Did I ever tell you I graduated with honors from high school? Yeah, I was a real brainy kid. Very precocious. I don't know, I thought I'd go into writing because it interested me. But I gotta tell you, the environment at the networks is just not that exciting. I'd rather be in music, you know, but I don't play an instrument. Maybe I could learn, though. I feel *now* like I could learn an instrument. Do you play an instrument? That's interesting, that's very interesting. We both don't play any instruments. But, you know, I feel that you, like me, we have the *spirit* of musicians. You know, sitting around communicating. I think *artists* do that.

"That girl in black, maybe she's an artist. I've always wanted to meet someone who wrote poetry and went to jazz clubs, and she'd draw me into her life and we'd become soulmates. I wonder if I have a soulmate.

"Can I have some more blow? One more hit, 'cause I'm like really cresting now. Maybe we could just buy a little, what the hell? This is a party. I have not been getting loaded. This is a reason to celebrate.

"(sniff) Aaahh! (sniff) Ooohhh! There is like an edge on this, though, don't you think? Am I sweating? I look all right, don't I? I don't look paranoid, do I? Sometimes I get paranoid that I look paranoid. I don't want anyone to think I'm paranoid. It's not like I care what people think, but sometimes I do. I admit it. I'm a human being. I've always cared a little bit what people think.

"But anyway, I like it when it's like this, you know, and we're just talking. This is a great conversation, man. We should be taping this. So, what do you do? You're writing? What are you writing about? Articles on stereo equipment. That's fascinating. So should we go buy some more of this blow? He's out? Well, let's go to Brentwood. No, that's true, he *usually* has shitty blow, but it's not that expensive and he's *always* there.

"Are my gums bleeding? It feels like my gums are bleeding. I don't know why, I must have cut myself talking. Maybe we could get a lude, too, because I'm starting to feel very . . . *unhappy.* I don't mean unhappy, literally, but it's like I wanna be somewhere else but I don't know where I wanna be . . . Let's go to Brentwood. Let's just, fuck it, let's go to Brentwood. Leave your car here, I'll drive you back later. How many toots do we have left? Shit, well, let's go to Brentwood.

"God, I wish I hadn't had that wheatgrass juice. I feel *awful.* Shit, they really should give you instructions with health food. Anything taken to excess can be unhealthy, even healthy stuff. But forget about excess, I don't even think it's that good for you in moderation. Nothing *green* can be good for you, can it? Uuugghh! Give me some more. Let's just do the last hit, just so we can get into the car and get to the next stop. (sniff) (sniff).

"What's the matter with you? You look tense. Are you okay? God, what time is it? Sometimes I get so nervous and I don't know why, you know? I heard this phrase once, 'contentless fear,' and I think that's what I have now. 'Cause there's no reason why I should be this jumpy. I mean, I'm comfortable with you, or I *was* comfortable with you. I'm sorry I'm talking so much. I don't know, it just must be the night. God, what a night.

"*Jesus!* Where did that guy come from, I almost ran him over. *Jesus!* Jesus. Okay, okay, I *am* slowing down. I don't know, somehow it got up to seventy-five. Jesus. Let's do the rest of the blow in case we're stopped. What did you do, *hog* it all?

"God, man. I should never have done this. I should never have done all this blow. I *hate* myself. Why did I do this? Now I have an upset stomach from the wheatgrass juice *and* the fuckin' thing with the blow. I wonder if that girl with the black dress is still at the . . . Here we are, this is his block.

"I feel so dumb now. Why did I *do* that? Well, I didn't do anything dumb. It was probably the blow. That blow *did* burn a little bit. Now we'll get some better blow. I hope he has some *good* blow. I hope he has some *blow*. Maybe he has a lude, though. You know, if I could . . . Well, now I'm maybe in kind of a two-lude mode . . .

"What do you mean, I'm talking to myself? Well, obviously I'm talking to myself. I can't talk to *you*. What do I have in common with someone who writes articles about stereo equipment? Jesus.

"All right, let's just get inside, we'll get inside. How much cash do I have? Hundred and ten, a hundred and ten bucks, that's good. Maybe he'll take a check, that'd be okay. I don't like to do that, though. What if they . . .

"Alex. It's *Alex!*"

What is this asshole, deaf?

"Hi! Hi, man, how ya doin'? Yeah, yeah, I know it's late. Yeah, well, we were just drivin' around and . . . You know Steve. Yeah. Well, can we come in? Thanks.

"So do you have any coke? Half a gram? What do you mean? I thought you were a *dealer*. Can you get more?"

Oh, shit. Oh, *shit!*

"Well, do you have any ludes or anything? I'm really on edge now, I'm *so* on edge. Well, yeah, get the half a gram, and see if . . . Whatever you have. Anything you have. I just want *anything* you have. And Steve wants whatever else there is."

God*damn* it, why did I do this? Just give me that half a gram, and then I'll take the half a gram, and then I'll try and decide what to do. I've gotta figure out how I'm gonna get down . . . I don't want to be with these people. Who *are* these people? I *loathe* these people. Look at the *skin* on that guy, God it's enough to drive anyone *insane*. What is that, a *bug* on the floor? Look at this place. God, what a dive. What a miserable dive.

I hear people. Why do I always hear people? Wait, now, this is the coke, just calm down. What's the big deal? Just *calm down*. I can't believe this, I'm not gonna be able to drive. I feel like digging a hole in the carpet. Oh, Jesus. Oh, Jesus.

Is that the *sun* coming up? No, it's probably just . . . It is, it's the streetlight. I just hope those *birds* don't come out. I'll kill myself, I will, I'll *kill* myself if those fuckin' birds come out. I've gotta have those ludes, gotta have a set of ludes just to get me down. Maybe I should check his medicine cabinet, but he's a dealer so wouldn't he be smart about that? Nah!

"Can I use your bathroom?"

I *loathe* this guy. Let's see, what's he got? Anacin. Afrin. Actifed. Lomotil—sure, 'cause he's got the runs all the time from the baby laxative in his fuckin' blow. Percodan! *Jesus!* Two. Two's not usually enough, but fuck it, I'll take the two. Endo 333, *oooh*, my favorite. I better run the water so they don't hear me close this. Aaahh, that's good, that'll be good. I've taken so much blow, though. Two Percodan on all this blow won't even matter. Maybe I should go get health food . . . Tomorrow I'm really . . .

That's it man, this is *it*. I'm gonna remember this, I'm *always* gonna remember this. That I'm sitting here in Brentwood with two loser guys that I have nothing in common with, doing drugs and trying to make conversation. I could kill myself. I *loathe* my life.

I'll *never* feel those Percodan. Goddamn it, I hope he's got some ludes. *Please* let him have ludes.

"Oh, man, I feel a little better after going to the john. Hey, listen, man, you wouldn't have any *ludes* or anything? I mean, I know I asked you already, but I had like a very tense day. I had some bad wheatgrass juice and . . . I don't know, maybe it's an astrological thing, but . . .

"Ecstasy? No, but I've heard of it. Yeah, right, who hasn't? Aren't you supposed to be with girls or something? Really? It just puts you in a good mood? Well, great, give me some. A *good* mood? Oh, great. No, no, I'm in a good mood now, I'm just in too *strong* of a mood. No, let's, let's . . . Give me one of those. Sorry, I didn't mean to grab.

"Great! They're big, aren't they? Do you have anything to wash it down? Any tequila or anything? Yeah, beer's fine. Oh, wow. So how long do these take to kick in? No, not since that juice this afternoon. Really? That quick? What's in it, do you know? Somebody said there was heroin in it. Not this stuff? Okay, good, 'cause that's the one thing I don't wanna do. Well, one time I snorted some, but I would *never* do any needles. I really think that makes you a drug addict, and me, I'm like a neck-up person."

I feel a little nauseous all of a sudden. It's probably the juice.

"Hey, this is a nice place. I've never really noticed that you have a nice apartment. It's like, kind. I don't know if that's an appropriate way to describe decor, but it seems so . . . friendly. Particularly for a dealer's house. *What* is this music? This is *fantastic* music. Really? I usually *hate* Led Zeppelin. It's so interesting, *so* interesting. Do you mind if I lie down near the speakers? Do you have a pillow or anything?"

God! I feel like I'm making such a fool of myself. I don't even know these guys and I love them. I guess it's gotta be the drug, but it doesn't *seem* like the drug. Maybe this is the Percodan. I know it's not good to mix so much, but this feels like such a good blend. Maybe this is *exactly right*. Maybe from now on I should only do a little cocaine, a couple of Percodan maybe, and then that Ecstasy, and listen to Led Zeppelin. And that'll be my recipe. Like when I've been good, like I have for the past whatever. I've been straight . . . I mean, I was drinking, but I don't count that. When I've been straight for this kind of a while and I really get on edge, the way to take it off is to be with *these* guys. I *love* these guys.

I mean, I don't want to have *sex* with them, but that idea is not totally repellent to me, either. Steve, even though he has bad skin, is a great guy, and he's got an ass like a girl. I never noticed that before. Oh, I'm so *happy*. I think I've really turned this experience around.

"Steve. Don't ever leave me. I can't imagine being separated from you people. *Ever.*"

I want to bond with them on some level. I want to show them how I feel. Maybe this is too excessive. Yeah, I should just get more into the music.

That girl at the party in black . . . Even the party seems nice now. Maybe we should . . . No, I'd have to move. Maybe I could call the party and tell them to send the girl here. *That* would be perfect.

I just feel at one with everything. I remember the time I took acid, and I took the wrong end of the cardboard and it never came on. Maybe this is like acid. But everything looks the same, it just looks *nicer*. Nicer to be with. Maybe I should decorate *my* apartment like this.

My nose still hurts, though. Maybe I should never take cocaine again. Yeah, from now on I'll just take Ecstasy every so often. It's probably better *for* me. They only just made it illegal, so how bad could it be? And they haven't even said it's *bad* for you. They just don't really know yet what it does to you.

How could I not have found this before? I'm so happy. Maybe I should just call the party and ask for that girl. What'd he say her name was? No, maybe I'll just . . . is it rude to jerk off in people's houses? I'll just get up and . . .

"No, no, no, I'm okay, man. I just wanna use your can. What? No, I've snorted heroin, but I would never shoot it. Oh, you would do it *for* me. Well, I suppose that doesn't count, then, right? But I wouldn't have to . . . ? And it'd just be a little bit, right?"

It seems like it would be good. Heroine's like the *natural* drug. I don't know, though. This is so weird.

"You wouldn't do anything bad to me, would you? You have such a great expression on your face right now. All right, sure, I'll trust you. But just give me a little bit. And Steve, you're driving us back, right? Well, maybe I'll just crash here then. That's cool, right? I like Brentwood."

I can't believe this. I'm tying off. This is *so weird*. I never thought I would do this. But I'm just gonna do it *once*.

"Okay."

Oh, *my God!* Now I understand everything. This is so intensely great. Smack. It sounds like a breakfast cereal. It sure doesn't *feel* like a breakfast cereal. Shit, I *love* this. It's like floating down the Nile in your mind. Deep sea diving in your head. This must be well-being.

Does this make me a drug addict? No, I'm just celebrating tonight. What a great night this is.

I'll never do cocaine again. Uh-uh. Maybe a little Ecstasy, a little heroin, but I'll never do cocaine again. And I'm gonna start working out tomorrow. I'm gonna start an aerobic workout tomorrow on my bike. Maybe tomorrow afternoon. I wish I'd never had that wheatgrass juice, though. I feel sort of nauseous.

"Oops, sorry man. Let me clean it up."

God, that was the easiest puke I've ever had. I wish I could have always thrown up that way. That felt almost good.

"Sure, take my car. I'll wait here. I'll just . . . be . . . here . . ."

What a nice, kind apartment this is. I think everyone should just love each other. That's what I think.

I don't know when I've felt this rested. I've never truly been relaxed. I'm finally relaxed. I feel like Jesus slipped me in the pocket of his robe, and we're walking over long, long stretches of water.

My parents were so fabulous to have had me. This is just . . . *everything.* My teeth feel so soft. *This* is why people take this. It wouldn't even be so bad to *die* of really good heroin. I wouldn't mind just living two more weeks and dying at the end of it if I could have two weeks like this. Although it would be much better to have years and years. I don't think you can even call this a drug. This is just a response to the conditions we live in.

I wonder what that art student at the party is doing. She had such soft, silky hair. She seemed so invested in everything, like the now was exactly where she wanted to be. And now I know how she feels. This is perfect.

If she were here now, it would be like Adam and Eve. We would make this the Garden of Eden, this apartment. Anywhere we were would be the Garden of Eden. And I could really communicate with my heart. It's just a question of finding the right person. If she were here now, I would just hold her and hold her and hold her, like we were twins waiting to be born out of this apartment in Brentwood.

She's probably my soulmate. What if I met my soulmate and now I'll never see her again? But we met and kissed on the astral plane. We flew in the astral plane, and now I'm flying toward her. If she's my soulmate, and I truly believe she is, we'll meet again. We're always meeting. There is no meeting for soulmates. They're always together and never apart.

We'll have a child, and we'll bring it up on heroin so that it'll have a happy childhood. And I'll buy her lots and lots of black shirts and sweaters. And she'll play the bongo drums in a jazz club in the East Village, while I recite stream-of-consciousness poetry that everyone thinks is brilliant. I am brilliant. I'm everything.

Sometimes I wonder if I really am Jesus, but I just haven't grown into it yet.

I wonder what color Jesus' eyes were. And if he needed glasses.

He had the sweetest face . . .

CHARLES DICKENS

❖

THE MYSTERY OF EDWIN DROOD

ALTHOUGH MR. CRISPARKLE and John Jasper met daily under the Cathedral roof, nothing at any time passed between them having reference to Edwin Drood, after the time, more than half a year gone by, when Jasper mutely showed the Minor Canon the conclusion and the resolution entered in his Diary. It is not likely that they ever met, though so often, without the thoughts of each reverting to the subject. It is not likely that they ever met, though so often, without a sensation on the part of each that the other was a perplexing secret to him. Jasper as the denouncer and pursuer of Neville Landless, and Mr. Crisparkle as his consistent advocate and protector, must at least have stood sufficiently in opposition to have speculated with keen interest on the steadiness and next direction of the other's designs. But neither ever broached the theme.

False pretence not being in the Minor Canon's nature, he doubtless displayed openly that he would at any time have revived the subject, and even desired to discuss it. The determined reticence of Jasper, however, was not to be so approached. Impassive, moody, solitary, resolute, so concentrated on one idea, and on its attendant fixed purpose, that he would share it with no fellow-creature, he lived apart from human life. Constantly exercising an Art which brought him into mechanical harmony with others, and which could not have been pursued unless he and they had been in the nicest mechanical relations and unison, it is curious to consider that the spirit of the man was in moral accordance or interchange with nothing around him. This indeed he had confided to his lost nephew, before the occasion for his present inflexibility arose.

That he must know of Rosa's abrupt departure, and that he must divine its cause, was not to be doubted. Did he suppose that he had terrified her into silence? or did he suppose that she had imparted to any one—to Mr. Crisparkle himself, for instance—the particulars of his last interview with her? Mr. Crisparkle could not determine this in his mind. He could not but admit, however, as a just man, that it was not, of itself, a crime to fall in love with Rosa, any more than it was a crime to offer to set love above revenge.

The dreadful suspicion of Jasper, which Rosa was so shocked to have received into her imagination, appeared to have no harbour in Mr. Crisparkle's. If it ever haunted Helena's thoughts or Neville's, neither gave it one spoken word of utterance. Mr. Grewgious took no pains to conceal his implacable dislike of Jasper, yet he never referred it, however distantly to such a source. But he was a reticent as well as an eccentric man; and he made no mention of a certain evening when he warmed his hands at the gatehouse fire, and looked steadily down upon a certain heap of torn and miry clothes upon the floor.

Drowsy Cloisterham, whenever it awoke to a passing reconsideration of a story above six months old and dismissed by the bench of magistrates, was pretty equally divided in opinion whether John Jasper's beloved nephew had been killed by his treacherously passionate rival, or in an open struggle; or had, for his own purposes, spirited himself away. It then lifted up its head, to notice that the bereaved Jasper was still ever devoted to discovery and revenge; and then dozed off again. This was the condition of matters, all round, at the period to which the present history has now attained.

The Cathedral doors have closed for the night; and the Choir-master, on a short leave of absence for two or three services, sets his face towards London. He travels thither by the means by which Rosa travelled, and arrives, as Rosa arrived, on a hot, dusty evening.

His travelling baggage is easily carried in his hand, and he repairs with it on foot, to a hybrid hotel in a little square behind Aldersgate Street, near the General Post Office. It is hotel, boarding-house, or lodging-house, at its visitor's option. It announces itself, in the new Railway Advertisers, as a novel enterprise, timidly beginning to spring up. It bashfully, almost apologetically, gives the traveller to understand that it does not expect him, on the good old constitutional hotel plan, to order a pint of sweet blacking for his drinking, and throw it away; but insinuates that he may have his boots blacked instead of his stomach, and may also have bed, breakfast, attendance, and a porter up all night, for a certain fixed charge. From these and similar premises, many true Britons in the lowest spirits deduce that the times are levelling times, except in the article of high roads, of which there will shortly be not one in England.

He eats without appetite, and soon goes forth again. Eastward and still eastward through the stale streets he takes his way, until he reaches his destination: a miserable court, especially miserable among many such.

He ascends a broken staircase, opens a door, looks into a dark stifling room, and says: "Are you alone here?"

"Alone, deary; worse luck for me, and better for you," replies a croaking voice. "Come in, come in, whoever you be: I can't see you till I light a match, yet I seem to know the sound of your speaking. I'm acquainted with you, ain't I?"

"Light your match, and try."

"So I will, deary, so I will; but my hand that shakes, as I can't lay it on a match all in a moment. And I cough so, that, put my matches where I may, I never find 'em there. They jump and start, as I cough and cough, like live things. Are you off a voyage, deary?"

"No."

"Not seafaring?"

"No."

"Well, there's land customers, and there's water customers. I'm a mother to both. Different from Jack Chinaman t' other side the court. He ain't a father to neither. It ain't in him. An he ain't got the true secret of mixing, though he charges as much as me that has, and more if he can get it. Here's a match, and now where's the candle? If my cough takes me, I shall cough out twenty matches afore I gets a light."

But she finds the candle, and lights it, before the cough comes on. It seizes her in the moment of success, and she sits down rocking herself to and fro, and gasping at intervals: "O, my lungs is awful bad! my lungs is wore away to cabbage-nets!" until the fit is over. During its continuance she has had no power of sight, or any other power not absorbed in the struggle; but as it leaves her, she begins to strain her eyes, and as soon as she is able to articulate, she cries, staring:

"Why, it's you!"

"Are you so surprised to see me?"

"I thought I never should have seen you again, deary. I thought you was dead, and gone to Heaven."

"Why?"

"I didn't suppose you could have kept away, alive, so long, from the poor old soul with the real receipt for mixing it. And you are in mourning too! Why didn't you come and have a pipe or two of comfort? Did they leave you money, perhaps, and so you didn't want comfort?"

"No."

"Who was they as died, deary?"

"A relative."

"Died of what, lovey?"

"Probably, Death."

"We are short to-night!" cries the woman, with a propitiatory laugh. "Short and snappish we are! But we're out of sorts for want of a smoke. We've got the all-overs, haven't us, deary? But this is the place to cure 'em in; this is the place where the all-overs is smoked off."

"You may make ready, then," replies the visitor, "as soon as you like."

He divests himself of his shoes, loosens his cravat, and lies across the foot of the squalid bed, with his head resting on his left hand.

"Now you begin to look like yourself," says the woman approvingly. "Now I begin to know my old customer indeed! Been trying to mix for yourself this long time, poppet?"

"I have been taking it now and then in my own way."

"Never take it your own way. It ain't good for trade, and it ain't good for you. Where's my ink-bottle, and where's my thimble, and where's my little spoon? He's going to take it in a artful form now, my deary dear!"

Entering on her process, and beginning to bubble and blow at the faint spark enclosed in the hollow of her hands, she speaks from time to time, in a tone of snuffling satisfaction, without leaving off. When he speaks, he does so without looking at her, and as if his thoughts were already roaming away by anticipation.

"I've got a pretty many smokes ready for you, first and last, haven't I, chuckey?"

"A good many."

"When you first come, you was quite new to it; warn't ye?"

"Yes, I was easily disposed of, then."

But you got on in the world, and was able by and by to take your pipe with the best of 'em, warn't ye?"

"Ah; and the worst."

"It's just ready for you. What a sweet singer you was when you first come! Used to drop your head, and sing yourself off like a bird! It's ready for you now, deary."

He takes it from her with great care, and puts the mouthpiece to his lips. She seats herself beside him, ready to refill the pipe. After inhaling a few whiffs in silence, he doubtingly accosts her with:

"Is it as potent as it used to be?"

"What do you speak of, deary?"

"What should I speak of, but what I have in my mouth?"

"It's just the same. Always the identical same."

"It doesn't taste so. And it's slower."

"You've got more used to it, you see."

"That may be the cause, certainly. Look here." He stops, becomes dreamy, and seems to forget that he has invited her attention. She bends over him, and speaks in his ear.

"I'm attending to you. Says you just now, Look here. Says I now, I'm attending to ye. We was talking just before of your being used to it."

"I know all that. I was only thinking. Look here. Suppose you had something in your mind; something you were going to do."

"Yes, deary; something I was going to do?"

"But had not quite determined to do."

"Yes, deary."

"Might or might not do, you understand."

"Yes." With the point of a needle she stirs the contents of the bowl.

"Should you do it in your fancy, when you were lying here doing this?"

She nods her head. "Over and over again."

"Just like me! I did it over and over again. I have done it hundreds of thousands of times in this room."

"It's to be hoped it was pleasant to do, deary."

"It *was* pleasant to do!"

He says this with a savage air, and a spring or start at her. Quite unmoved she retouches and replenishes the contents of the bowl with her little spatula. Seeing her intent upon the occupation, he sinks into his former attitude.

"It was a journey, a difficult and dangerous journey. That was the subject in my mind. A hazardous and perilous journey, over abysses where a slip would be destruction. Look down, look down! You see what lies at the bottom there?"

He has darted forward to say it, and to point at the ground, as though at some imaginary object far beneath. The woman looks at him, as his spasmodic face approaches close to hers, and not at his pointing.

She seems to know what the influence of her perfect quietude would be; if so, she has not miscalculated it, for he subsides again.

"Well; I have told you I did it here hundreds of thousands of times. What do I say? I did it millions and billions of times. I did it so often, and through such vast expanses of time, that when it was really done, it seemed not worth the doing, it was done so soon."

"That's the journey you have been away upon," she quietly remarks.

He glares at her as he smokes; and then, his eyes becoming filmy, answers: "That's the journey."

Silence ensues. His eyes are sometimes closed and sometimes open. The woman sits beside him, very attentive to the pipe, which is all the while at his lips.

"I'll warrant," she observes, when he has been looking fixedly at her for some consecutive moments, with a singular appearance in his eyes of seeming to see her a long way off, instead of so near him: "I'll warrant you made the journey in a many ways, when you made it so often?"

"No, always in one way."

"Always in the same way?"

"Ay."

"In the way in which it was really made at last?"

"Ay."

"And always took the same pleasure in harping on it?"

"Ay."

For the time he appears unequal to any other reply than this lazy monosyllabic assent. Probably to assure herself that it is not the assent of a mere automaton, she reverses the form of her next sentence.

"Did you never get tired of it, deary, and try to call up something else for a change?"

He struggles into a sitting posture, and retorts upon her: "What do you mean? What did I want? What did I come for?"

She gently lays him back again, and before returning him the instrument he has dropped, revives the fire in it with her own breath; then says to him, coaxingly:

"Sure, sure, sure! Yes, yes, yes! Now I go along with you. You was too quick for me. I see now. You come o' purpose to take the journey. Why, I might have known it, through its standing by you so."

He answers first with a laugh, and then with a passionate setting of his teeth: "Yes, I came on purpose. When I could not bear my life, I came to get the relief, and I got it. It WAS one! It WAS one!" This repetition with extraordinary vehemence, and the snarl of a wolf.

She observes him very cautiously, as though mentally feeling her way to her next remark. It is: "There was a fellow-traveller, deary."

"Ha, ha, ha!" He breaks into a ringing laugh, or rather yell.

"To think," he cries, "how often fellow-traveller, and yet not know it! To think how many times he went the journey, and never saw the road!"

The woman kneels upon the floor, with her arms crossed on the coverlet of the bed, close by him, and her chin upon them. In this crouching attitude she watches him. The pipe is falling from his mouth. She puts it back, and laying her hand upon his chest, moves him slightly from side to side. Upon that he speaks, as if she had spoken.

"Yes! I always made the journey first, before the changes of colours and the great landscapes and glittering processions began. They couldn't begin till it was off my mind. I had no room till then for anything else."

Once more he lapses into silence. Once more she lays her hand upon his chest, and moves him slightly to and fro, as a cat might stimulate a half-slain mouse. Once more he speaks, as if she had spoken.

"What? I told you so. When it comes to be real at last it is so short that it seems unreal for the first time. Hark!"

"Yes, deary. I'm listening."

"Time and place are both at hand."

He is on his feet, speaking in a whisper, and as if in the dark.

"Time, place, and fellow-traveller," she suggests, adopting his tone, and holding him softly by the arm.

"How could the time be at hand unless the fellow-traveller was? Hush! The journey's made. It's over."

"So soon?"

"That's what I said to you. So soon. Wait a little This is a vision. I shall sleep it off. It has been too short and easy. I must have a better vision than this; this is the poorest of all. No struggle, no consciousness of peril, no entreaty—and yet I never saw *that* before." With a start.

"Saw what, deary?"

"Look at it! Look what a poor, mean miserable thing it is! *That* must be real. It's over."

He has accompanied this incoherence with some wild unmeaning gestures; but they trail off into the progressive inaction of stupor, and he lies a log upon the bed.

The woman, however, is still inquisitive. With a repetition of her cat-like action she stirs his body again, and listens; stirs again, and listens; whispers to it, and listens. Finding it past all rousing for the time, she slowly gets upon her feet, with an air of disappointment, and flicks the face with the back of her hand in turning from it.

But she goes no further away from it than the chair upon the hearth. She sits in it, with an elbow on one of its arms, and her chin upon her hand, intent upon him. "I heard ye say once," she croaks under her breath, "I heard ye say once, when I was lying where you're lying, and you were making your speculations upon me, 'Unintelligible!' I heard you say so, of two more than me. But don't ye be too sure always; don't ye be too sure, beauty!"

Unwinking, cat-like, and intent, she presently adds: "Not so potent as it once was? Ah! Perhaps not at first. You may be more right there. Practice makes perfect. I may have learned the secret how to make ye talk, deary."

He talks no more, whether or no. Twitching in an ugly way from time to time, both as to his face and limbs, he lies heavy and silent. The wretched candle burns down; the woman takes its expiring end between her fingers, lights another at it, crams the guttering frying morsel deep into the candlestick, and rams it home with the new candle, as if she were loading some ill-savoured and unseemly weapon of witchcraft; the new candle in its turn burns down; and still he lies insensible. At length what remains of the last candle is blown out, and daylight looks into the room.

It has not looked very long, when he sits up, chilled and shaking, slowly recovers consciousness of where he is, and makes himself ready to depart. The woman receives what he pays her with a grateful, "Bless ye, bless ye, deary!" and seems, tired out, to begin to make herself ready for sleep as he leaves the room.

But seeming may be false or true. It is false in this case; for, the moment the stairs have ceased to creak under his tread, she glides after him, muttering emphatically: "I'll not miss ye twice!"

There is no egress from the court but by its entrance. With a weird peep from the doorway, she watches for his looking back. He does not look back before disappearing, with a wavering step. She follows him, peeps from the court, sees him still faltering on without looking back, and holds him in view.

He repairs to the back of Aldersgate Street, where a door immediately opens to his knocking. She crouches in another doorway, watching that one, and easily comprehending that he puts up temporarily at that house. Her patience is unexhausted by hours. For sustenance she can, and does, buy bread within a hundred yards, and milk as it is carried past her.

He comes forth again at noon, having changed his dress, but carrying nothing in his hand, and having nothing carried for him. He is not going back into the country, therefore, just yet. She follows him a little way, hesitates, instantaneously turns confidently, and goes straight into the house he has just quitted.

"Is the gentleman from Cloisterham indoors?"

"Just gone out."

"Unlucky. When does the gentleman return to Cloisterham?"

"At six this evening."

"Bless ye and thank ye. May the Lord prosper a business where a civil question, even from a poor soul, is so civilly answered!"

"I'll not miss ye twice!" repeats the poor soul in the street, and not so civilly. "I lost ye last, where that omnibus you got into nigh your journey's end plied betwixt the station and the place. I wasn't so much as certain that you even went right on to the place. Now I know ye did. My gentleman from Cloisterham, I'll be there before ye, and bide your coming. I've swore my oath that I'll not miss ye twice!"

Accordingly, that same evening the poor soul stands in Cloisterham High Street, looking at the many quaint gables of the Nuns' House, and getting through the time as best she can until nine o'clock; at which hour she has reason to suppose that the arriving omnibus passengers may have some interest for her. The friendly darkness, at that hour, renders it easy for her to ascertain whether this be so or not; and it is so, for the passenger not to be missed twice arrives among the rest.

"Now let me see what becomes of you. Go on!"

An observation addressed to the air, and yet it might be addressed to the passenger, so compliantly does he go on along the High Street until he comes to an arched gateway, at which he unexpectedly vanishes. The poor soul quickens her pace; is swift, and close upon him entering under the gateway; but only sees a postern staircase on one side of it, and on the other side an ancient vaulted room, in which a large-headed, gray-haired gentleman is writing, under the odd circumstances of sitting open to the thoroughfare and eyeing all who pass, as if he were toll-taker of the gateway: though the way is free.

"Halloa!" he cries in a low voice, seeing her brought to a standstill: "who are you looking for?"

"There was a gentleman passed in here this minute, sir."

"Of course there was. What do you want with him?"

"Where do he live, deary?"

"Live? Up that staircase."

"Bless ye! Whisper. What's his name, deary?"

"Surname Jasper, Christian name John. Mr. John Jasper."

"Has he a calling, good gentleman?"

"Calling? Yes. Sings in the choir."

"In the spire?"

"Choir."

"What's that?"

Mr. Datchery rises from his papers, and comes to his doorstep. "Do you know what a cathedral is? he asks, jocosely.

The woman nods.

"What is it?"

She looks puzzled, casting about in her mind to find a definition, when it occurs to her it is easier to point out the substantial object itself, massive against the dark blue sky and the early stars.

"That's the answer. Go in there at seven tomorrow morning, and you may see Mr. John Jasper, and hear him too."

"Thank ye! Thank ye!"

The burst of triumph in which she thanks him does not escape the notice of the single buffer of an easy temper living idly on his means. He glances at her; clasps his hands behind him, as the wont of such buffers is; and lounges along the echoing Precincts at her side.

"O," he suggests, with a backward hitch of his head, "you can go up at once to Mr. Jasper's rooms there."

The woman eyes him with a cunning smile, and shakes her head.

"O! you don't want to speak to him?"

She repeats her dumb reply, and forms with her lips a soundless "No."

"You can admire him at a distance three times a day, whenever you like. It's a long way to come for that, though."

The woman looks up quickly. If Mr. Datchery thinks she is to be so induced to declare where she comes from, he is of a much easier temper than she is. But she acquits him of such an artful thought, as he lounges along, like the chartered bore of the city, with his uncovered gray hair blowing about, and his purposeless hands rattling the loose money in the pockets of his trousers.

The chink of the money has an attraction for her greedy ears. "Wouldn't you help me to pay for my traveller's lodging, dear gentleman, and to pay my way along? I am a poor soul, I am indeed, and troubled with a grievous cough."

"You know the travellers' lodging, I perceive, and are making directly for it," is Mr. Datchery's bland comment, still rattling his loose money. "Been here often, my good woman?"

"Once in all my life."

"Ay, ay?"

They have arrived at the entrance to the Monks' Vineyard. An appropriate remembrance, presenting an exemplary model for imitation, is revived in the woman's mind by the sight of the place. She stops at the gate, and says energetically:

"By this token though you mayn't believe it, That a young gentleman gave me three-and-sixpence as I was coughing my breath away on this very grass. I asked him for three-and sixpence, and he gave it me."

"Wasn't it a little cool to name your sum?" hints Mr. Datchery still rattling. "Isn't it customary to leave the amount open? Mightn't it have had the appearance, to the young gentleman—only the appearance—that he was rather dictated to?"

"Look 'ee here, deary," she replies, in a confidential and persuasive tone, "I wanted the money to lay it out on a medicine as does me good, and as I deal in. I told the young gentleman so, and he gave it me, and I laid it out honest to the last brass farden. I want to lay out the same sum in the same way now; and if you'll give it me, I'll lay it out honest to the last brass farden again, upon my soul!"

"What's the medicine?"

"I'll be honest with you beforehand, as well as after. It's opium."

Mr. Datchery, with a sudden change of countenance, gives her a sudden look.

"It's opium, deary. Neither more nor less. And it's like a human creetur so far, that you always hear what can be said against it, but seldom what can be said in its praise."

Mr. Datchery begins very slowly to count out the sum demanded of him. Greedily watching his hands, she continues to hold forth on the great example set him.

"It was last Christmas Eve, just arter dark, the once that I was here afore, when the young gentleman gave me the three-and-six."

Mr. Datchery stops in his counting, finds he has counted wrong, shakes his money together, and begins again.

"And the young gentleman's name," she adds, "was Edwin."

Mr. Datchery drops some money, stoops to pick it up, and reddens with the exertion as he asks:

"How do you know the young gentleman's name?"

"I asked him for it, and he told me. I only asked him the two questions, what was his Chris'en name, and whether he'd a sweetheart? And he answered Edwin, and he hadn't."

Mr. Datchery pauses with the selected coins in his hand, rather as if he were falling into a brown study of their value, and couldn't bear to part with them. The woman looks at him distrustfully, and with her anger brewing for the event of his thinking better of the gift; but he bestows it on her as if he were abstracting his mind from the sacrifice, and with many servile thanks she goes her way.

John Jasper's lamp is kindled, and his lighthouse is shining when Mr. Datchery returns alone towards it. As mariners on a dangerous voyage, approaching an iron-bound coast, may look along the beams of the warning light to the haven lying beyond it that may never be reached, so Mr. Datchery's wistful gaze is directed to this beacon, and beyond.

His object in now revisiting his lodging is merely to put on the hat which seems so superfluous an article in his wardrobe. It is half-past ten by the Cathedral clock when he walks out into the Precincts again; he lingers and looks about him, as though, the enchanted hour when Mr. Durdles may be stoned home having struck, he had some expectation of seeing the Imp who is appointed to the mission of stoning him.

In effect, that Power of Evil is abroad. Having nothing living to stone at the moment, he is discovered by Mr. Datchery in the unholy office of stoning the dead, through the railings of the churchyard. The Imp finds this a relishing and piquing pursuit; firstly, because their resting-place is announced to be sacred; and secondly, because the tall headstones are sufficiently like themselves, on their beat in the dark, to justify the delicious fancy that they are hurt when hit.

Mr. Datchery hails him with: "Halloa, Winks!"

He acknowledges the hail with: "Halloa, Dick!" Their acquaintance seemingly having been established on a familiar footing.

"But I say," he remonstrates, "don't yer go a-making my name public. I never means to plead to no name, mind yer. When they says to me in the Lock-up, a-going to put me down in the book, 'What's your name?' I says to them, 'Find out.' Likeways when they says, 'What's your religion?' I says, 'Find out.' "

Which, it may be observed in passing, it would be immensely difficult for the State, however statistical, to do.

"Asides which," adds the boy, "there ain't no family of Winkses."

"I think there must be."

"Yer lie, there ain't. The travellers give me the name on account of my getting no settled sleep and being knocked up all night; whereby I gets one eye roused open afore I've shut the other. That's what Winks means. Deputy's the nighest name to indict me by: but yer wouldn't catch me pleading to that, neither."

"Deputy be it always, then. We two are good friends; eh, Deputy?"

"Jolly good."

"I forgave you the debt you owed me when we first became acquainted, and many of my sixpences have come your way since; eh, Deputy?"

"Ah! And what's more, yer ain't no friend o' Jarsper's. What did he go a-histing me off my legs for?"

"What indeed! But never mind him now. A shilling of mine is going your way to-night, Deputy. You have just taken in a lodger I have been speaking to; an infirm woman with a cough."

"Puffer," assents Deputy, with a shrewd leer of recognition, and smoking an imaginary pipe, with his head very much on one side and his eyes very much out of their places: "Hopeum Puffer."

"What is her name?"

" 'Er Royal Highness the Princess Puffer."

"She has some other name than that; where does she live?"

"Up in London. Among the Jacks."

"The sailors?"

"I said so; Jacks; and Chayner men; and hother Knifers."

"I should like to know, through you, exactly where she lives."

"All right. Give us 'old."

A shilling passes; and, in that spirit of confidence which should pervade all business transactions between principals of honour, this piece of business is considered done.

"But here's a lark!" cries Deputy. "Where did yer think 'Er Royal Highness is a-goin' to to-morrow morning? Blest if she ain't a-going to the KIN-FREE-DER-EL!" He greatly prolongs the word in his ecstasy, and smites his leg, and doubles himself up in a fit of shrill laughter.

"How do you know that, Deputy?"

"Cos she told me so just now. She said she must be hup and hout o' purpose. She ses, 'Deputy, I must 'ave a early wash, and make myself as swell as I can, for I'm a-goin' to take a turn at the KIN-FREE-DER-EL!' " He separates the syllables with his former zest, and, not finding his sense of the ludicrous sufficiently relieved by stamping about on the pavement, breaks into a slow and stately dance, perhaps supposed to be performed by the Dean.

Mr. Datchery receives the communication with a well-satisfied though pondering face, and breaks up the conference. Returning to his quaint lodging, and sitting long over the supper of bread-and-cheese and salad and ale which Mrs. Tope has left prepared for him, he still sits when his supper is finished. At length he rises, throws open the door of a corner cupboard, and refers to a few uncouth chalked strokes on its inner side.

"I like," says Mr. Datchery, "the old tavern way of keeping scores. Illegible except to the scorer. The scorer not committed, the scored debited with what is against him. Hum; ha! A very small score this; a very poor score!"

He sighs over the contemplation of its poverty, takes a bit of chalk from one of the cupboard shelves, and pauses with it in his hand, uncertain what addition to make to the account.

"I think a moderate stroke," he concludes, "is all I am justified in scoring up"; so, suits the action to the word, closes the cupboard, and goes to bed.

A brilliant morning shines on the old city. Its antiquities and ruins are surpassingly beautiful, with a lusty ivy gleaming in the sun, and the rich trees waving in the balmy air. Changes of glorious light from moving boughs, songs of birds, scents from gardens, woods, and fields—or, rather, from the one great garden of the whole cultivated island in its yielding time—penetrate into the Cathedral, subdue its earthy odour, and preach the Resurrection and the Life. The cold stone tombs of centuries ago grow warm; and flecks of brightness dart into the sternest marble corners of the building, fluttering there like wings.

Comes Mr. Tope with his large keys, and yawningly unlocks and sets open. Come Mrs. Tope and attendant sweeping sprites. Come, in due time, organist and bellows-boy, peeping down from the red curtains in the loft, fearlessly flapping dust from books up at that remote elevation, and whisking it from stops and pedals. Come sundry rooks, from various quarters of the sky, back to the great tower; who may be presumed to enjoy vibration, and to know that bell and organ are going to give it them. Come a very small and straggling congregation indeed: chiefly from Minor Canon Corner and the Precincts. Come Mr. Crisparkle, fresh and bright; and his ministering brethren, not quite so fresh and bright. Come the Choir in a hurry (always in a hurry, and struggling into their nightgowns at the last moment, like children shirking bed), and comes John Jasper leading their line. Last of all comes Mr. Datchery into a stall, one of a choice empty collection very much at his service, and glancing about him for Her Royal Highness the Princess Puffer.

The service is pretty well advanced before Mr. Datchery can discern Her Royal Highness. But by that time he has made her out, in the shade. She is behind a pillar, carefully withdrawn from the Choirmaster's view, but regards him with the closest attention. All unconscious of her presence, he chants and sings. She grins when he is most musically fervid, and—yes, Mr. Datchery sees her do it!—shakes her fist at him behind the pillar's friendly shelter.

Mr. Datchery looks again, to convince himself. Yes, again! As ugly and withered as one of the fantastic carvings on the under brackets of the stall seats, as malignant as the Evil One, as hard as the big brass eagle holding the sacred books upon his wings (and, according to the sculptor's representation of his ferocious attributes, not at all converted by them), she hugs herself in her lean arms, and then shakes both fists at the leader of the Choir.

And at that moment, outside the grated door of the Choir, having eluded the vigilance of Mr. Tope by shifty resources in which he is an adept, Deputy peeps, sharp-eyed, through the bars, and stares astounded from the threatener to the threatened.

The service comes to an end, and the servitors disperse to breakfast. Mr. Datchery accosts his last new acquaintance outside, when the Choir (as much in a hurry to get their bedgowns off, as they were but now to get them on) have scuffled away.

"Well, mistress. Good morning. You have seen him?"

"*I*'ve seen him, deary; *I*'ve seen him!"

"And you know him?"

"Know him! Better far than all the Reverend Parsons put together know him."

Mrs. Tope's care has spread a very neat, clean breakfast for her lodger. Before sitting down to it, he opens his corner-cupboard door; takes his bit of chalk from its shelf; adds one thick line to the score, extending from the top of the cupboard door to the bottom; and then falls to with an appetite.

J. Moreau de Tours

❀

ON HASHISH AND MENTAL ALIENATION

THURSDAY, DECEMBER 5—I had already taken hashish, and I knew about the effects [of dawamesk], not from experience but from what a person who had visited the Orient had told me of them, so I waited calmly for the happy madness that was to descend upon me. I sat down at table—I wouldn't say, as some people do, after savoring this dough, because I in fact found it revolting, but after swallowing it with some effort. While I was eating oysters, there came to me an attack of uncontrollable laughter, which subsided when I focused my attention on two other persons who, like me, had wanted to taste the oriental substance, and who were already seeing a lion's head in their plates. I remained quite calm until dinner was over; but then I seized a spoon and began to joust against the pot of dried fruit with which I imagined myself to be dueling, then left the dining room in a burst of laughter.

I began to play a song from the Black Domino, but interrupted myself after a few bars, as I observed a truly diabolical sight: I believed the portrait of my brother above the piano had come to life, complete with a black forked tail ending in three lanterns—red green and white. This apparition came to me several times that evening.

I was sitting on a sofa. "Why do you nail down my limbs?" I cried out suddenly. "I'm turning into lead, I know it. God, I'm heavy." People took my hands to lift me up, and I fell heavily to the ground; I prostrated myself like a Muslim, saying, "Father, I am guilty" and so on, as if I were beginning a confession. People raised me up, and suddenly I changed again. I danced the polka with a foot-warmer; I imitated the voice and gestures of several actors; then my thoughts transported me from the theater to the ball at the Opera; the world, the noise, the lights exalted me, and after a thousand incoherent speeches, I went off—gesticulating and crying out like all the masked dancers I thought I was seeing—in the direction of an unlit room next door.

And then an appalling thing happened to me: I was suffocating, asphyxiating, falling into a bottomless pit—the Bicêtre well. Like a drowning man who seeks salvation from the frail reed just out of reach, I tried to grasp the rocks that surrounded the well, but they fell with me into these infinite depths. The feeling was awful, but it didn't last long, because when I cried out, "I'm falling down a well!" I was brought back into the room I'd left. My first words were, "I'm such a fool! I thought it was a well, and I'm at the Opera Ball." I knocked against a stool, and it seemed to be a masked man lying on the ground, dancing in a most unseemly way, and I asked a policemen to arrest him. I asked for a drink: a lemon was called for, to make lemonade, and I told the maid not to bring one as yellow as her face, which appeared almost orange.

I ran my hands through my hair. I could feel millions of insects devouring my head. The female of one of these insects was suffering labor-pains and had chosen for her lying-in the third hair to the left of my forehead. I sent for an obstetrician, but he was occupied with looking after Madame B., and after long labor, the animal gave birth to seven little creatures. . . .

When I saw my child, my beloved son, in a blue and silver sky, I was intoxicated with happiness, a madness that only the heart of a mother can understand. He had white wings bordered with pink; he smiled at me and showed me the two pretty little white teeth whose birth I had been anticipating with such solicitude; he was surrounded by lots of children who had wings, like him, and flew about in this pure blue sky; but my son was the most beautiful. There had never been a purer joy. He smiled at me and held out his two little arms as if calling me to him.

But this sweet vision faded like the others, and I fell from the heights of the hashish sky to the land of lanterns. It was a land where the people, the houses, the trees, the streets, were lanterns, exactly like the colored glass that festooned the Champs-Elysées last July 29. These lanterns walked and danced, and in the middle, brighter than the others, were the three lanterns from my brother's supposed tail; I saw one light in particular dancing constantly in front of my eyes (it was caused by the flames of the coal burning in the fireplace) . . .

My eyes were closed, by a kind of nervous contraction, and they burned; I sought the cause and lost no time discovering that the valet had coated my eyes with beeswax and that he was polishing them with a brush. . . .

I drank a glass of lemonade, and then all at once, and for no reason at all, my imagination transported me to the Ouarnier Baths in the Seine. I wanted to swim, and was seized by a cruel emotion when I felt myself sink into the water; the more I wanted to cry out, the more water I swallowed, until a friend came to help me and brought me back up to the surface; and through the curtains hanging around the Baths I could see my brother, crossing the river at the Pont des Arts bridge.

I can't even describe the thousands of fantastical thoughts that crossed my mind during the three hours that I was under the influence of the hashish—they would seem bizarre beyond belief; even the people with me were skeptical, and they asked me if I weren't toying with them, because even in the midst of this strange madness, I retained my grasp on reason. My cries and song woke up my son, who was sleeping in my mother's lap. His little voice, crying out, brought me to my senses and I went to him, and kissed him as though I were in my normal state. But the others feared I would revert to my fits and took him from me, and I said then that he was not mine—that he was the child of a woman I know, who has none and envies me him. And then I went off visiting; I chatted (supplying both the questions and their answers), I went to cafes and asked for ice-cream, I found the waiters stupid, etc. And after much walking about, during which I met Mr. So-and-So or Mr. Such-and-Such (whose nose began stretching out longer and longer, even though it was already reasonably large), I went back home. I said, "Oh, look at the huge rat running through B's head"—and at that point the rat swelled up and became as large as the rat in the show *The Seven Castles of the Devil*. I saw it; I could have sworn that rat was walking on B.'s head; yet I was watching the bonnet of one of the women present. I knew it was she, really, who was present, while B. was just an imaginary being. And yet I can affirm that I saw him, too.

ALAN WATTS

L S D

BACK THROUGH THE tunnels, through the devious status-and-survival strategy of adult life, through the interminable passes which we remember in dreams . . . all the streets, the winding pathways between the legs of tables and chairs where one crawled as a child, the tight and bloody exit from the womb, the fountainous surge through the channel of the penis, the timeless wandering through ducts and spongy caverns. Down and back through ever narrowing tubes to the point where the passage itself is the traveler . . . relentlessly back and back through endless and whirling dances to the astronomically proportioned spaces which surround the original nuclei of the world, the centers of centers, as remotely distant on the inside as the nebulae beyond our galaxy on the outside.

E L I Z A B E T H   B A R R E T T   B R O W N I N G

❀

O P I U M   N I G H T S

I TOOK TWO draughts of opium last night—but even the second failing to bring sleep. It *is* a blessed thing!—that sleep!—one of my worst sufferings being the want of it. Opium—opium—night after night—! and some nights, during east winds, even opium won't do. . . .

SEAN ELDER

❖

ON ECSTASY

THE FIRST THING I heard about "Ecstasy" was that it was the designer drug of the eighties. I had never been sure what exactly "designer drugs" were, but I imagined that, like designer jeans, they would cost more than regular drugs for no reason but the name.

But no. The word on the street for the new drug in town was, well, ecstatic. People said it gave the user the confidence of cocaine and the insight of LSD. (There are, of course, problems with that analogy, as anyone who's ever seen a cokehead crawling on the carpet looking for a grain no bigger than a pinpoint can testify; confidence is not the word that comes to mind. As for acid, I can't help but recall the title of a drug propaganda film they used to show us in high school: *LSD: Insight or Insanity?* But more on that later.) Not only that, the high lasted only about four hours, your thinking remained lucid and coherent throughout, and you were erotically energized. Oh, and there were no bad side effects either. Seriously.

Then there were the conscientious proponents of the drug, therapists and spiritual seekers who claimed that it gave the user a great sense of peace and contentment, that it melted the fear in people's hearts and opened them to love in a way that they never felt possible. These advocates often refer to MDMA (Ecstasy's true call letters) as an empathogenic substance because of its "empathy generating" properties. Great for couples counseling, some therapists have testified. Helpful for those overcoming a cocaine addiction, others have said. Also wonderful in grief counseling, accelerating the long and painful process of grappling with the death of a loved one. It had also been successfully used in treating victims of rape and violent accidents, helping them face their horrible memories without fear or anxiety.

So if this drug was so fucking wonderful, so fun and liberating and harmless, why had the federal Drug Enforcement Agency outlawed it two years ago? I decided to try it myself (anything for a story) and suss out a few of the experts, pro and con, in the meanwhile.

Conveniently, the Haight-Ashbury Free Clinic and Merritt Hospital were co-sponsoring an interdisciplinary conference on the drug. It turned out to be a big draw, a sea of beards and Ph.D.'s with all the honchos of MDMA in attendance, the Learys and Alperts and even Owsleys of Ecstasy. Such a varied confab gathered to confer on LSD would have been unthinkable twenty years ago. Even more unthinkable would have been the presence of a government representative there to tell the assembled weirdos why the feds were taking their sunshine away.

But here was Frank Sapienza, a chemist from the DEA, standing at the podium, looking like a Christian prepared to address a group of very Roman lions. Clearing his throat, Sapienza began his address.

"Hi," he said. "Uh, any questions?"

MDMA, MORE POPULARLY known as Ecstasy, "XTC," or "Adam," is the abbreviation for the drug's chemical name, 3, 4-methylenedioxymethamphetamine. It was originally developed by E. Merck, a German pharmaceutical firm, in 1914 as an appetite suppressant but never marketed. Had it been, all of Eastern Europe might now be thinner and happier, and the Archduke Ferdinand might be summering in Cannes.

The drug made its reappearance in the later 1970s as one of the new designer drugs—or, in its case, a redesigner drug. "Designer drugs" was the phrase coined to describe the flurry of narcotic analgesics being produced at the time, drugs that had, basically, three things in common: They were hard to detect, hard to test for, and—most significantly—chemically different from psychedelics outlawed under the Controlled Substance Act of 1970. The idea was to design and manufacture new, fun drugs faster than the feds could outlaw them.

MDMA, brother to the longer lasting, speedier and illegal MDA, was the newest and funnest of the bunch.

In fact, MDMA was so much fun, so too-good-to-be-true, that the DEA canned it but good in the summer of 1984, placing it under Schedule I, a category of controlled substances that includes heroin and LSD. (Indeed, it was almost exactly twenty years ago that the feds gave acid the same kibosh.) According to the DEA, Schedule I drugs have a high potential for abuse, no safety standards accepted by the Food and Drug Administration and no accepted medical use. What this meant to the potential dealer was that trafficking in MDMA could land him fifteen years in prison and a $125,000 fine. Very unecstatic.

What this meant to the therapeutic community, though, the psychologists and spiritualists who had been quietly using the drug for years in search of contentment and "individuation," was that their activities were now illegal. It was the "no accepted medical use" part of the DEA's definition that really rankled them. A wave of protests from the medical community caught the DEA by surprise, and in August of '84 they granted a series of hearings before banning the drug. Among those protesting the proposed ban was San Francisco psychiatrist Jack Downing, who had good things to say about the effects of MDMA on the troubled psyche.

"In general, it gives patients some release from the fear and anxiety that pattern everyone's life," says Downing now. "They can approach whatever it is—the fact that their parents didn't love them, the fact that they themselves have acted in a way they were ashamed of, almost anything. Practically everybody has done something so distressing that they prefer to hide it in the closet, the emotional closet, rather than express it."

Needless to say, the pleas of Downing and his comrades fell on deaf ears. As Sapienza said at the conference, "Even if the DEA had been aware of the drug's therapeutic use, it would have not been considered accepted medical use." Accepted medical use means the treatment of some physical ailment, and the testimony of a therapist and his patient—or a thousand therapists and a thousand patients—is not admissible. What the government found admissible were the experiments done with MDMA on rats and dogs. Large, human-sized doses of the drug were administered to these beasts, and hyperactivity and heart failure were the result. Go ask a dog about his state of mind. (Or, as one of the animal researchers at the conference remarked, "My rats are all atheists.")

But it wasn't the psychiatric community with its controlled, introspective use of the drug that had attracted the DEA's attention. It had been (shades of LSD!) thrill-seeking youngsters, blowing their gourds in public, that had excited the feds into action. Bars in Dallas were dispensing the stuff the way other taverns sell lottery tickets and the young folk were acting strange, dancing, hugging, getting all emotional. Of course the government banned it.

I TOOK ACID for the first time when I was fifteen, not long before my sixteenth birthday, in the company of a gang of like-minded imbeciles. We had come together not so much through choice as by social exclusion. We didn't fit in. We hated school—that was a given—but we also hated sports and beer parties and fights and dating and all the other standard small-town high school diversions. Aside from shooting pool and swimming in the American River in the summertime, the only thing we really shared was a love of drugs.

I ended up doing acid once or twice a week for the next year or so. It became a way of life for me and my friends; we'd do it on weekends, at parties, even in school, waiting to see who would notice. I started wearing weird gear to classes—capes, goggles, rubber waders—hoping to get a rise, or at least a look, out of someone. A friend and I even ran for school office under a "Joint Ticket." I put up a big painted poster in the cafeteria that read "Let Sean Decide," with the first letters of each word painted in bright, fluorescent orange.

It wasn't long after I was elected to the office of Junior Boy (yes, that was the title) that I had my first bad acid experience. I had cut school with another fellow to spend the winter day tripping down in the canyons of the North Fork. Suddenly, all of nature, which had seemed so beckoning before, turned menacing and insatiable. Time was turning on some wheel that now had teeth, and my friend and I were going to be ground down and consumed, little legumes in the garbage disposal of life.

We sped out of that canyon like insects out of a drain, thankful to be still alive but equally sure that our lives were meaningless, expendable. We wandered back toward town, where, my friend kept telling me, we were sure to be caught and hung by our thumbs. I had already spent time in Juvenile Hall for drug offenses; why risk eternal incarceration, he reasoned, by wandering around all lit up like a goddamned Christmas tree? Why not stay put in the hills where at least the chances of being noticed were considerably less?

The demarcation point between rural relief and community consumption came at an irrigation ditch above our school. In my friend's mind, it was the point of no return. If we crossed the little bridge that went over that ditch, we were finished, history. And in my stoned mind there seemed to be only one alternative: I leapt into the water, fully clothed, in the middle of February, thinking that I was somehow beating the preordained events that conspired against me.

My friend beat a hasty retreat, figuring at that point that I was too far gone for any recollection, and no doubt dealing with some demons of his own. I emerged, soaking wet in my blue jeans and work shirt, a hundred feet down the canal and every bit as amped as I was when I went in. I sloshed my way down into town back to my mother's house, where my little brother was watching a rerun of *Gomer Pyle, U.S.M.C.* on television.

"Are you okay?" he asked as I entered the living room.

On the TV screen Jim Nabors squinted, smiled, and spoke. "Gollleee, Sarge! It's hepalah arn foor shorn nah gebalah?"

I walked in a trance into my bedroom and changed my clothes to go to work. For some reason, I was convinced I had to go to my after-school job, repairing educational films for the county school district. I arrived there not long afterwards, still wet, still blasted.

"It just keeps going around and around," I announced profoundly to the first person I saw. I was immediately escorted back home.

Later that evening, considerably saner, I forswore drugs for all time, even flushing a lid of fine grass down the toilet. I kept to this new lifestyle for at least a couple of days, in the course of which I decided that the only way to deal with my acid paranoia was to—well, do more acid!

And so I did, like some idiot who keeps flinging himself against the wall, thinking there's some hidden door there. I kept having bad trips, seeing things that weren't there, laughing at the shadows, making a fool of myself. And through it all I was poison, socially speaking, as welcome as a leper at a Twister party. It wasn't until years later that I heard acid-trailblazer Richard Alpert's dictum against repeated use: "When you get the message, hang up the phone."

GIVEN MY DRUG-SCARRED psyche and my increasing skepticism about the potential of any wonder drug to provide anything but a portal to other possibilities, I seemed like a logical candidate to take the MDMA test. (I don't feel comfortable calling it Adam; that's my son's name and he is far from an ephemeral experience. And I don't believe in ecstasy outside of sex or death.)

I took it by myself, outdoors, in the Marin Headlands, between forts Berry and Cronkhite. (I did give some thought to my choice of location; I wanted to be able to move about, I like the openness of that area and I'm comfortable near the ocean.) And though I had no specific issues I wanted to deal with, my psychic closet certainly needed cleaning. I'd been divorced in the last year. One of my best friends wasn't speaking to me. And I wasn't making enough money at my chosen profession to buy myself a new pair of shoes.

I set out on my excursion as though I were going to camp for the weekend, making a list of things to bring with me in my daypack: suntan lotion, a pair of shorts, a sweater, a canteen of water, smokes, matches, money, a Walkman and some tapes I thought I might want to hear, a notebook and portable tape recorder to take down any profound thoughts I might have. I did everything but sew my name in my underwear.

It had been raining the morning I set out on my trip, though the weather service assured me that it would clear by mid-day. Sure enough, by the time I reached Fort Berry, the clouds had all blown away and the sun was burning off the residual fog. I parked my car, hoisted my daypack, took my pill (a 150-mg dose of MDMA), duly recorded the time (11:30 a.m.) on my tape recorder and set out in search of the unknown.

Within fifteen minutes I discovered that all the trails leading away from Ft. Berry are in a cloverleaf and kept leading me back to the same spot, one of the many cement fortresses built by the Army in anticipation of a Japanese invasion during World War II. Since I was told that the drug should take effect in thirty minutes, I decided to drive a little further down the road before I was incapable. Besides, the clearing weather was bringing out clusters of tourists, whom I didn't want to deal with.

As I drove down the access road I dutifully recorded my unchanging perceptions on my little Sony: "11:50 and still no difference," I muttered into the litttle metal box, one hand on the wheel. "If nothing changes soon, I'll take another hit." (I had thoughfully brought a second.) I parked my car away past the path that leads down to Black Sand Beach, near another cement cannon housing. As I climbed out of my auto and checked my belongings I felt a slight rush, as though I were coming on to speed. Probably just anxiety, I figured grimly, anticipation of something that's not going to happen. The whole thing might be a hoax, I thought as I trudged off toward the bluffs, a sort of mass hysteria that's been built up around no-big-deal, like Kohoutek or the traveling K-Paul's kitchen.

There were other nature lovers gathered around the sight, basking in the sun, reading the Sunday paper, picnicking on blankets. After walking out to the cliffs and realizing there was still no clearly marked trail that led down the coast, I rethought my route for a second time. About half a mile down the road, on a green lawned area near Point Bonita, I could see a wedding party gathering. A little greenery, perhaps, or at least the trail out to the lighthouse; that was the way to go. I decided to drive again, still feeling straight and figuring that when the drugs did finally kick in, I'd want to be close to my car. So I hiked back to the road, looking at the graffiti spraypainted large across the cement walls.

It was about a quarter after noon as I approached my car, and I still figured nothing was happening. A little anxiety, probably the result of too much coffee. I should have stayed home, I thought, I should have brought some pot. Then I realized, as I gazed plaintively through the window of my car, that I'd locked my keys inside.

Now, I won't say that I've never locked my keys in my car before; I have, at a time of great duress. But generally getting out of the car with my keys in my hand is second nature to me, like walking out of the house with my pants on. As I stood there, metaphorically bare-assed, looking at my own sorry reflection in the windshield, I thought of a story a friend had told me about the time she and her lover had locked the keys in their van while tripping on acid. With the engine running. And a dog inside. And I found myself thinking that it was too bad you couldn't teach dogs to do simple things like unlock car doors, and that if it had been Lassie inside that car, she would have gotten behind the wheel and driven back to the ranch for help.

Suddenly I felt very stoned. It wasn't just the image of Lassie on the CB that convinced me. It was my complete lack of concern for my predicament. Sure, I was a good ways from home—San Francisco shimmered off in the distance like the Emerald City—but, like a good

Boy Scout, I had come prepared. It was the shank of a beautiful day and it wouldn't be dark for another seven hours. My car was a rolling dumpster and easily accessible (it had been broken into before). All I needed was a coat hanger, which didn't seem too much to ask. I set off down the road toward Point Bonita, in search of pliable wire.

As I walked I gauged my perceptions. I wasn't hallucinating: I stared at the stones before me and found them to be just stones, unchanging. I felt slightly speedy, but not wired for sound. I had been told that MDMA had aphrodisiacal properties, but making love at that moment would have been physically impossible: My member had done the incredible disappearing act familiar to any man who's ever done speed. Looking out over the whole San Francisco Bay glistening in the sun, the world seemed a perfect pearl, and I felt impossibly serene.

I reached the green at Point Bonita and observed the wedding party for a moment. It was a well-heeled crowd, dressed in formal pastels, emerging from expensive German automobiles—the sort of people I would ordinarily despise. But as I watched them awkwardly greet each other, anticipating the ceremony, I felt an unexpected compassion for them. Just try to be happy, I thought, floundering around like everyone else, without a clue. I noted "love-of-yuppie" as a new symptom.

I passed a portable restroom where a young father was having trouble with his recently toilet-trained son, who was refusing to come out of the john. The father lost his patience and began banging on the door.

"If you don't come out of there right now," he yelled, "we're going straight home, do you hear me? We'll turn the car around and go straight home!"

I was amazed to find that parents still used this chestnut. I thought of my own father—impatient, occasionally cruel—using this line on us, a hundred miles from home ("Now this vacation doesn't mean so much to me, but your mother. . . ."). As I walked past this scenario, one being played out in cars and parks across the country, I felt a great empathy, not just for the poor kid trying to pee, but for his shortsighted dad, doing what he learned from his father. Would the kid go on to yell at his son like that?

I walked out to the end of the point, through the tunnel that led to the lighthouse, marveling that I had never been out there before. If I was stoned on acid, I told myself, this tunnel would take on some symbolic portent, as would the light at the end of it and the lighthouse. But now all just seemed right. Darkness, good. Light, good.

I passed couples sitting quietly in the sun, small children running up the stairs that led to the lighthouse. Out at the crest I stood alone, looking out over the ocean while a warm breeze blew through my hair. Ships were passing out of the bay into the ocean, sailing away, some forever. And I thought about loss.

Everybody's afraid of losing. Friends and lovers leave, things fall apart, people die. Then you die. (Ouch.) And nobody wants to go. The Buddhists believe that it's our attachment to things that makes us unhappy. At that moment I felt very unattached. Nothing really went anywhere, it seemed at that moment; friends, wives, children went out the door, but they don't really go anywhere: there is nowhere to go. Time passed, sure, but where did it go? For an instant I felt I understood the notion of the "eternal now" that Claudio Naranjo had spoken of in his writings on empathogenic drugs. And in short I was unafraid.

I was still broke, it occurred to me as I walked away from the lighthouse—there are some things that even wonder drugs won't change. But who would judge me by my shoes? The world was very beautiful and God inhabited it fully. In the bay the buoys were singing their warnings to the clear ocean air.

I walked back inland, over the narrow wooden bridge that led toward the park. I had given up on getting back into my car. Seven maids with seven mops had swept this area for half a year; the ground was cleaner than the floor of my house. I walked up a trail out over the bluffs, farther and farther from the people below. I knew there was a bus that went from Fort Cronkhite back to the city; my car wasn't going anywhere. It just meant embarrassment, perhaps. And there, far from everything, I found it.

A coat hanger.

I WASN'T EXACTLY praying for a coat hanger that day; I was, rather, musing that a benignly indifferent universe might just spit up an odd bit of wire that it had no use for, a hanger that, in fact, had no business being there. And, lo: what was needed had been produced. No reasonable offer refused, the universe seemed to be saying. Se habla español.

I walked back to my car feeling that all was in balance. I got the wire inside the wind-wing and was inches away from getting a loop of it around the door-latch when a park ranger pulled up in a truck.

"Locked out of my car," I said, rather sheepishly. When she failed to respond I added, "Doesn't look like the kind of car you'd want to steal, does it?"

"No," she said (a little too matter-of-factly, I thought). She produced a slim-jim and in a matter of moments had my door open.

It should be noted that a non-stoned person might have thought of finding a park ranger immediately. But I seldom think of searching out people in uniforms, no matter the stripe, when under the influence of illegal substances. But then the non-stoned person probably wouldn't have locked himself out of his car.

Once the door was open I produced some proof of ownership and then we chatted amiably for a moment or two, her telling me which trails led where. Talking was no problem: I felt as lucid as a linguist, as shameless as a priest. I had been told that this was the drug you could call your mother on, and though I didn't feel like calling Mom, I was quite content to chat up this park ranger. She seemed so *pleasant,* fascinating, really, a wonderful person. . . .

From there I hiked down to the Black Sand beach, thinking it time for a rest. Once down there I removed my clothes and sat contentedly, watching the ships again. I was coming down, nearly four hours after taking the capsule.

In the end, taking MDMA seemed a transient glimpse at our transient existence, an experience as delicate and ephemeral as breath on a glass. I didn't feel as though I had learned anything new, but that I had been reminded of something important.

Before I left the beach that day to make the long climb back up the road, I went down the shore to write my son's name in the sand. I was thinking of him more than anyone else at the end of it all. He was my anchor, my earth and his presence seemed palpable. I wrote his name, Adam, in the black sand and then watched in perfect contentment as the waves washed the words away.

OSCAR WILDE

❖

THE PICTURE OF DORIAN GRAY

A COLD RAIN began to fall, and the blurred street-lamps looked ghastly in the dripping mist. The public-houses were just closing, and dim men and women were clustering in broken groups round their doors. From some of the bars came the sound of horrible laughter. In others, drunkards brawled and screamed.

Lying back in the hansom, with his hat pulled over his forehead, Dorian Gray watched with listless eyes the sordid shame of the great city, and now and then he repeated to himself the words that Lord Henry had said to him on the first day they had met, "To cure the soul by means of the senses, and the senses by means of the soul." Yes, that was the secret. He had often tried it, and would try it again now. There were opium-dens, where one could buy oblivion, dens of horror where the memory of old sins could be destroyed by the madness of sins that were new.

The moon hung low in the sky like a yellow skull. From time to time a huge misshapen cloud stretched a long arm across and hid it. The gas-lamps grew fewer, and the streets more narrow and gloomy. Once the man lost his way, and had to drive back half a mile. A steam rose from the horse as it splashed up the puddles. The side-windows of the hansom were clogged with a grey-flannel mist.

"To cure the soul by means of the senses, and the senses by means of the soul!" How the words rang in his ears! His soul, certainly, was sick, to death. Was it true that the senses could cure it? Innocent blood had been spilt. What could atone for that? Ah! for that there was no atonement; but though forgiveness was impossible, forgetfulness was possible still, and he was determined to forget, to stamp the thing out, to crush it as one would crush the adder that had stung one.

Indeed, what right had Basil to have spoken to him as he had done? Who had made him a judge over others? He had said things that were dreadful, horrible, not to be endured.

On and on plodded the hansom, going slower, it seemed to him, at each step. He thrust up the trap, and called the man to drive faster. The hideous hunger for opium began to gnaw at him. His throat burned, and his delicate hands twitched nervously together. He struck at the horse madly with his stick. The driver laughed, and whipped up. He laughed in answer, and the man was silent.

The way seemed interminable, and the streets like the black web of some sprawling spider. The monotony became unbearable, and, as the mist thickened, he felt afraid.

Then they passed by lonely brickfields. The fog was lighter here, and he could see the strange bottle-shaped kilns with their orange fan-like tongues of fire. A dog barked as they went by, and far away in the darkness some wandering seagull screamed. The horse stumbled in a rut, then swerved aside, and broke into a gallop.

After some time they left the clay road, and rattled again over rough-paven streets. Most of the windows were dark, but now and then fantastic shadows were silhouetted against some lamp-lit blind. He watched them curiously. They moved like monstrous marionettes, and made gestures like live things. He hated them. A dull rage was in his heart. As they turned a corner a woman yelled something at them from an open door, and two men ran after the hansom for about a hundred yards. The driver beat at them with his whip.

It is said that passion makes one think in a circle. Certainly with hideous iteration the bitten lips of Dorian Gray shaped and reshaped those subtle words that dealt with soul and sense, till he had found in them the full expression, as it were, of his mood, and justified, by intellectual approval, passions that without such justification would still have dominated his temper. From cell to cell of his brain crept the one thought; and the wild desire to live, most terrible of all man's appetites, quickened into force each trembling nerve and fibre. Ugliness that had once been hateful to him because it made things real, became dear to him now for that very reason. Ugliness was the one reality. The coarse brawl, the loathsome den, the crude violence of disordered life, the very vileness of thief and outcast, were more vivid, in their intense actuality of impression, than all the gracious shapes of Art, the dreamy shadows of Song. They were what he needed for forgetfulness. In three days he would be free.

Suddenly the man drew up with a jerk at the top of a dark lane. Over the low roofs and jagged chimney-stacks of the houses rose the black masts of ships. Wreaths of white mist clung like ghostly sails to the yards.

"Somewhere about here, sir, ain't it?" he asked huskily through the trap.

Dorian started, and peered round. "This will do," he answered, and, having got out hastily, and given the driver the extra fare he had promised him, he walked quickly in the direction of the quay. Here and there a lantern gleamed at the stern of some huge merchantman. The light shook and splintered in the puddles. A red glare came from an outward-bound steamer that was coaling. The slimy pavement looked like a wet mackintosh.

He hurried on towards the left, glancing back now and then to see if he was being followed. In about seven or eight minutes he reached a small shabby house, that was wedged in between two gaunt factories. In one of the top-windows stood a lamp. He stopped, and gave a peculiar knock.

After a little time he heard steps in the passage, and the chain being unhooked. The door opened quietly, and he went in without saying a word to the squat misshapen figure that flattened itself into the shadow as he passed. At the end of the hall hung a tattered green curtain that swayed and shook in the gusty wind which had followed him in from the street. He dragged it aside, and entered a long, low room which looked as if it had once been a third-rate dancing-saloon. Shrill flaring gas-jets, dulled and distorted in the fly-blown mirrors that faced them, were ranged round the walls. Greasy reflectors of ribbed tin backed them, making quivering discs of light. The floor was covered with ochre-coloured sawdust, trampled here and there into mud, and stained with rings of spilt liquor. Some Malays were crouching by a little charcoal stove playing with bone counters, and showing their white teeth as they chattered. In one corner with his head buried in his arms, a sailor sprawled over a table, and by the tawdrily-painted bar that ran across one complete side stood two haggard women mocking an old man who was brushing the sleeves of his coat with an expression of disgust. "He thinks he's got red ants on him," laughed one of them, as Dorian passed by. The man looked at her in terror, and began to whimper.

At the end of the room there was a little staircase, leading to a darkened chamber. As Dorian hurried up its three rickety steps, the heavy odour of opium met him. He heaved a deep breath, and his nostrils quivered with pleasure. When he entered, a young man with smooth yellow hair, who was bending over a lamp lighting a long thin pipe, looked at him, and nodded in a hesitating manner.

"You here, Adrian?" muttered Dorian.

"Where else should I be?" he answered, listlessly. "None of the chaps will speak to me now."

"I thought you had left England."

"Darlington is not going to do anything. My brother paid the bill at last. George doesn't speak to me either. . . . I don't care," he added, with a sigh. "As long as one has this stuff, one doesn't want friends. I think I have had too many friends."

Dorian winced, and looked round at the grotesque things that lay in such fantastic postures on the ragged mattresses. The twisted limbs, the gaping mouths, the staring lustreless eyes, fascinated him. He knew in what strange heavens they were suffering, and what dull hells were teaching them the secret of some new joy. They were better off than he was. He was prisoned in thought. Memory, like a horrible malady, was eating his soul away. From time to time he seemed to see the eyes of Basil Hallward looking at him. Yet he felt he could not stay. The presence of Adrian Singleton troubled him. He wanted to be where no one would know who he was. He wanted to escape from himself.

"I am going on to the other place," he said, after a pause.

"On the wharf?"

"Yes."

"That mad-cat is sure to be there. They won't have her in this place now."

Dorian shrugged his shoulders. "I am sick of women who love one. Women who hate one are much more interesting. Besides, the stuff is better."

"Much the same."

"I like it better. Come and have something to drink. I must have something."

"I don't want anything," murmured the young man.

"Never mind."

Adrian Singleton rose up wearily, and followed Dorian to the bar. A half caste, in a ragged turban and a shabby ulster, grinned a hideous greeting as he thrust a bottle of brandy and two tumblers in front of them. The women sidled up, and began to chatter. Dorian turned his back on them, and said something in a low voice to Adrian Singleton.

A crooked smile, like a Malay crease, writhed across the face of one of the women. "We are very proud to-night," she sneered.

"For God's sake, don't talk to me," cried Dorian, stamping his foot on the ground. "What do you want? Money? Here it is. Don't ever talk to me again."

Two red sparks flashed for a moment in the woman's sodden eyes, then flickered out, and left them dull and glazed. She tossed her head, and raked the coins off the counter with greedy fingers. Her companion watched her enviously.

"It's no use," sighed Adrian Singleton. "I don't care to go back. What does it matter? I am quite happy here."

"You will write to me if you want anything, won't you?" said Dorian, after a pause.

"Perhaps."

"Good-night, then."

"Good-night," answered the young man, passing up the steps, and wiping his parched mouth with a handkerchief.

Dorian walked to the door with a look of pain on his face. As he drew the curtain aside a hideous laugh broke from the painted lips of the woman who had taken the money. "There goes the devil's bargain!" she hiccoughed, in a hoarse voice.

"Curse you," he answered, "don't call me that."

She snapped her fingers. "Prince Charming is what you like to be called, ain't it?" she yelled after him.

The drowsy sailor leapt to his feet as she spoke, and looked wildly around. The sound of the shutting of the hall door fell on his ear. He rushed out as if in pursuit.

Dorian Gray hurried along the quay through the drizzling rain. His meeting with Adrian Singleton had strangely moved him, and he wondered if the ruin of that young life was really to be laid at his door, as Basil Hallward had said to him with such infamy of insult. He bit his lip, and for a few seconds his eyes grew sad. Yet, after all, what did it matter to him? One's days were too brief to take the burden of another's errors on one's shoulders. Each man lived his own life, and paid his own price for living it. The only pity was one had to pay so often for a single fault. One had to pay over and over again, indeed. In her dealings with man Destiny never closed her accounts.

There are moments, psychologists tell us, when the passion for sin, or for what the world calls sin, so dominates a nature, that every fibre of the body, as every cell of the brain, seems to be instinct with fearful impulses. Men and women at such moments lose the freedom of their will. They move to their terrible end as automatons move. Choice is taken from them, and conscience is either killed, or, if it lives at all, lives but to give rebellion its fascination, and disobedience its charm. For all sins, as theologians weary not of reminding us, are sins of disobedience. When that high spirit, that morning-star of evil, fell from heaven, it was as a rebel that he fell.

Callous, concentrated on evil, with stained mind, and soul hungry for rebellion, Dorian Gray hastened on, quickening his step as he went, but as he darted aside into a dim archway, that had served him often as a short cut to the ill-famed place where he was going, he felt himself suddenly seized from behind, and before he had time to defend himself he was thrust back against the wall, with a brutal hand round his throat.

He struggled madly for life, and by a terrible effort wrenched the tightening fingers away. In a second he heard the click of a revolver, and saw the gleam of a polished barrel pointing straight at his head, and the dusky form of a short thick-set man facing him.

"What do you want?" he gasped.

"Keep quiet," said the man. "If you stir, I shoot you."

"You are mad. What have I done to you?"

"You wrecked the life of Sibyl Vane," was the answer, "and Sibyl Vane was my sister. She killed herself. I know it. Her death is at your door. I swore I would kill you in return. For years I have sought you. I had no clue, no trace. The two people who could have described you were dead. I knew nothing of you but the pet name she used to call you. I heard it tonight by chance. Make your peace with God, for to-night you are going to die."

Dorian Gray grew sick with fear. "I never knew her," he stammered. "I never heard of her. You are mad."

"You had better confess your sin, for as sure as I am James Vane, you are going to die." There was a horrible moment. Dorian did not know what to say or do. "Down on your knees!" growled the man. "I give you one minute to make your peace—no more. I go on board to-night for India, and I must do my job first. One minute. That's all."

Dorian's arms fell to his side. Paralyzed with terror, he did not know what to do. Suddenly a wild hope flashed across his brain. "Stop," he cried. "How long ago is it since your sister died? Quick, tell me!"

"Eighteen years," said the man. "Why do you ask me? What do years matter?"

"Eighteen years," laughed Dorian Gray, with a touch of triumph in his voice. "Eighteen years! Set me under the lamp and look at my face."

James Vane hesitated for a moment, not understanding what was meant. Then he seized Dorian Gray and dragged him from the archway.

Dim and wavering as was the windblown light, yet it served to show him the hideous error, as it seemed, into which he had fallen, for the face of the man he had sought to kill had all the bloom of boyhood, all the unstained purity of youth. He seemed little more than a lad of twenty summers, hardly older, if older indeed at all, than his sister had been when they had parted so many years ago. It was obvious that this was not the man who had destroyed her life.

He loosened his hold and reeled back. "My God! my God!" he cried, "and I would have murdered you!"

Dorian Gray drew a long breath. "You have been on the brink of committing a terrible crime, my man," he said, looking at him sternly. "Let this be a warning to you not to take vengeance into your own hands."

"Forgive me, sir," muttered James Vane. "I was deceived. A chance word I heard in that damned den set me on the wrong track."

"You had better go home, and put that pistol away, or you may get into trouble," said Dorian, turning on his heel, and going slowly down the street.

James Vane stood on the pavement in horror. He was trembling from head to foot. After a little while a black shadow that had been creeping along the dripping wall, moved out into the light and came close to him with stealthy footsteps. He felt a hand laid on his arm and looked round with a start. It was one of the women who had been drinking at the bar.

"Why didn't you kill him?" she hissed out, putting her haggard face quite close to his. "I knew you were following him when you rushed out from Daly's. You fool! You should have killed him. He has lots of money, and he's as bad as bad."

"He is not the man I am looking for," he answered, "and I want no man's money. I want a man's life. The man whose life I want must be nearly forty now. This one is little more than a boy. Thank God, I have not got his blood upon my hands."

The woman gave a bitter laugh. "Little more than a boy!" she sneered. "Why, man, it's nigh on eighteen years since Prince Charming made me what I am."

"You lie!" cried James Vane.

She raised her hand up to heaven. "Before God I am telling the truth," she cried.

"Before God!"

"Strike me dumb if it ain't so. He is the worst one that comes here. They say he has sold himself to the devil for a pretty face. It's nigh on eighteen years since I met him. He hasn't changed much since then. I have though," she added, with a sickly leer.

"You swear this?"

"I swear it," came in hoarse echo from her flat mouth. "But don't give me away to him," she whined; "I am afraid of him. Let me have some money for my night's lodging."

He broke from her with an oath, and rushed to the corner of the street, but Dorian Gray had disappeared. When he looked back, the woman had vanished also.

GÉRARD DE NERVAL

❖

THE STORY OF CALIPH HAKEM

ON THE RIGHT bank of the Nile, some distance from the port of Fostat where the ruins of old Cairo lie, not far from Mount Mokatam that overlooks the new city, there could be found, some time after the Christian year 1,000 (which corresponds to the fourth century of the Muslim Hegira), a little village inhabited mainly by people of the Sabian sect.

A charming view is to be had from the last houses along the river; the waves of the Nile caress the island of Roddah, which the river appears to support, much like a bouquet of flowers that a slave might carry in his arms. Gizah can be seen on the other bank, and in the evening, just as the sun has gone down, the gigantic triangles of the pyramids tear through the violet mist of dusk. The tops of the doum palms, the sycamores and the Pharaoh's fig trees become black silhouettes against this light backdrop. Herds of water buffalo, seemingly guarded from afar by the Sphinx stretched out on the plain like a pointer dog, come down to the watering-hole in single file, and the lights of the fishermen dot the opaque shadows of the riverbanks with pinprick stars.

In the Sabian village, the place where this view could be most appreciated, was a white-walled *okel* surrounded by carob trees, whose terrace went down to the water-side, where, nightly, boatmen traveling up or down the Nile watched little lights flicker in puddles of oil.

A curious person sitting in a fishing boat in the middle of the river could easily have discerned inside the *okel* the travelers and the regulars, sitting on palm-wood boxes in front of little tables, or on divans covered in woven leaves, and he would certainly have been surprised by their strange appearance. Their extravagant gestures followed by stupid immobility, the senseless laughter, the inarticulate cries that escaped periodically from their chests, all this would have allowed him to guess that this was one of those houses where, braving the prohibitions, infidels go to intoxicate themselves on wine, *bouza* (beer), or hashish.

One evening, a boat, navigated with the certitude of long familiarity with the area, came to moor in the shadow of the terrace, at the foot of a stairway whose first few steps were kissed by water, and from it stepped out a young man with a fresh face, who might have been a fisherman, and who, ascending the stairs with a firm and rapid step, sat down in a corner of the room in a spot that appeared to be his own. No one paid any attention to his arrival; he was manifestly a regular visitor.

At the same moment, by the opposite, landward door, there entered a man wearing a black wool tunic, his hair worn uncustomarily long underneath a *takieh* (white skull-cap).

His unexpected appearance caused some surprise. He sat in the shadows, and, inebriation once again dominating the room, no one paid him any further attention. Although his clothes were in a sorry state, the newcomer's face did not display the worried humility of misery. His firmly drawn features had the severe lines of a lion's. His eyes, as dark blue as sapphire, had an indefinable strength; they simultaneously terrified and charmed.

Yousouf, the name of the young man brought by the fishing boat, immediately felt a secret sympathy for the newcomer, whose unusual presence he hadn't failed to notice. Having not yet participated in the general merry-making, he approached the divan where the stranger crouched.

"Brother," said Yousouf, "you seem weary; doubtless you have traveled a long way? Would you care to take some refreshment?"

"My road has indeed been long," replied the stranger. "I came into this *okel* to rest, but what could I drink here, where only forbidden beverages are served?"

"You Muslims dare not wet your lips with anything but pure water, but we of the Sabian sect may, without offending our law, refresh ourselves with the generous blood of the vine or the blond liquor of hops."

"And yet I see before you no fermented drink."

"Oh! I have long disdained their coarse drunkenness," said Yousouf, signalling to a black man who placed on the table two little silver-filigreed glasses and a box filled with greenish dough, with an accompanying ivory spatula. "Within the hour I will put you in the arms of the *houris* without your having passed across the al-Sirat bridge."

"But this dough is hashish, if I am not mistaken," replied the stranger, pushing back the cup in which Yousouf had deposited a portion of the fantastic mixture. "And hashish is forbidden."

"Everything that is agreeable is forbidden," said Yousouf, swallowing a first spoonful.

The stranger fixed on him his dark azure pupils, his forehead contracted with such violent folds that his hairline followed its waves; for a moment it was as if he had wanted to throw himself at the thoughtless young man and tear him to pieces; but he contained himself, his features relaxed, and, suddenly changing his mind, he stretched out his hand, took the cup, and began slowly to taste the green dough.

After a few minutes the effects of the hashish began to make themselves felt on Yousouf and the stranger; a sweet languor flowed through their limbs and a vague smile floated on their lips. Although they had in fact spent but a half-hour together, it seemed to them they had known each other for a thousand years. As the drug acted more forcefully on them, they began to laugh, to become agitated and to talk with extreme volubility, especially the stranger, a strict observer of the prohibitions who had never before tasted the preparation, and keenly felt its effects. He seemed prey to an extraordinary exaltation; swarms of new, outrageous, inconceivable thoughts crossed his soul in fiery whirlwinds; his eyes shone as though lit from within by the reflections of an unknown world, and then the vision dimmed, and he gave himself up slackly to all the beatitudes of *kif.*

"So, my companion!" said Yousouf, seizing on this intermittence in the stranger's inebriation, "what do you think of this honest pistachio pastry? Will you still curse the good people who gather quietly in low-ceilinged rooms to be happy in their own way?"

"Hashish makes you like God," replied the stranger in a slow, deep voice.

"Yes," said Yousouf with enthusiasm. "Water drinkers know only the coarse, material aspect of things. Hashish, by obscuring the body's eyes, enlightens those of the soul; the spirit is disengaged from the body, its heavy jailer, and escapes like a prisoner whose guard has fallen asleep after leaving the key in the door of the cell. It roams, joyful and free in space and light, chatting familiarly with the genii it meets, who dazzle it with sudden, charming revelations. It crosses atmospheres of unspeakable happiness with an easy stroke of the wing, in the space of one minute that seems eternal, so rapidly do these sensations succeed each other. I personally have a dream that reappears incessantly, always the same yet always changing: I am going back to my fishing boat, staggering under the splendor of my visions, closing my eyelids to the perpetual trickle of hyacinths, carbuncles, emeralds, rubies, which form the backdrop against which hashish draws its marvelous fantasies; then, in the very heart of the infinite, I perceive a celestial figure, more beautiful than all the creations of the poets, who smiles at me with a penetrating tenderness and leaves the skies to come down to me. Is it an angel, a genie? I do not know. She sits beside me in my boat, whose coarse wood is transformed immediately to mother-of-pearl, and which floats on a river of silver, pushed along by breezes charged with perfume."

"A happy and singular vision," murmured the stranger, nodding his head.

"That is not all," continued Yousouf. "One night, I had taken a weaker dose; I awoke from my drunkenness as my fishing boat passed the tip of the island of Roddah. A woman like that in my dream looked upon me with eyes that, though human, nonetheless contained a celestial spark; inside her half-opened veil a garment thick with precious stones shone up to the moon's rays. My hand met hers; her skin, soft and fresh as a flower petal, and her rings, whose facets brushed against me, convinced me of her reality.

"Near the island of Roddah?" asked the stranger with a meditative air.

"I didn't dream it," Yousouf continued, ignoring the remark of his impromptu confidant. "Hashish merely brought out a memory hidden deep within my soul, for this divine face was known to me. But where had I seen it? In what world had we met? What previous existence had linked us to each other? That I do not know, but this strange meeting, this bizarre adventure did not surprise me: it seemed completely natural that this woman, who so completely corresponded to my ideal, was to be found there, in my fishing-boat, in the middle of the Nile, as if she had been thrown up from the calyx of one of the wide flowers which rise to the surface of the waters. Without asking her for any explanation, I threw myself at her feet, and as to the genie of my dream, I gave her all the fiery and sublime sentiments that love in its exaltation can imagine; there came to me words of immense significance, expressions that contained a universe of thoughts, mysterious phrases wherein vibrated the echo of forgotten worlds. My soul grew larger in the past and in the future; I was convinced that I had felt for all eternity the love that I expressed.

"As I spoke, I saw her large eyes light up and throw out emanations; her transparent hands stretched out to me, disappearing in the rays of light. I felt myself enveloped in a network of flames and, despite myself, I fell back into the dream of the previous day. When I was able to shake off the invincible and delicious torpor that held my limbs, I was on the opposite bank, at Gizah, sitting against a palm tree, and my black slave slept quietly beside the boat, which he had pulled up on the sand. A pink light fringed the horizon; daylight was coming."

"This is a love that bears little resemblance to earthly love," said the stranger, without objecting in any way to the many improbabilities of Yousouf's tale, as hashish makes one easily credulous of miracles.

"I have never told this incredible story to anyone; why then did I confide it in you, whom I have never seen? It is difficult to explain. Some mysterious attraction drew me to you. When you entered the room, a voice cried from within my soul, 'Here he is, at last.' Your arrival calmed a secret anxiety that left me without rest. You are he whom I have been awaiting without knowing it. My thoughts sprang out before you, and I was obliged to tell you all the mysteries of my heart."

"What you are feeling," responded the stranger, "I also feel, and I will tell you what I had not even dared admit to myself until now. You have an impossible passion, I have a monstrous one; you love a genie, and I love—you will tremble—my sister! And yet, strangely, I feel no remorse for this illegitimate inclination; however much I condemn myself, I am absolved by a mysterious power I feel within me. My love has nothing of earthly impurities. It is not lust that pushes me toward my sister, though she equals in beauty the phantom of my visions; it is an indefinable attraction, an affection deep as the sea, vast as the sky, and so large it could be felt by a god. The idea that my sister could unite with a man inspires in me the disgust and horror of a sacrilege; there is in her something celestial that I divine through the veil of her flesh. Despite the name they give it on earth, she is the bride of my immortal soul, the virgin destined for me from the first days of creation. At times I believe I am recapturing, across the ages and the shadows of appearances, our secret union. Scenes that happened before the appearance of men on earth come up from my memory, and I see myself under the golden boughs of Eden, sitting beside her, served by obedient spirits. In uniting myself with another woman, I would fear prostituting and dissipating the soul of the world that palpitates within me. By the concentration of our divine blood-lines, I wish to found an immortal race, a definitive god, more powerful than all those who have manifested themselves until now under various names and changing appearances!"

While Yousouf and the stranger exchanged these long confidences, the regular visitors to the *okel*, affected by inebriation, had been agitated by extravagant contortions, inane laughter, ecstatic swoons, convulsive dances; but little by little, the force of the hemp dissipated, calm returned to them, and they lay on their divans in the state of prostration that typically follows such excesses.

A man of patriarchal bearing, whose beard flooded his flowing robe, entered the *okel* and advanced to the middle of the room.

"My brothers, get up," he said in a sonorous voice; "I have just observed the sky; the hour is favorable for the sacrifice of a white rooster before the Sphinx, in honor of Hermes and Agathodaemon."

The Sabians stood up and seemed ready to follow their priest; but the stranger, hearing this proposal, changed color two or three times: the blue of his eyes became black, terrible folds criss-crossed his face, and from his chest escaped a deafening roar, making the assembled group tremble with terror, as if a real lion had fallen into the middle of the *okel*.

"Heretics! Blasphemers! Vile brutes! Idolaters!" he cried in a thunderous voice.

The crowd was amazed at this explosion of anger. The stranger had such an air of authority, and raised the folds of his garment with gestures so proud, that none dared respond to his insults.

The old man approached and said to him, "What evil do you find, brother, in the sacrifice of a rooster, according to the rites, to the good genies of Hermes and Agathodaemon?"

The stranger gritted his teeth at the mere mention of the two names.

"If you do not share the beliefs of the Sabians, what brought you here? Are you of the sect of Jesus or of Mohammed?"

"Mohammed and Jesus are impostors," cried out the stranger with an incredible blasphemous power.

"Doubtless you are of the religion of the Parsis, who worship fire . . ."

"All that is fantasies, mockeries, lies," interrupted the man in the black tunic with redoubled indignation.

"Then whom do you worship?"

"He asks me whom I worship! . . . I worship no one, as I am God myself! The one, the true, the only God, before whom all others are merely shadows."

At this inconceivable, outrageous, insane assertion, the Sabians threw themselves on the blasphemer, who would have suffered great ill if Yousouf, covering him with his own body, had not led him out to the terrace beside the Nile, though the stranger fought and cried out like a madman. Then, with a vigorous kick to the riverbank, Yousouf launched the boat out to the middle of the river. When they caught the current, Yousouf asked his friend, "Where should I take you?"

"There, to the island of Roddah, where you see those lights shining," replied the stranger, who had been calmed by the night air.

In a few oar-strokes, they reached the island, and the man in the black tunic, before jumping on land, said to his savior, offering him an old ring that he pulled from his finger, "In whatever place you meet me, you have only to show me this ring, and I will do for you whatever you wish." Then he walked off and disappeared under the trees at the river's edge.

TERRY SOUTHERN

❋

THE BLOOD OF A WIG

MY MOST OUTLANDISH drug experience, now that I think about it, didn't occur with beat Village or Harlem weirdos, but during a brief run with the ten-to-four Mad Ave crowd.

How it happened, this friend of mine who was working at *Lance* ("The Mag for Men") phoned me one morning—he knew I was strapped.

"One of the fiction editors is out with syph or something," he said. "You want to take his place for a while?"

I was still mostly asleep, so I tried to cool it by shooting a few incisive queries as to the nature of the gig—which he couldn't seem to follow.

"Well," he said finally, "you won't have to *do* anything, if that's what you mean." He had a sort of blunt and sullen way about him—John Fox his name was, an ex-Yalie and would-be writer who was constantly having to "put it back on the shelf," as he expressed it (blunt, sullen), and take one of these hot-shot Mad Ave jobs, and always for some odd reason—like at present, paying for his mom's analysis.

Anyway, I accepted the post, and now I had been working there about three weeks. It wasn't true, of course, what he'd said about not having to do anything—I mean the way he had talked I wouldn't even have to get out of bed—but after three weeks my routine was fairly smooth: up at ten, wash face, brush teeth, fresh shirt, dex, and make it. I had this transistor-shaver I'd copped for five off a junky-booster, so I would shave with it in the cab, and walk into the office at ten-thirty or so, dapper as Dan and hip as Harry. Then into my own small office, lock the door, and start stashing the return postage from the unsolicited mss. We would get an incredible amount of mss.—about two hundred a day—and these were divided into two categories: (1) those from agents, and (2) those that came in cold, straight from the author. The ratio was about 30 to 1, in favor of the latter—which formed a gigantic heap called "the shit pile," or (by the girl-readers) "the garbage dump." These always contained a lot of return postage—so right away I was able to supplement my weekly wage by seven or eight dollars a day in postage stamps. Everyone else considered the "shit pile" as something heinously repugnant, especially the sensitive girl ("garbage") readers, so it was a source of irritation and chagrin to my secretary when I first told her I wished to read "*all* unsolicited manuscripts and *no* manuscripts from agents."

John Fox found it quite in comprehensible.

"You must be out of your nut!" he said. "Ha! Wait until you try to read some of that crap in the shit pile!"

I explained however (and it was actually true in the beginning) that I had this theory about the existence of a *pure, primitive, folklike* literature—which, if it did exist, could only turn up among the unsolicited mss. Or *weird*, something really *weird*, even insane, might turn up there—whereas I knew the stuff from the agents would be the same old predictably competent tripe. So, aside from stashing the stamps, I would read each of these shit-pile ms. very carefully—reading subtleties, insinuations, multilevel *entendre* into what was actually just a sort of flat, straightforward simplemindedness. I would think each was a put-on—a fresh and curious parody of some kind, and I would read on, and on, all the way to the end, waiting for the payoff . . . but, of course, that never happened, and I gradually began to revise my theory and to refine my method. By the second week, I was able to reject a ms. after reading the opening sentence, and by the third I could often reject on the basis of *title* alone—the principle being if an author would allow a blatantly dumbbell title, he was incapable of writing a story worth reading. (This was thoroughly tested and proved before adopting.) Then instead of actually *reading* mss., I would spend hours, days really, just thinking, trying to refine and extend my method of blitz-rejection. I was able to take it a little farther, but not much. For example, any woman author who used "Mrs." in her name could be rejected out of hand—*unless* it was used with only one name, like "by Mrs. Carter," then it might be a weirdie. And again, any author using a middle initial or a "Jr." in his name, shoot it right back to him! I knew I was taking a chance with that one (because of Connell and Selby), but I figured what the hell, I could hardly afford to gear the sort of fast-moving synchro-mesh operation I had in mind to a couple of exceptions—which, after all, only went to prove the consarn rule, so to speak. Anyway, there it was, the end of the third week and the old job going smoothly enough, except that I had developed quite a little dexie habit by then—not actually a *habit*, of course, but a sort of very real dependence . . . having by nature a nocturnal metabolism whereby my day (pre-*Lance*) would ordinarily begin at three or four in the afternoon and finish at eight or nine in the morning. As a top staffer at *Lance*, however, I had to make other arrangements. Early on I had actually asked John Fox if it would be possible for me to come in at four and work until midnight.

"Are you out of your *nut*? (That was his standard comeback). "Don't you know what's happening here? This is a *social* scene, man— these guys want to *see* you, they want to get to *know* you!"

"What are they, faggots?"

"No, they're not *faggots*," he said stoutly, but then seemed hard pressed to explain, and shrugged it off. "It's just that they don't have very much, you know, *to do*."

It was true in a way that no one seemed to actually *do* anything—except for the typists, of course, always typing away. But the guys just sort of hung out, or around, buzzing each other, sounding the chicks, that sort of thing.

The point is though that I had to make in by ten, or thereabouts. One reason for this was the "pre-lunch conference," which Hacker, or the "Old Man" (as, sure enough, the publisher was called), might decide to have on any given day. And so it came to pass that on this particular—Monday it was—morning, up promptly at nine-three-oh, wash face, brush teeth, fresh shirt, all as per usual, and reach for the dex . . . no dex, out of dex. This was especially inopportune because it was on top of two straight white and active nights, and it was somewhat as though an 800-pound bag, of loosely packed sand, began to settle slowly on the head. No panic, just immediate death from fatigue.

At Sheridan Square, where I usually got the taxi, I went into the drugstore. The first-shift pharmacist, naturally a guy I had never seen before, was on duty. He looked like an aging efficiency expert.

"Uh, I'd like to get some Dexamyl, please."

The pharmacist didn't say anything, just raised one hand to adjust his steel-rimmed glasses, and put the other one out for the prescription.

"It's on file here," I said, nodding toward the back.

"What name?" he wanted to know, then disappeared behind the glass partition, but very briefly indeed.

"Nope," he said, coming back, and was already looking over my shoulder to the next customer.

"Could you call Mr. Robbins?" I asked, "he can tell you about it." Of course this was simply whistling in the dark, since I was pretty sure Robbins, the night-shift man, didn't know me by name, but I had to keep the ball rolling.

"I'm not gonna wake Robbins at this hour—he'd blow his stack. Who's next?"

"Well, listen, can't you just *give* me a couple—I've, uh, got a long drive ahead."

"You can't get dexies without a script," he said, rather reproachfully, wrapping a box of Tampax for a teenybopper nifty behind me, "*you* know that."

"Okay, how about if I get the doctor to phone you?"

"Phone's up front," he said, and to the nifty: "That's seventy-nine."

The phone was under siege—one person using it, and about

five waiting—all, for some weird reason, spade fags and prancing gay. Not that I give a damn about who uses the phone, it was just one of those absurd incongruities that seem so often to conspire to undo sanity in times of crisis. What the hell was going on? They were obviously together, very excited, chattering like magpies. Was it the Katherine Dunham contingent of male dancers? Stranded? Lost? Why out so early? One guy had a list of numbers in his hand the size of a small flag. I stood there for a moment, confused in pointless speculation, then left abruptly and hurried down West Fourth to the dinette. This was doubly to purpose, since not only is there a phone, but the place is frequented by all manner of heads, and a casual score might well be in order—though it was a bit early for the latter, granted.

And this did, in fact, prove to be the case. There was no one there whom I knew—and, worse still, halfway to the phone, I suddenly remembered my so-called doctor (Dr. Friedman, his name was) had gone to California on vacation a few days ago. Christ almighty! I sat down at the counter. This called for a quick think-through. Should I actually call him in California? Have him phone the drugstore from there? Quite a production for a couple of dex. I looked at my watch, it was just after ten. That meant just after seven in Los Angeles—Friedman would blow his stack. I decided to hell with it and ordered a cup of coffee. Then a remarkable thing happened. I had sat down next to a young man who now quite casually removed a small transparent silo-shaped vial from his pocket, and without so much as a glance in any direction, calmly tapped a couple of the belovedly familiar green-hearted darlings into his cupped hand, and tossed them off like two salted peanuts.

Deus ex machina!

"Uh, excuse me," I said, in the friendliest sort of way, "I just happened to notice you taking a couple of, ha ha, Dexamyl." And I proceeded to lay my story on him—while he, after one brief look of appraisal, sat listening, his eyes straight ahead, hands still on the counter, one of them half covering the magic vial. Finally he just nodded and shook out two more on the counter. "Have a ball," he said.

I REACHED THE office about five minutes late for the big pre-lunch confab. John Fox made a face of mild disgust when I came in the conference room. He always seemed to consider my flaws as his responsibility since it was he who had recommended me for the post. Now he glanced uneasily at old Hacker, who was the publisher, editor-in-chief, etc. etc. A man of about fifty-five, he bore a striking resemblance to Edward G. Robinson—an image to which he gave further credence by frequently sitting in a squatlike manner, chewing an unlit cigar butt, and mouthing coarse expressions. He liked to characterize himself as a "tough old bastard," one of his favorite prefaces being: "I know most of you guys think I'm a *tough old bastard*, right? Well, maybe I am. In the quality-Lit game you *gotta* be tough!" And bla-bla-bla.

Anyway as I took my usual seat between Fox and Bert Katz, the feature editor, Old Hack looked at his watch, then back at me.

"Sorry," I mumbled.

"We're running a *magazine* here, young man, not a *whorehouse*."

"Right and double right," I parried crisply. Somehow Old Hack always brought out the schoolboy in me.

"If you want to be *late*," he continued, "be late at the *whorehouse*—and do it on your own time!"

Part of his design in remarks of this sort was to get a reaction from the two girls present—Maxine, his cutiepie private sec, and Miss Rogers, assistant to the art director—both of whom managed, as usual, a polite blush and half-lowered eyes for his benefit.

The next ten minutes were spent talking about whether to send our own exclusive third-rate photographer to Viet Nam or to use the rejects of a second-rate one who had just come back.

"Even with the rejects we could still run our *E.L. trade*," said Katz, referring to an italicized phrase *Exclusively Lance* which appeared under photographs and meant they were not being published elsewhere—though less through exclusivity, in my view, than general crappiness.

Without really resolving this, we went on to the subject of "Twiggy," the British fashion-model who had just arrived in New York and about whose boyish hair and bust-line raged a storm of controversy. What did it mean philosophically? Aesthetically? Did it signal a new trend? Should we adjust our center-spread requirements (traditionally 42-24-38) to meet current taste? Or was it simply a flash fad?

"Come next issue," said Hack, "we don't want to find ourselves holding the wrong end of the shit-stick, now do we?"

Everyone was quick to agree.

"Well, *I* think she's absolutely *delightful*," exclaimed Ronnie Rondell, the art director (prancing gay and proud of it), "she's so much more . . . sensitive-looking and . . . *delicate* than those awful . . . *milk-factories!*" He gave a little shiver of revulsion and looked around excitedly for corroboration.

Hack, who had a deep-rooted antifag streak, stared at him for a moment like he was some kind of weird lizard, and he seemed about to say something cruel and uncalled for to Ron, but then he suddenly turned on me instead.

"Well, Mister Whorehouse man, isn't it about time we heard from you? Got any ideas that might conceivably keep this operation out of the shithouse for another issue or two?"

"Yeah, well I've been thinking," I said, winging it completely, "I mean, Fox here and I had an idea for a series of interviews with unusual persons. . . ."

"Unusual *persons*?" he growled, "what the hell does that mean?"

"Well, you know, a whole new department, like a regular feature. Maybe call it, uh, 'Lance Visits. . . .' "

He was scowling, but he was also nodding vigorously. " 'Lance Visits. . . .' Yeh, yeh, you wantta gimme a fer instance?"

"Well, you know, like, uh, . . . 'Lance Visits a Typical Teenybopper'—cute teenybopper tells about cute teen-use of Saran Wrap as a contraceptive, etcetera . . . and uh, let's see . . . 'Lance Visits a Giant Spade Commie Bull-Dike' . . . 'Lance Visits the Author of *Masturbation Now!*', a really fun-guy."

Now that I was getting warmed up, I was aware that Fox, on my left, had raised a hand to his face and was slowly massaging it, mouth open, eyes closed. I didn't look at Hack but I knew he had stopped nodding. I pressed on . . . "You see, it could become a sort of regular department, we could do a 'T.L.' on it . . . *'Another Exclusive Lance Visit.'* How about this one: 'Lance Visits a Cute Junkie Hooker' . . . 'Lance Visits a Zany Ex-Nun Nympho' . . . 'Lance Visits the Fabulous Rose Chan, beautiful research and development technician for the so-called French Tickler . . .'"

"Okay," said Hack, "how about *this* one: 'Lance Visits Lance,'—know where? Up shit-creek without a paddle! Because that's where we'd be if we tried any of that stuff." He shook his head in a lament of disgust and pity. "Jeez, that's some sense of humor you got, boy." Then he turned to Fox. "What rock you say you found him under? Jeez."

Fox, as per usual, made no discernible effort to defend me, simply pretended to suppress a yawn, eyes averted, continuing to doodle on his "Think Pad," as it was called, one of which lay by each of our ashtrays.

"Okay," said Hack, lighting a new cigar, "suppose *I* come up with an idea? I mean, I don't wantta *surprise* you guys, cause any *heart attacks* . . . by *me* coming up with an *idea*," he saying this with a benign serpent smile, then adding in grim significance, "*after twenty-seven years in this goddam game!*" He took a sip of water, as though trying to cool his irritation at being (as per usual) "the only slob around here who delivers." "Now let's just stroke this one for a while," he said, "and see if it gets stiff. Okay, lemme ask you a question: what's the hottest thing in mags at this time? What's raising all the stink and hullabaloo? The *Manchester* book, right? The suppressed passages, right?" He was referring, of course, to a highly publicized account of the assassination of President Kennedy—certain passages of which had allegedly been deleted. "Okay, now all this stink and hullabaloo—I don't like it, *you* don't like it. In the first place, it's infringement on freedom of the press. In the second, they've exaggerated it all out of proportion. I mean, what the hell was *in* those passages? See what I mean? All right, suppose we do a *takeoff* on those same passages?"

He gave me a slow look, eyes narrowed—ostensibly to protect them from his cigar smoke, but with a Mephistophelian effect. *He* knew that *I* knew that his "idea" was actually an idea I had gotten from Paul Krassner, editor of *The Realist*, a few evenings earlier, and had mentioned, *en passant* so to speak, at the last prelunch confab. He seemed to be wondering if I would crack. A test, like. I avoided his eyes, doodled on the "Think Pad." He exhaled in my direction, and continued:

"Know what I mean? Something *light*, something *zany*, kid the pants off the guys who suppressed it in the first place. A satire like. Get the slant?"

No one at the table seemed to. Except for Hack we were all in our thirties or early forties, and each had been hurt in some way by the President's death. It was not easy to imagine any particular "zaniness" in that regard.

Fox was the first to speak, somewhat painfully it seemed. "I'm, uh, not quite sure I follow," he said. "You mean it would be done in the style of the book?"

"Right," said Hack, "but get this, we don't say it *is* the real thing, we say it *purports* to be the real thing. And editorially we *challenge* the *authenticity* of it! Am I getting through to you?"

"Well, uh, yeah," said Fox, "but I'm not sure it can be, you know, uh, *funny*."

Hack shrugged. "So? *You're* not sure, *I'm* not sure. Nobody's sure it can be funny. We all take a crack at it—just stroke it a while and see if we get any jism—right?"

Right.

AFTER WORK THAT evening I picked up a new Dexamyl prescription and stopped off at Sheridan Square to get it filled. Coming out of the drugstore, I paused momentarily to take in the scene. It was a fantastic evening—late spring evening, warm breeze promise of great summer evenings imminent—and teenies in minies floating by like ballerinas, young thighs flashing. Summer, I thought, will be the acid test for minies when it gets too warm for tights, bodystockings, that sort of thing. It should be quite an interesting phenomenon. On a surge of sex-dope impulse I decided to fall by the dinette and see if anything of special import was shaking, so to speak.

Curious that the first person I should see there, hunched over his coffee, frozen saintlike, black shades around his head as though a hippy crown of thorns, should be the young man who had given me the dex that very morning. I had the feeling he hadn't moved all day. But this wasn't true because he now had on a white linen suit and was sitting in a booth. He nodded in that brief formal way it is possible to nod and mean more than just hello. I sat down opposite him.

"I see you got yourself all straightened out," he said with a wan smile, nodding again, this time at my little paper bag with the pharmacy label on it.

I took out the vial of dex and popped a quick one, thinking to do a bit of the old creative Lit later on. Then I shook out four or five and gave them to the young man.

"Here's some interest."

"Anytime," he said, dropping them in his top pocket, and after a pause, "You ever in the mood for something beside dexies?"

"Like what?"

He shrugged, "Oh, you know," he said, raising a vague limp hand, then added with a smile, "I mean you know your moods better than I do."

During the next five minutes he proved to be the most acquisitive pusher, despite his tender years, I have ever encountered. His range was extensive—beginning with New Jersey pot, and ending with something called a "Frisco Speedball," a concoction of heroin and cocaine, with a touch of acid ("gives it a little color"). While we were sitting there, a veritable parade of his far-flung connections commenced, sauntering over, or past the booth, pausing just long enough to inquire if he wanted to score—for sleepers, leapers, creepers . . . acid in cubes, vials, capsules, tablets, powder . . . "hash, baby, it's black as O" . . . mushrooms, mescalin, buttons . . . cosanyl, codeine, coke . . . coke in crystals, coke in powder, coke that looked like karo syrup . . . red birds, yellow jackets, purple hearts . . . "liquid-0, it comes straight from Indochina, stamped right on the can" . . . and from time to time the young man ("Trick" he was called) would turn to me and say: "Got eyes?"

After committing to a modest (thirty dollars) score for crystals, and again for two ounces of what was purported to be 'Panamanian Green' ("It's 'one-toke pot', baby."), I declined further inducement. Then an extremely down-and-out type, a guy I had known before whose actual name was Rattman, but who was known with simple familiarity as "Rat," and even more familiarly, though somehow obscurely, as "The Rat-Prick Man," half staggered past the booth, clocked the acquisitive Trick, paused, moved uncertainly towards the booth, took a crumpled brown paper bag out of his coat pocket, and opened it to show.

"Trick," he muttered, almost without moving his lips, ". . . Trick, can you use any Lights? Two-bits for the bunch." We both looked in, on some commodity quite unrecognizable—tiny, dark cylinder-shaped capsules, sticky with a brown-black guk, flat on each end, and apparently made of plastic. There was about a handful of them. The young man made a weary face of distaste and annoyance.

"Man," he asked softly, plaintively, looking up at Rattman, "*when* are you going to get buried?"

But the latter, impervious, gave a soundless guffaw, and shuffled on.

"What," I wanted to know, "were those things?" asking this of the young man half in genuine interest, half in annoyance at not knowing. He shrugged, raised a vague wave of dismissal. "Lights they're called . . . they're used nicotine-filters. You know, those nicotine filters you put in a certain kind of cigarette holder."

"*Used* nicotine-filters? What do you do with them?"

"Well, you know, drop two or three in a cup of coffee—gives you a little buzz."

"A little *buzz*" I said, "are you kidding? How about a little *cancer?* That's all tar and nicotine in there, isn't it?"

"Yeah, well you know . . ." he chuckled dryly, "anything for kicks. Right?"

Right, right, right.

And it was just about then he sprung it—first giving me his look of odd appraisal, then the sigh, the tired smile, the haltering deference: "Listen, man . . . you ever made red-split?"

"I beg your pardon?"

"Yeah, you know—the blood of a wig."

"No," I said, not really understanding, "I don't believe I have."

"Well, it's something else, baby, I can tell you that."

"Uh, well, *what* did you call it—I'm not sure I understood. . . ."

" 'Red-split,' man, it's called 'red-split'—it's schizo-juice . . . *blood* . . . the blood of a wig."

"Oh, I see." I had, in fact, read about it in a recent article in the *Times*—how they had shot up a bunch of volunteer prisoners (very normal, healthy guys, of course) with the blood of schizophrenia patients—and the effect had been quite pronounced . . . in some cases, manic; in other cases, depressive—about 50/50 as I recalled.

"But that can be a big bring-down, can't it?"

He shook his head somberly. "Not with *this* juice it can't. You know who this is out of?" Then he revealed the source—Chin Lee, it was, a famous East Village resident, a Chinese symbolist poet, who was presently residing at Bellevue in a straightjacket. "Nobody," he said, "and I mean *nobody,* baby, has gone anywhere but *up, up, up* on *this* taste!"

I thought that it might be an interesting experience, but using caution as my watchword (the *Times* article had been very sketchy) I had to know more about this so-called red-split, blood of a wig. "Well, how long does it, uh, you know, *last?*"

He seemed a little vague about that—almost to the point of resenting the question. "It's a *trip,* man—four hours, six if you're lucky. It all depends. It's a question of *combination*—how your blood makes it with his, you dig?" He paused and gave me a very straight look. "I'll tell you this much, baby, *it cuts acid and STP . . . * " He nodded vigorously. "That's right, cuts both them. *Back, down,* and *sideways.*"

"Really?"

He must have felt he was getting a bit too loquacious, a bit too much on the old hard-sell side, because then he just cooled it, and nodded. "That's right," he said, so soft and serious that it wasn't really audible.

"How much?" I asked, finally, uncertain of any other approach.

"I'll level with you," he said, "I've got this connection—a ward attendant . . . you know, a male nurse . . . has, what you might call *access* to the hospital pharmacy . . . does a little trading with the guards on the fifth floor—that's where the *monstro*-wigs are— 'High Five' it's called. That's where Chin Lee's at. Anyway, he's operating at cost right now—I mean, he'll cop as much M, or whatever other hard-shit he can, from the pharmacy, then he'll go up to High Five and trade for the juice—you know, just fresh, straight, uncut wig-juice—90 c.c.'s, that's the regular hit, about an ounce, I guess . . . I mean, that's what they hit the wigs for, a 90 c.c. syringeful, then they cap the spike and put the whole outfit in an insulated wrapper. Like it's supposed to stay at body temperature, you dig? They're very strict about that—about how much they tap the wig for, and about keeping it fresh and warm, that sort of thing. Which is okay, because that's the trip—90 c.c.'s, 'piping hot,' as they say." He gave a tired little laugh at the curious image. "Anyway the point is, he never knows in front what the *price* will be, my friend doesn't, because he never knows what kind of M score he'll make. I mean like if he scores for half-a-bill of M, then that's what he charges for the split, you dig?"

To me, with my Mad Ave savvy, this seemed fairly illogical.

"Can't he hold out on the High Five guys?" I asked, ". . . you know, tell them he only got half what he really got, and save it for later?"

He shrugged, almost unhappily. "He's a very ethical guy," he said, "I mean like he's pretty weird. He's not really interested in narcotics, just *changes*. I mean, like he lets *them* do the count on the M—they tell him how much it's worth and that's what he charges for the split."

"That *is* weird," I agreed.

"Yeah, well it's like a new market, you know. I mean there's no established price yet, he's trying to develop a clientele—can you make half-a-bill?"

While I pondered, he smiled his brave tired smile, and said: "There's one thing about the cat, being so ethical and all—he'll never burn you."

So in the end it was agreed, and he went off to complete the arrangements.

THE EFFECT OF red-split was "as advertised" so to speak—in this case, quite gleeful. Sense-derangementwise, it was unlike acid in that it was not a question of the "Essential I" having new insights, but of becoming a different person entirely. So that in a way there was nothing very scary about it, just extremely weird, and as it turned out, somewhat mischievous (Chin Lee, incidentally, was not merely a great wig, but also a great wag). At about six in the morning I started to work on the alleged "Manchester passages." Krassner might be cross, I thought, but what the hell, you can't copyright an idea. Also I intended to give him full and ample credit. "Darn good exposure for Paul" I mused benignly, taking up the old magic quill.

The first few passages were fairly innocuous, the emphasis being on a style identical to that of the work in question. Towards the end of Chapter Six, however, I really started cooking: ". . . wan, and wholly bereft, she steals away from the others, moving trancelike towards the darkened rear-compartment where the casket rests. She enters, and a whispery circle of light shrouds her bowed head as she closes the door behind her and leans against it. Slowly she raises her eyes and takes a solemn step forward. She gasps, and is literally slammed back against the door by the sheer impact of the outrageous horror confronting her: i.e., the hulking Texan silhouette at the casket, its lid half raised, and he hunching bestially, his coarse animal member thrusting into the casket, and indeed into the neck-wound itself.

"*Great God*," she cries, "how heinous! It must be a case of . . . of . . . *NECK*-ROPHILIA!"

I FINISHED AT about ten, dexed, and made it to the office. I went directly into Fox's cubicle (the "Lair" it was called).

"You know," I began, lending the inflection a childlike candor, "I could be wrong but I think I've *got* it," and I handed him the ms.

"Got what?" he countered dryly, "the clap?"

"You know, that Manchester thing we discussed at the last prelunch confab." While he read, I paced about, flapped my arms in a gesture of uncertainty and humble doubt. "Oh, it may need a little tightening up, brightening up, granted, but I hope you'll agree that the *essence* is there."

For a while he didn't speak, just sat with his head resting on one hand staring down at the last page. Finally he raised his eyes; his eyes were always somehow sad.

"You really *are* out of your nut, aren't you?"

"Sorry, John," I said. "Don't follow."

He looked back at the ms., moved his hands a little away from it as though it were a poisonous thing. Then he spoke with great seriousness:

"I think you ought to have your head examined."

"My *head* is swell," I said, and wished to elaborate, "my *head* . . ." but suddenly I felt very weary. I had evidently hit on a cow sacred even to the cynical Fox.

"Look," he said, "I'm not a *prude* or anything like that, but this . . ."—he touched the ms. with a cough which seemed to stifle a retch— . . . "I mean, *this* is the most . . . *grotesque* . . . *obscene* . . . well, I'd rather not even discuss it. Frankly, I think you're in very real need of psychiatric attention."

"Do you think Hack will go for it?" I asked in perfect frankness.

Fox averted his eyes and began to drum his fingers on the desk.

"Look, uh, I've got quite a bit of work to do this morning, so, you know, if you don't mind. . . ."

"Gone too far, have I, Fox? Is that it? Maybe you're missing the point of the thing—ever consider that?"

"Listen," said Fox stoutly, lips tightened, one finger raised in accusation, "you show this . . . *this thing* to anybody else, you're liable to get a *big smack in the kisser!*" There was an unmistakable heat and resentment in his tone—a sort of controlled hysteria.

"How do you know I'm not from the C.I.A.?" I asked quietly. "How do *you* know this isn't a *test?*" I gave him a shrewd narrow look of appraisal. "Isn't it just possible, Fox, that this quasi-indignation of yours is, in point of fact, simply an *act? A farce? A charade? An act,* in short, to *save your own skin!?!*"

He had succeeded in putting me on the defensive. But now, steeped in Chink poet cunning, I had decided that an offense was the best defense, and so plunged ahead. "Isn't it true, Fox, that in this parable you see certain underlying homosexual tendencies which you unhappily recognize in yourself? Tendencies, I say, which to confront would bring you to the very brink of, 'fear and trembling,' so to speak." I was counting on the Kierkegaard allusion to bring him to his senses.

"You crazy son of a bitch," he said flatly, rising behind his desk, hands clenching and unclenching. He actually seemed to be moving towards me in some weird menacing way. It was then I changed my tack. "Well listen," I said, "what would you say if I told you that it wasn't actually *me* who did that, but a Chinese poet? Probably a Commie . . . an insane Commie-fag-spade-Chinese poet. Then we could view it objectively, right?"

Fox, now crazed with his own righteous adrenalin, and somewhat encouraged by my lolling helplessly in the chair, played his indignation to the hilt.

"Okay, Buster," he said, towering above me, "keep talking, but make it good."

"Well, uh, let's see now. . . ." So I begin to tell him about my experience with the red-split. And speaking in a slow, deliberate, very serious way, I managed to cool him. And then I told him about an insight I had gained into Viet Nam, Cassius Clay, Chessman, the Rosenbergs, and all sorts of interesting things. He couldn't believe it. But, of course, no one ever really does—do they?

S A M U E L
T A Y L O R   C O L E R I D G E

❊

K U B L A   K H A N

THE FOLLOWING FRAGMENT *is here published at the request of a poet of great and deserved celebrity [Lord Byron], and, as far as the Author's own opinions are concerned, rather as a psychological curiosity, than on the ground of any supposed poetic merits.*

In the summer of the year 1797, the Author, then in ill health, had retired to a lonely farm-house between Porlock and Linton, on the Exmoor confines of Somerset and Devonshire. In consequence of a slight indisposition, an anodyne had been prescribed, from the effects of which he feel asleep in his chair at the moment that he was reading the following sentence, or words of the same substance, in "Purchas's Pilgrimage": "Here the Khan Kubla commanded a palace to be built, and a stately garden thereunto. And thus ten miles of fertile ground were inclosed with a wall." The Author continued for about three hours in a profound sleep, at least of the external senses, during which time he has the most vivid confidence, that he could not have composed less than from two to three hundred lines; if that indeed can be called composition in which all the images rose up before him as things, *with a parallel production of the correspondent expressions, without any sensation or consciousness of effort. On awaking he appeared to himself to have a distinct recollection of the whole, and taking his pen, ink, and paper, instantly and eagerly wrote down the lines that are here preserved. At this moment he was unfortunately called out by a person on business from Porlock, and detained by him above an hour, and on his return to his room, found, to his no small surprise and mortification, that though he still retained some vague and dim recollection of the general purport of the vision, yet, with the exception of some eight or ten scattered lines and images, all the rest had passed away like the images on the surface of a stream into which a stone has been cast, but, alas! without the after restoration of the latter!*

In Xanadu did Kubla Khan
A stately pleasure-dome decree:
Where Alph, the sacred river, ran
Through caverns measureless to man
   Down to a sunless sea.
So twice five miles of fertile ground
With walls and towers girdled round:
And there were gardens bright with sinuous rills,
Where blossomed many an incense-bearing tree;
And here were forests ancient as the hills,
Enfolding sunny spots of greenery.

But oh! that deep romantic chasm which slanted
Down the green hill athwart a cedarn cover!
A savage place! as holy and enchanted
As e'er beneath a waning moon was haunted
By woman wailing for her demon-lover!
And from this chasm, with ceaseless turmoil seething,
As if this earth in fast thick pants were breathing,
A mighty fountain momently was forced:
Amid whose swift half-intermitted burst
Huge fragments vaulted like rebounding hail,
Or chaffy grain beneath the thresher's flail:
And 'mid these dancing rocks at once and ever
It flung up momently the sacred river.
Five miles meandering with a mazy motion
Through wood and dale the sacred river ran,

Then reached the caverns measureless to man,

And sank in tumult to a lifeless ocean:

And 'mid this tumult Kubla heard from far

Ancestral voices prophesying war!

    The shadow of the dome of pleasure

    Floated midway on the waves;

    Where was heard the mingled measure

    From the fountain and the caves.

It was a miracle of rare device,

A sunny pleasure-dome with caves of ice!

    A damsel with a dulcimer

    In a vision once I saw:

    It was an Abyssinian maid,

    And on her dulcimer she played,

    Singing of Mount Abora.

Could I revive within me

Her symphony and song,

To such a deep delight 'twould win me,

That with music loud and long,

I would build that dome in air,

That sunny dome! those caves of ice!

And all who heard should see them there,

And all should cry, Beware! Beware!

His flashing eyes, his floating hair!

Weave a circle round him thrice,

And close your eyes with holy dread,

For he on honey-dew hath fed,

And drunk the milk of Paradise.

NELSON ALGREN (1909-81) grew up in the slums of Chicago, the
setting for his most famous novel, *The Man with the Golden Arm*. The
title refers to Frankie Machine (played by Frank Sinatra in the classic
1955 film), a decorated war veteran and poker dealer renowned for his
facility with a deck of cards and a spoonful of morphine. Frankie finds
his dope habit more difficult to break than the neck of his supplier, Nifty
Louie Fomorowski.

CHARLES BAUDELAIRE's sole book of poems, *Les Fleurs du Mal*, is
recognized as a cornerstone of all that is modern in modern poetry.
Equally important, though less widely known, are his later "prose
poems," which include "La Chambre Double (The Double Room)."
His interest in decadence as a way of life and art led him to opium and
hashish (which he called "paradis artificiels") and to an early death of
syphilis in 1867.

PAUL BOWLES, New York-born composer, poet, and novelist (*The
Sheltering Sky*), lived for many years in Tangier. His remarkable
household there served as gateway-to-the-East for Allen Ginsberg,
William Burroughs, and subsequent waves of peripatetic hipsters. As
Without Stopping (his 1972 autobiography) attests, Majoun (edible
hashish) was never in short supply.

In her native England, ELIZABETH BARRETT BROWNING (1806–1861)
was constrained by a jealous father and an immobilizing spinal injury.
Then she found love, a new home in Italy, and success as a poet, but
little rest without the aid of opiates. Her husband, poet Robert Browning,
recalled that "sleep only came to her in a red hood of poppies."

WILLIAM S. BURROUGHS, who would come to prominence in the 1960s with his autobiographical dispatches from Junkie Hell (particularly *Naked Lunch*), farmed marijuana in Texas, shot his wife in Mexico, and consorted with gangsters in Tangier before he arrived in South America in 1953, looking for new kicks. He chronicled his introduction to ayahuasca, the "vision vine" from which yage is brewed, in a series of letters to Allen Ginsberg.

LEWIS CARROLL (1832–1898) was an unlikely progenitor of psychedelia. A stalwart Christian who lectured on mathematics at Christ Church, Oxford, his stories written for Alice Liddell have nonetheless served as a compass-point for a generation of LSD-takers. The famous mushroom scene in *Alice in Wonderland* (1865) may have been inspired by Carroll's reading of *Cooke's Plain and Easy Account of British Fungi*, published three years prior to Alice.

After three months in a Saint-Cloud clinic, JEAN COCTEAU (1889–1963) emerged with the finished manuscript of *Les Enfants Terribles;* a sheath of terrifying drawings; and a notebook that would become a classic text on the subject of addiction, *Opium: Journal d'Une Désintoxication.* This "cure," paid for by Cocteau's friend Coco Chanel, left the prolific French artist feeling reinvigorated but still pining for his beloved opium.

SAMUEL TAYLOR COLERIDGE (1772–1834) first took laudanum (the alcoholic tincture of opium) to relieve rheumatic pain caused by the damp of the Lake District. Whatever the nature of his "slight indisposition," he had the drug to thank for "Kubla Khan," the finest poem he ever wrote.

LAURIE COLWIN published four novels, two short books of essays, and three collections of short fiction, including *The Lone Pilgrim*.

In 1890, novelist MARIE CORELLI took it upon herself to singlehandedly keep "the morbid modern French mind" far from England's shores. To this end, she published *Wormwood: A Drama of Paris*, a morality tale about Gaston Beauvais, a well-bred banker, and his absinthe-soaked descent into hell. Absinthe, Corelli ventured, was the perfect symbol of "the open atheism, heartlessness, flippancy and flagrant immorality of the whole French school of thought. "

MILES DAVIS, legendary bebop innovator and pioneer of "cool jazz," was introduced to heroin and cocaine in the late 1940s, but unlike Bud Powell, Charlie Parker, Billie Holiday, and so many others, he outlived the bebop era. "I was never into that trip that if you shot heroin you might be able to play like Bird," he wrote in his 1989 autobiography. "What got me strung out was the depression I felt when I got back to America [from Paris]." Miles died in 1992.

In 1804, THOMAS DE QUINCEY, essayist and pioneer of the English romantic movement, went to a London chemist looking for a simple pain-reliever, as Coleridge had done a few years earlier. He came out with a shilling's worth of laudanum and wound up the nineteenth-century's most famous "opium-eater."

PHILIP K. DICK, whose 36 novels and five short-story collections once seemed forever doomed to the ghetto of the sci-fi shelves, has undergone a thorough literary rehabilitation since his death in 1982. This excerpt is from the 1964 cult classic, *The Three Stigmata of Palmer Eldritch*.

The real mystery of Edwin Drood is that the novel has no ending—CHARLES DICKENS (1812–70) died in the midst of writing it. The sinister choirmaster, John Jasper, secretly loves Rosa, and he may have killed her fiancée, Edwin. That may explain why Jasper is trying to pin the murder on Edwin's arch-rival, Neville Landless. But as Edwin's body hasn't turned up, one can't be sure he was murdered at all. Hadn't he been spotted in the same opium den frequented by Jasper? We'll never know for sure.

During a London dinner party in September 1889, SIR ARTHUR CONAN DOYLE sold his second Sherlock Holmes story, "The Sign of Four," to Philadelphia publisher J. M. Stoddart. (That same evening, Stoddart arranged with Oscar Wilde to publish the as-yet-unfinished *The Picture of Dorian Gray.*) Holmes, of course, is one of the best-known dope-fiends in modern literature. The detective found "a seven-percent solution" of cocaine to be "transcendently stimulating."

SEAN ELDER's writing has appeared in several publications, including *Vogue, Elle,* and *Mother Jones.* He is the author of a novel, *Everything Must Go,* and a play, *Lost in Flight,* which he has adapted for the screen. Elder's Ecstasy joyride was originally chronicled for the *Berkeley Monthly* in 1986.

Among the FANG PEOPLE in northwestern Africa, a religious movement known as the Bwiti cult relies heavily on the powerful psychotropic properties of the eboka bush. Initiates into the cult ingest the plant in order to "see" the Bwiti, a divine spirit. Depending upon the quality of the hallucinatory visions, the initiate may be admitted to Akum, the sect's inner circle. The origin myth excerpted here reflects the religion's role as a response to the hardships imposed by colonialism (". . . the misery in which the blackman was living") as well as the belief that the Fang originally received *eboka* as a gift from the Pygmies.

CARRIE FISHER's autobiographical novel, *Postcards from the Edge* (1987), chronicles Hollywood's peculiar fascination with drugs in the 1980s. Another actor, Steve Martin, suggested that *Postcards* made *Moby Dick* "seem like a big, fat, dumb book."

SIGMUND FREUD (1856–1939) spent much of his life codifying his study of the mind into a form of science; similarly, he sought a scientific explanation for his pronounced taste for cocaine. *Über Coca* was published in 1884, three years after Freud graduated in medicine from the University of Vienna, and its advocacy of the drug's usefulness in fighting everything from indigestion to hysteria, syphilis, and typhoid gave Freud his first taste of medical renown.

Reduced to plastering handbills on the walls of Paris to pay the bills, PAUL GAUGUIN (1848–1903) fled to Arles for a few famous weeks in September 1888. He found his friend, Vincent Van Gogh, hanging around in absinthe bars, like the Café de l'Alcazar, which both of them wound up portraying on canvas.

ROGER GILBERT-LECOMTE (1907–43) abruptly threw over his medical studies in 1927 and devoted the rest of his life to the pursuit of a radical, single-minded experimentation with spiritism, medium-like trances, and drugs. *Monsieur Morphée: Empoisonneur Public* was written when Gilbert-Lecomte was 22, in the brief period when his madness and talent had made him a hot young thing on the Paris literary scene.

JIM HOGSHIRE published "Poor Man's PCP" in the Spring 1993 issue of *Pills-a-go-go*, his Seattle-based "journal of pills."

ALDOUS HUXLEY died in Los Angeles at 69, on the same 1963 afternoon that John F. Kennedy was assassinated. Huxley's last request was for a 100 gm. injection of LSD, which his wife, Laura, administered to him while reading from *The Tibetan Book of the Dead.* Though he was ridiculed in some corners for embracing hallucinogens as a leg up on "the visionary experience," his intellectual pedigree and his talent—which, after all, had produced *Brave New World*—confounded these same critics. Had anyone else written *Doors of Perception*, one reviewer noted, it would have been called, "the woolgathering of a misguided crackpot." As it was, the reviewer had to admit the book deserved "more careful scrutiny."

In the spring of 1961, Harvard faculty members TIMOTHY LEARY and RICHARD ALPERT (later known as Ram Dass) conducted a series of highly controversial psilocybin experiments. RALPH METZNER, a Social Relations doctoral candidate, was their star pupil. By the following summer, the three were conducting evangelical LSD cocktail parties in a seedy hotel in Zihuatanejo, Mexico. They intended *The Psychedelic Experience* to be their updated version of the *Bardo Thodol, The Tibetan Book of the Dead.*

Prescient naturalist PETER MATTHIESSEN has written ecologically sensitive stories since the early sixties. His most popular book, *The Snow Leopard* (1978), is an account of a Nepalese journey to find the rare albino leopard. For Matthiessen, this was an equally important spiritual quest—one buoyed by routine use of LSD.

In 1971, TERENCE MCKENNA and a small gypsy-like band ventured deep into Amazonian jungles in search of the mystical hallucinogens of the Witoto people. The blow-by-blow is recorded in *True Hallucinations*, McKenna's latest in a string of studies of "the ethnopharmacology of spiritual transformation."

J. MOREAU DE TOURS, a celebrated physician to the literati, created a furor with the publication of his *Du Hachisch et de l'Alienation Mentale* in 1845. One of the earliest documents describing the action of this drug, this excerpt is an amusing record of the kind of hallucinations that might come to a respectable member of society in Paris 150 years ago.

GÉRARD DE NERVAL (born Gérard Labrunie) was a well-known writer of pleasant poetry until 1841 when, at the age of 32, he suffered his first attack of madness. That "overflowing of dream into real life," as he later put it, inspired the best of his work. As his intense bouts of insanity recurred, travel-writing became a kind of therapy. In 1842 he took his first extended trip to the Orient (the Greek Islands, Egypt, Syria, Lebanon, and Turkey); *Histoire du Calife Hakem* was first published in 1847.

FLORENCE NIGHTINGALE (1820–1910) set up a hospital for the wounded in the Crimean War and became known, to those who saw her making her nightly rounds, as the Lady with the Lamp. It's wrong to say she was also the Lady with the Pipe—there is no evidence she had an opium habit, but she did sample the drug to help with her back pain and the boredom she felt after returning from the war.

Among the 1,000 hymns contained in the *RIG VEDA*, the ancient Hindu scripture dating back at least 3,000 years, 120 of them praise soma, a magical plant credited for engendering Hatha Yoga. Aldous Huxley borrowed the term *soma* to describe the drug of choice in his *Brave New World*, but the nature of the actual historical substance is still the subject of debate. Worshippers in the cult believed soma was bestowed upon them by Varuna, a member of the early Hindu pantheon. Modern ethnobotanists contend that soma is likely to have been a vine or mushroom that accompanied Aryan invaders from Central Asia around 1,500 B.C.

ARTHUR RIMBAUD (1854–1891) determinedly steered himself into extreme situations all his life in search of forbidden fruit, producing visionary poetry and a career whose strangeness has obsessed scholars for a century. By the age of 16, Rimbaud had run away from his boring hometown to Paris and was haunting absinthe bars with his mentor and most famous lover, the poet Paul Verlaine.

Novelist, screenwriter, and general satirist TERRY SOUTHERN is the author of several monumentally sixties books and films, including *The Magic Christian, Dr. Strangelove, Barbarella,* and *Easy Rider.* "Blood of a Wig" is from his classic 1955 collection of short stories, *Red Dirt Marijuana and Other Tastes.*

When the *Atlantic Monthly* published BAYARD TAYLOR's cannabis-induced rhapsodies in 1854, he earned his place as the first American to wax hallucinatory for publication.

HUNTER S. THOMPSON's scattershot irreverence has targeted presidents and posers for the past three decades and has spared neither his own work nor his chosen profession. He calls *Fear and Loathing in Las Vegas* "a failed experiment in gonzo journalism" and "a vile epitaph for the drug culture of the sixties."

AMOS TUTUOLA was born in Lagos in 1920. Choosing to write in English rather than Yoruba, he typically blends traditional folktales and personal mythology, pioneering what has been called "a new type of Afro-English literature." After *The Palm-Wine Drinkard* (1953), he wrote *My Life in the Bush of Ghosts.*

ALAN WATTS was an ordained Anglican minister who turned up at Harvard's Divinity School, fell in with Leary and company, and later lived on a houseboat in Sausalito, California. He could be counted on to lead LSD sessions that contained elements of Zen, Christianity, and mime. Writing the introduction to Watts's *The Joyous Cosmology,* Timothy Leary and Richard Alpert heaped on the praise: "Watts follows Huxley's lead and pushes beyond," compiling "the best statement on the subject of space-age mysticism."

Of OSCAR WILDE (1854–1900), a jealous contemporary said that, "while he ate—and he ate little—he never stopped smoking opium-tainted Egyptian cigarettes." The same drug provides cold comfort for Dorian Gray. Wilde's protagonist heads for an opium den after murdering Basil Hallward, the artist who painted the fiendish picture and who loves Dorian to excess.

In *The Electric Kool-Aid Acid Test,* TOM WOLFE wrote about novelist Ken Kesey's adventures as a "guinea pig" for LSD and other drug research being conducted in Menlo Park at the Palo Alto Veterans Hospital in 1957. Kesey would go on to become a psychiatric aide there, using his experiences as the basis for *One Flew over the Cuckoo's Nest.* Wolfe wasn't there—he just wrote that way.

A C K N O W L E D G M E N T S

Excerpt from *The Yage Letters* by William S. Burroughs and Allen Ginsburg ©1975 by William S. Burroughs and Allen Ginsburg. Reprinted by permission of City Lights.

Excerpt from *Postcards from the Edge* by Carrie Fisher ©1987 by Carrie Fisher. Reprinted by permission of Simon & Schuster.

Excerpt from *The Psychedelic Experience* by Timothy Leary, Ralph Metzner, Richard Alpert ©1964 by Timothy Leary, Ralph Metzner, Richard Alpert. Reprinted by permission of Citadel Press, a division of Lyle Stuart, Inc.

Excerpt from *Without Stopping* by Paul Bowles ©1972 by Paul Bowles. Reprinted by permission of Ecco Press.

Excerpt from "On Ecstasy" by Sean Elder was first published in *The Berkeley Monthly*. ©1986 by Sean Elder. Reprinted by permission of the author.

Excerpt from *The Doors of Perception* by Aldous Huxley ©1965 by Aldous Huxley. Reprinted by permission of HarperCollins Publishers.

Excerpt from *True Hallucinations* by Terence McKenna ©1993 by Terence McKenna. Reprinted by permission of HarperCollins Publishers.

Excerpt from *Miles* by Miles Davis ©1989 Miles Davis. Reprinted by permission of Simon & Schuster.

Excerpt from *The Great Shark Hunt* by Hunter S. Thompson ©1979 by Hunter S. Thompson. Reprinted by permission of Summit Books, a division of Simon & Schuster.

Excerpt from *The Palm-Wine Drinkard* by Amos Tutuola ©1953 by George Braziller. Reprinted by permission of George Braziller.

"The Electric Cough Syrup Acid Test" from "Poor Man's PCP" by Jim Hogshire ©1993 by Jim Hogshire. Reprinted by permission of the author.

"The Achieve of, the Mastery of the Thing" by Laurie Colwin ©1981 by Laurie Colwin. Reprinted by permission of Washington Square Press, a division of Pocket Books.

Excerpt from *The Three Stigmata of Palmer Eldritch* by Philip K. Dick ©1964 by Philip K. Dick. Reprinted by permission of Vintage Books, a division of Random House, Inc.

Excerpt from *The Man with the Golden Arm* by Nelson Algren ©1949 by Nelson Algren. Reprinted by permission of Four Walls Eight Windows.

Excerpt from *The Electric Kool Aid Acid Test* by Tom Wolfe ©1968 by Tom Wolfe. Reprinted by permission of Farrar, Straus, and Giroux, Inc.

Excerpt from *The Snow Leopard* by Peter Matthiessen. ©1978 by Peter Matthiessen. Reprinted by permission of Viking Penguin.

"The Blood of a Wig" from *Red Dirt Marijuana and Other Tales* by Terry Southern. ©1967 by Terry Southern. Reprinted by permission of Carol Publishing.

Excerpt from *The Joyous Cosmology* by Alan Watts. Copyright ©1962 by Alan Watts. Reprinted by permission of Vintage Books, a division of Random House.

"Opium" by Jean Cocteau, "Mister Morpheus" by Roger Gilbert-Lecomte, "The Double Room" by Charles Baudelaire, excerpt from *The Story of Caliph Hakem* by Gérard de Nerval, and "On Hashish and Mental Alienation" by J. Moreau de Tours all translations ©1993 by Randall Koral and Ruth Marshall.